New Day at the Beach House

Diamond Beach Book 3

MAGGIE MILLER

D1414105

NEW DAY AT THE BEACH HOUSE: Diamond Beach, book 3
Copyright © 2023 Maggie Miller

All she wanted was one last summer at the beach house...

It's a new day in Diamond Beach and things are looking good for all of the Thompson women, upstairs and down. In part because Bryan Thompson's will has finally been read. It's not quite what the families were expecting, but that seems to follow with everything else that's happened. Ultimately, everyone's happy with the outcome.

Claire Thompson's made a new friend. Her next-door neighbor, Danny Rojas. He's not only helped her come to terms with some of her feelings, he's offered her an incredible opportunity. But can she afford to be part of it?

Roxie Thompson is struggling to find her place in this new reality. Helping her daughter, Trina, start a business is great, but Roxie wants more. Her mom, Willie, isn't letting anything hold her back. Maybe Roxie should be more like her?

Regardless of some small obstacles, the future looks brighter than it ever did before. For all of them. But when a stranger shows up at the beach house with incredible news, will it change everything again? Or will they find the courage to keep moving forward?

Claire can only pray things work out for them during their last summer at the beach house.

Chapter One

Trina glanced around at everyone gathered in Claire's living room. Maybe the outcome of the will being read was still settling over everyone, because no one said a word. She'd expected some kind of response to her comment about no one going anywhere, meaning that no one would have to leave the beach house now that she and Kat each owned half of it. But nope. Nothing.

Maybe, she thought, they hadn't heard her. She had sort of been speaking to Roxie, her mom. Or it could be that they were all still dealing with how the reading of the will had left them feeling.

For instance, Trina found it kind of surprising that she and Kat had gotten the beach house, and not either of their mothers.

Either way, Trina figured it was worth saying again, so she stood, glancing at Kat. "Since Kat and I each get a half share of this house, then I see no reason for anyone to go anywhere. We can all just stay right here."

Kat nodded and got to her feet. "I agree." Then she made a little face. "Except we're using more than fifty percent of it, since Cash is staying on the third floor."

Trina shrugged. "Doesn't matter to me." She smiled at Cash, her Aunt Jules's son and, technically, Trina's cousin. "I'm happy you're here. You're family. You can stay as long as you want."

"Thanks, cuz." He grinned back at her. "You're all right."

Being called "cuz" made Trina feel good. Especially from a member of her newly discovered family. She glanced at Kat. "I can't believe Dad gave us the house."

Kat nodded. "It is kind of surprising, isn't it?"

Trina had a feeling she knew why their father had left them the house. Probably because he'd known they wouldn't fight over it like their mothers would.

Trina's grandmother, Willie, got to her feet. "Well, that's that. At least this place won't have to be sold now."

"Maybe," Claire, Kat's mother, said. "Even split in

half, the upkeep and utilities on this place aren't going to be free."

Roxie, Trina's mom, shot her a look. "We're getting the life insurance money. That'll help."

"And the salon will be open before too long," Trina said. "Hopefully, once that happens, I'll be able to contribute something." She said that assuming her mom and Mimi would take care of things until she had the money to do so herself.

"Don't you worry," her Mimi said. "Your half of things will be taken care of, my girl."

Trina kissed her grandmother on the cheek. "Thanks, Mimi." Considering that her grandmother had just inherited seven million dollars from her last husband, Trina had sort of thought she might say something like that.

Not that Trina expected her grandmother to foot the bill for everything just because of that new money. Her grandmother had already bought a small strip mall for the sole purpose of giving Trina a place to open her own salon. That was far and above anything Trina could have dreamed anyone would do for her.

She certainly didn't want her grandmother to think that she'd become a blank check to her grand-daughter. Trina very much wanted to get her place open and operational as soon as possible so that she could start paying her grandmother back.

That was important to her. Even if all she could afford was a hundred dollars a month, she was going to do it.

Claire just shook her head as she got up. "It would help if I knew how much that life insurance check was going to be. That would give me some piece of mind. Or let me know how soon I need to go back to work."

For once, Trina's mom seemed to agree. "Yeah, it would be nice to know that."

Claire pulled out her phone. "I'll call Kinnerman's office and see what I can find out. I'll let you know."

"Thanks," Roxie said. "I really don't want to have to live off of savings. Or my mom's money."

"Neither do I," Claire said.

Margo, who'd been quiet up until now, spoke up. "I don't mind contributing to my portion of the bills."

Trina didn't love all the talk about money and bills. It made her worry that things might get ugly. That there might be fighting. She wanted them all to get along and be friends, despite the circumstances.

She didn't think her mom and Claire would ever

be best friends, but if they could just be civil, she'd settle for that. She understood, though. It was a big shock to find out the man you'd been married to for most of your adult life had secretly had another family. Another house, another wife, another daughter.

It was a lot of hurt feelings, lying, and betrayal to get past, that was for sure. So far, they seemed to be doing all right. Her mom and Claire were still a little chilly toward each other, but they weren't calling each other names or acting like the other one didn't exist, either. Trina was okay with that. But she hoped things would warm between them a bit.

Especially since they were all going to be living in this house together.

"Hey," Kat said softly. "I need to get ready. I have an interview in a bit and I want to study up on the company before I go in. I want to be prepared, you know?"

"Right," Trina said. "That is so smart to do. I never would have thought of that. I hope it goes really well."

Kat smiled nervously. "Me, too. I'll let you know."

"Thanks." As Kat went off to her room, Trina looked at her mom and grandmother. "I guess we should head downstairs and see what's next on the list for the salon."

"Good thinking," her Mimi called out as she got up and headed for the stairs. "Margo, don't forget about the play tonight."

"I won't," Margo said.

"Well, I'm off, too, then." Trina's mom took a few steps after Mimi before glancing at Trina. "You coming?"

"I am," Trina said. She really thought the rest of them would have had more to say. "Bye, everyone. See you later." She waved at Aunt Jules, Cash, Margo, and Claire, but only Aunt Jules and Cash waved back. Claire was on the phone and Margo's only response was a nod.

Trina pulled out her phone and sent Miles a quick text to tell him everything had gone well, and she'd fill him in later, then she caught up to her mom. They went down the steps together, but her mom didn't say a word until they were back on the first floor.

Then her mother exhaled as if she'd been holding her breath. "I am so glad you got half the house. I was so worried Claire was going to get it and that she'd throw us out." She put her hand on her heart. "I feel like a weight has been lifted off me."

Trina frowned. "Claire wouldn't have done that."

Roxie shook her head, smiling tightly. "Trina, I love that you always think the best of people, but there are some folks in this world who don't deserve that. I'm not saying Claire's a bad person—in fact, I wouldn't have blamed her for sending us packing— but I have no doubt that's what she would have done. Maybe not today, but she would have given us a deadline. Mark my words."

"Maybe," Trina said. But she really didn't believe it. She didn't *want* to believe it. She changed the subject as they headed into the living room. "Can you call Ethan and see what we need to do next?"

"Gladly, but I have a feeling he's going to want your decision on the paint color and whether or not you want wallpaper on that accent wall."

"Right," Trina said. "I'll go pull out all those samples again and have a look at them on the deck. I want to see them in natural light."

"Smart," Willie said. She was already sitting on the couch, phone in her hands. "I'll come out and look at them with you just as soon as I text Miguel. I want to remind him about the play tonight, too."

Trina's mom gave her mother a look. "When did you invite him?"

"Don't worry about it," Willie shot back.

Trina just shrugged. "The more the merrier."

"Yeah, but what if we can't get tickets?"

Willie shook her head. "I've already emailed about needing another one."

"Good thinking, Mimi." Trina glanced at her mother. "Ma, it's a play at the seniors center. I doubt it's going to be sold out. Even on the day of."

"You're probably right. Come on, let's go have a look at those samples again."

Trina gathered everything from her room: the paint samples, the wallpaper book, the lighting book, a pen, and her binder where she was keeping track of things for the salon. She carried it all out to the deck. She put everything on the couch, then spread the paint samples out on the table. "There they are."

Her mom sat on the couch, put her elbows on her knees, then leaned her chin in her hands as she studied them. "They're all pretty."

"That's the problem," Trina said. She sat by her mom and started flipping through the wallpaper book. She had a few samples bookmarked. She looked at all of those and managed to eliminate one of them right off the bat. What had she been thinking with that one?

But there was one she kept coming back to. It

was a bright, scrolling design that was sort of floral but also geometric. To Trina, the hot pink on magenta pattern looked bold and fresh without being completely over the top. She put her finger on it. "I really, *really* like this one. Am I crazy?"

Her mom looked at it. "It's bright."

"I know. But it's only going to be on that one wall. And maybe in the bathroom, because why not?"

Her mom smiled. "It's happy and colorful and really makes a statement." She laughed softly. "It's very you."

Trina wasn't sure what to think about that. "Is that a good thing?"

"It's a great thing. A Cut Above is your salon. It should reflect you. If that's what you like, that's what you should have. I think it'll look fantastic. And I bet you'll have clients taking photos in front of it for their social media."

Trina hadn't thought about that. "Maybe I should add the salon name to that wall, too."

"You could do it in brushed-gold letters."

Trina's grandmother joined them on the porch. "Miguel said he'd get an Uber to drive us to the play tonight. Isn't that sweet of him? That way we can all have a glass of champagne at intermission."

Roxie snorted. "You really think they're going to

serve champagne at the seniors center? I don't think they have a liquor license, Ma."

Willie took a seat in her usual chair. "Hmm. I'd better bring my flask."

"Mimi! Don't cause trouble," Trina said, laughing. "What do you think of this wallpaper?"

Her grandmother looked over at the book. "That's a humdinger, that one. I love it. Is that what you're going with?"

Trina took a breath. "Yeah, I think it is."

Her grandmother clapped her hands. "Fantastic. I love it."

Her mom tapped the sample. "Now you don't have to decide on a paint color. You can just have the paint store match one of the colors already in the wallpaper."

"That's good," Trina said. "Then that's settled, and we can place our order. After that, let's see if we can pick out some lighting now, too."

Willie grinned. "Let's do it. You know, I never realized how much fun it was to spend money, but then, until recently, I never had very much to spend."

Trina laughed. "I'm so glad you think so, Mimi."

Chapter Two

*J*ules and Cash had gone upstairs, but Margo stayed in her chair until Claire ended her phone call. Margo wanted to know what Claire had found out. She wanted to know that her daughter and granddaughter would be taken care of.

Claire had been standing, but now she sat back down on the couch and stared at her phone.

Margo stayed quiet for a moment as she waited, then finally said, "Well?"

Claire blinked and shook her head. "Sorry. Just lost in thought. His life insurance was for one point two million dollars. That means we'll each get six hundred thousand." She turned to better see her mother and finally smiled. "We're going to be okay."

"Well, you were *always* going to be okay," Margo

said. "But that amount will definitely make things easier."

"Easier for sure, but it's more than that. Mom, I can be a *real* partner in the bakery now. This will allow me to put some of my own money in and truly be an investor. Bryan did a lot of things I hate, but he got this one right."

Margo nodded. She'd never liked her son-in-law, but on this matter, she could agree. "I'm very happy for you. I know it'll take a lot of the worry away."

"It will." Claire sighed like that worry was just now leaving her. "I can't wait to tell Danny."

"I'm sure he'll be happy, too. What are your plans for the day?"

"I'm going to work on a new cookie idea. A popcorn sugar cookie. It just came to me when I realized I'd be able to be a true partner in the business." She smiled. "I'm more excited about it than ever."

"It's good to be excited about something, isn't it?" Margo knew of which she spoke. The book she and her new friend, Conrad, had started writing together had filled her with a whole new love for life. She got up from her chair to get ready.

"Are you off to Conrad's?"

"Soon, yes."

Claire held her mother's gaze for a moment as a soft smile curved her mouth. "We're really moving here, aren't we?"

Margo nodded. "We are. Which means we need to sort things out at home. Get those places up for sale, bring the cars over, deal with our belongings..."

Claire's smile disappeared as she blew out a breath. "It's a lot to think about."

"It is. And frankly, I don't want to just yet. Although it would be lovely to have my car." Maybe she'd ask Conrad if he'd be willing to drive her back to Landry to pick up her vehicle and some more of her things. She was going over to his place to work on the book with him shortly. But there was something else she wanted to discuss with her daughter before she headed off to his house.

"Claire?"

"Yes?"

"About staying here..." Margo wasn't sure how her daughter would react to Margo's decision, but she wasn't going to back down. "I will be here for a little while, but I'm eventually going to get my own place. I can't go on sharing a room with Jules indefinitely, no matter how much I love her."

"No, of course not." Claire started laughing, reacting very differently than Margo had anticipated. "I totally get it, Mom. You want a place where you can entertain Conrad."

"Claire." Margo pursed her lips. "I don't know what you're implying—"

"I'm not implying anything." Claire was still smiling. "You're a grown woman and a consenting adult and if you want a place of your own to have your boyfriend over to, then by all means, you should."

"He's not my boyfriend."

Claire got up as faint strains of music drifted down from the third floor. "So you haven't kissed him?"

"The nerve of you asking your mother a question like that."

Claire chuckled and nodded. "You *have* kissed him. You don't blush about much, but your cheeks have definitely gone pink. Good for you."

"Hmph." Margo got up and strode off to her room, shutting the door behind her. Toby, Jules's dachshund, was on the bed. He looked at Margo expectantly.

She shook her head. "I didn't come in here because I'm taking you for a—" She stopped before she uttered the word "walk." That would only get him all worked up. "This isn't about you, that's all

I'm saying."

She sat on her bed and texted Conrad. *I'm ready when you are.*

He answered so quickly he must have been waiting for her message. *On my way.*

She smiled as she got up and went into the bathroom to inspect her hair and makeup one more time. All good. She went back into the bedroom to get her purse, then out into the rest of the house.

Claire was nowhere to be found. Maybe in her room. Or maybe she'd gone next door to see Danny and tell him about her windfall.

Either way, Margo was glad for the reprieve. She didn't want to talk about her relationship with Conrad any more than they already had.

She knocked on her granddaughter's door. "Kat?"

"It's open."

Margo stuck her head in. Kat was on the bed, laptop in front of her. "Conrad's coming to get me. Jules and Cash are upstairs, and I have no idea where your mother is. Will you keep an eye on Toby in case he needs to go out?"

She nodded. "Sure."

"Thank you. Are you nervous about your interview?"

She nodded a second time, more rapidly than before. "Yes."

"Do you know what you're wearing?"

"I brought my tan pantsuit back with me from Landry. I'm going to wear that with a green top. Not sure about the accessories yet, though."

"Anything you want to borrow of mine, you're welcome to it."

"Thanks."

"You're going to do fine," Margo said. She was proud of her granddaughter for taking charge of her life. "Any company would be lucky to have you."

Kat smiled. "I hope they feel the same way."

"You're smart and beautiful and you deserve the kind of job that makes you happy. If they don't hire you, they're idiots."

Kat laughed. "I'll let them know."

"You do that. Text me if you find out anything, all right?"

"I will, but I don't know if they'll tell me right away or not."

"Good enough. I'll see you later this evening then."

"Have fun at Conrad's."

"Thank you. Should I leave the door open so you can hear Toby?"

"Yes."

Margo did that, then went to the elevator and took it to the ground floor. She still had a few minutes before Conrad arrived, but there were plenty of places to sit while she waited. She found a spot on the big outdoor couch and settled in.

She thought about the book and what they'd be writing today. She hoped they were able to get back into the same sort of rhythm they'd had yesterday. The words hadn't exactly been easy, but they'd flowed well enough.

She supposed it wouldn't always be that way. Writing a book was incredibly hard. If it wasn't, everyone would do it. She'd heard a statistic that something like only two percent of the people who ever tried to write a book actually finished it.

She certainly hoped she and Conrad were in that two percent. It would really be something to have her name on a book. Even if it was a pen name. Which was something they still needed to discuss.

Writing a book, actually finishing it, would make her feel like she'd done something important with her life. Not that her daughters weren't important. They were. But this would be important in a different way. In a way that was much more personal.

Certainly she wasn't looking for fame and fortune. She wasn't so deluded as to think one book was going to turn her into an overnight success. Not hardly. But to be able to say she was an author...

She smiled. It had such a nice ring to it. *Ladies and gentlemen, please welcome author Margo Bloom.* She laughed at her own imagination. No one was going to be introducing her to a crowd anytime soon. Maybe never.

But it was fun to daydream. When was the last time she'd done that? She wasn't sure, that's how long it had been.

The sound of a car approaching got her on her feet. Conrad was here, his vehicle pulling down the drive. She started walking toward his car.

He parked and got out, greeting her with a big smile. "Good morning. How did everything go?"

She nodded. "Well enough. My granddaughter got half of the house and my daughter is getting enough insurance money to take care of things. How are you?"

"I'm good. And ready to work." He went around to open her door.

She smiled as she got in. "So am I. Looking forward to it, too."

"Good." He closed her door, then went back to

his side and sat behind the wheel. He pulled out of the driveway. "I have a surprise for you."

"Oh?" She adjusted her seatbelt. "What is it?"

"I talked to Lynette Steadman. She owns Seaside Books in town, and she said she'd be happy to host a book signing for us when we get to that point."

Margo blinked, at a loss for words. She quickly found some, though. "You told someone we were writing a book? What if we don't finish it? And a book signing already? That's assuming a lot. Mostly that we're not only going to finish but that the book is actually going to get published. Conrad, that is the very definition of putting the cart before the horse."

He looked lost. "I thought you'd be happy about it."

"Happy?" She shook her head. "I...I don't know what I am, but it's not happy."

He sighed. "I'm sorry. I didn't do it to upset you."

She took a few breaths, surprised by her own reaction. "I know you didn't. And I didn't mean to respond so strongly. I'm sorry. It just feels like...I don't know how to describe it."

"Pressure," he said. "It makes you feel under pressure, doesn't it."

She exhaled and nodded. "I suppose it does. And I don't care for that feeling."

"Look, Lynette isn't going to say anything. She's a good friend. I've known her for years. It was just a conversation. It doesn't mean anything."

Margo nodded. "I overreacted. Again, I'm sorry." She offered him a quick smile. "Forgive me?"

He laughed softly. "They say creative types can be a little temperamental. You're just becoming the author you were meant to be."

She snorted. "I hope that's not true. Just be patient with me. This is all so new and I feel like at any moment someone is going to ask me what I think I'm doing. That I'm going to be found out. Silly, isn't it?"

"Not at all. It's called imposter syndrome. The belief that you'll be discovered as a phony when you attempt something new. It's perfectly natural."

"Good to know." She patted his arm. "I really am sorry. And I do genuinely love your enthusiasm."

"I'll do my best to rein it in a bit, all right?"

"No," she said. "Don't. I'm the one who needs to get over my insecurities. And this imposter syndrome business." She stared through the windshield, not really seeing the passing scenery. "Do you think we're actually going to finish?"

He let out a soft grunt. "Margo Bloom, have you ever quit anything?"

"No."

"Well, neither have I. If there were ever two people destined to write a book, it's us."

She smiled. And hoped with all her being that he was right.

Chapter Three

Jules loved playing music with her son. It wasn't something she'd had a chance to do in a long time and now that they were doing it again, it made her heart so happy. They played one of her oldest songs, *Coming Home*, to warm up and have a little fun.

Using the third floor as their studio, she sat on the sofa, while he sat in the chair at the end, both of them strumming along while she sang, although he mouthed the words with her. She'd been singing him this song since he'd been a baby in the cradle, so it was no wonder he knew the words as well as she did.

As they finished up the final notes, Cash grinned. "That sounded good. You've gotten better. I mean, you were amazing before, but you make it look so effortless."

She smiled. "I've played that song more times than I can count."

"I bet." Sunlight filtered through the sheers covering the sliding doors, giving him a golden glow. "So what's the new one you've been working on?"

She hesitated, sitting back slightly. "It's really different than the rest of my stuff. I've been kind of inspired by everything going on with your Aunt Claire, but I don't know what my audience is going to think."

"They love everything you do."

She nodded. "Mostly. But this is a lot more rock-n-roll. A lot more in your face."

"Yeah?" His eyes twinkled with curiosity. "Let me hear it."

She took a breath, surprised that she felt a little nervous about playing this new song in front of her own son. But that's how different it was. "It's not really polished yet."

He put his guitar aside. "No worries if it's still a work in progress. Everything starts somewhere, right?"

"Right. Needs refining. You know." And that was true, but it was so not the kind of song she was known for. She'd even thought about selling the song. Wouldn't be the first time. She'd made good money that way. A lot of it. But there was something about this song she loved so much she didn't want to let it go. It felt like it might be a brand-new path for her. The kind of thing that would get her new ears.

Or it might be a colossal failure.

"I do know." Cash sat back. "So let me hear what you've got. I won't judge."

He would, though. It would be impossible to hear the song and not think *something* about it.

All the same, she adjusted her fingers on the guitar strings and began to play the catchy, rollicking intro she'd come up with. Then she sang the first verse. "He shoulda been home already but it's half past ten. Dixie knows in her gut that he's done it again. He's down at that bar, taking things too far, making some other woman feel like a star."

Jules went into the chorus next. "Dixie's got her boots on, and she's headed to town. By the way she's walking, trouble's about to go down. Yeah, trouble's 'bout to go down."

She played the bridge, a softer, slower break from the fast pace of the rest of the song. It dropped lower, too, and when she sang it, she breathed out the words so that it sounded like the warning it was meant to be. "You'd better run, boy, run as fast as you can. There's a woman on her way with a gun in her hand."

She sang the next two verses and the chorus again, then strummed the last few chords. As the music faded, she looked at her son, half afraid of what he was going to say.

He was staring at her, mouth open, the expression on his face one she couldn't quite read. Did he hate it? Think it was the dumbest thing he'd ever heard?

"Well," she said quietly. "What do you think? Go on. I can take it."

"Mom, that was…"

"Not me. I know." She cringed inwardly, glancing down at the strings on her guitar.

"No, it wasn't. But it might be one of the best things you've ever done."

She looked up and laughed, not sure she'd heard him right. "What?"

"Look, you've written a lot of amazing songs, a lot of really great stuff. But this? This is something entirely new. It's like the kind of song that turns into an anthem. Women are going to go crazy for this. This might put you on the *Billboard* charts. I'm serious."

She hadn't been expecting that. "You really think so?"

He nodded. "I don't think it needs any work, either. It's got this kind of raw sound that really works. You need a band, obviously, because it needs a big sound. It's a lot of song. It's great acoustically, don't get me wrong, but this is the sort of story that needs more. But I love that about it. You know what I mean, right?"

She nodded. "I do. And I agree.

He smiled. "I'm telling you, people are going to go nuts. Has your agent heard this?"

"Not yet," Jules said. "Like I told you, it's still a work in progress. You're the first person who's heard it."

"That's pretty cool, by the way. Thanks for sharing. Your agent is going to freak."

She laughed. Billy Grimm had been her agent for years. He probably would freak, because she'd never written anything this bold. Most of her songs told stories, sure, but nothing like this. "I'm not sure he'll know what to do with it."

"Oh, I bet he will. This sort of sound is really breaking out in country right now. It's a lot more mainstream than you think." Cash tipped his head like he was thinking. "You should let Jesse hear it."

Jesse, who owned the Diamond Beach Dolphin Club, which was the best music venue in town, hands down, was also the man she'd sort of starting seeing. It wasn't anything official, but they definitely enjoyed each other's company.

What would Jesse think about this tune? She was curious. Maybe not curious enough just yet, though. "I'll consider it, but I'm not sure I'm ready."

"Mom, what's to lose? Jesse will give you an honest opinion. And if you really want feedback, play it at open mic night. I'm *telling* you, it's going to kill." Cash laughed suddenly. "No pun intended. But, yeah, you need to get this out there and then watch what happens. You're going to blow up."

"You know, I'm not exactly an unknown."

"No, you're not. But how many twenty-something things walk around singing your songs?"

She knew what he was saying and he wasn't wrong. Her demographic definitely skewed older. "Probably not that many."

He pointed at her guitar. "This song will change that. What's the title, by the way?"

"*Dixie's Got Her Boots On.*" She hadn't expected Cash's enthusiasm. It was pretty interesting. "You really think your age group would go for this?"

"Heck, yes. Call Billy. Let him hear it. And if he

doesn't get it, then ignore him and put it out your-self. You can do that now, you know. Then please, *please* do it for open mic night."

Encouraged by his excitement, she patted the body of her guitar. "I think I can be comfortable enough with it by then."

He grinned. "Yeah?"

She nodded. "Yeah. But give me a couple of days to really refine it, okay? I need to feel like it's the best it can be before I share it with the world."

"I get that. But I bet Jesse could set you up with some musicians. A drummer and a bass player, at least. Although I think a fiddle would work great on this."

"Wow, you're right. It would." When had Cash gotten so smart about such things? He was talking like a producer now.

"It would really underscore that kind of gritty, back-country thing you've got going on."

A little trill of excitement went through her. "You could play rhythm guitar."

He shook his head. "I'm not good en—"

"Don't you dare complete that sentence, Cash." She knew he was going through a bit of a life crisis, trying to find his way in the world and thinking he could never compare to his parents. But she thought a boost of confidence would help. Playing on stage with her could do just that. "You are absolutely good enough. And you're my son. I would love to have you on stage with me."

"That would be pretty fun." He grinned. "I guess we both have a lot of work to do before open mic night, then. Will you please talk to Jesse about getting you some session players? At least a drummer. Or I can do it. But you should really let him hear this."

"Billy first. Then I'll think about sharing it with Jesse. But if I'm doing open mic night with this song, you're going to be on stage with me. That's the deal."

"I don't know the song yet. I've only just heard it. But I guess I can try."

"That's all I'm asking. Well, that's not true. I'm asking you to try but I'm also asking you to be on stage with me. What do you say?"

He pulled out his phone. "I say I need to record a version of it so I can figure out the rhythm guitar part."

She adjusted her guitar on her lap. "How would you feel about adding your vocals to the bridge?"

"Really?" He picked up his guitar, settling the strap over his body. "We could at least try it. Give me the lyrics one more time."

"You'd better run, boy, run as fast as you can. There's a woman on her way with a gun in her hand."

Cash repeated it, then nodded. "I'll give it a shot."

Jules smiled and began to strum.

Chapter Four

*H*aving just left the paint and wallpaper store, Willie sat in the backseat of the car with Trina in front of her and Roxie behind the wheel. Roxie was driving them to the lighting place. Ethan was meeting them there to make sure what they'd picked out would work.

Well, that's what he'd said. She couldn't see how lights wouldn't work. That was the whole purpose of them. To be installable, or whatever you called putting new lights in.

It was probably more likely he was meeting them there because he wanted to see Roxie again. Just the thought made Willie a little tingly with happiness. Roxie deserved a good man and Ethan sure seemed like he was that guy. Of course, it was early days, but the same could be said for Willie and Miguel and he'd already offered to marry her if she needed him to.

If that didn't put a smile on her face, nothing would.

But she didn't need Miguel to marry her and give her a home. They were safe and secure right where they were, thanks to Bryan doing the right thing and giving Trina one half of the beach house. He'd done right by Roxie, too, making sure she got money from his life insurance.

They were all going to be just fine. It didn't hurt that Zippy, the last of her five husbands, had left her a little over seven million dollars, either. It was thanks to his amazing generosity that she'd been able to buy the Beachview Shopping Center where Trina would be opening her new salon.

What a dream come true that was, not just for Trina, but for Willie being able to make it happen for her granddaughter. Never would she have thought it possible in a million years, but now it was just a matter of time before the doors opened.

There was so much to do it made Willie's head spin. Thankfully, Trina, Roxie, and Ethan were on top of things.

And now that Miguel and his son, Danny, were taking over one of the shops to be their new bakery, things were really looking up. That only left the two middle spaces to be rented out. She wondered who'd end up taking over those spots.

Roxie parked at the lighting store, right next to Ethan's shiny black truck. They all got out and went in.

Willie went over to the coffee area and fixed herself a cup. They had a plate of cookies out, chocolate chip. Willie could tell just by looking at them that they were from a grocery store bakery. Probably Publix. No complaints there. She took two and went to sit down on the little sofa nearby, holding her cup in one hand and putting the second cookie down on the table on a napkin.

The girls didn't need her for the ordering. And when the time came, she'd put her credit card down and pay the bill. At this rate, she was going to rack up enough Air Miles to go somewhere fancy.

She dunked the first cookie in her coffee and wondered what Miguel would think about a trip back to Puerto Rico, his homeland. She'd bet he'd love to show her around. She already knew they'd have a great time. Just going out to dinner with him had been wonderful.

Could the two of them really take a trip like that? It was something to think about.

"Mimi, don't you want to see what we're getting?" Trina called over.

Willie gestured with her half-eaten cookie. "Whatever you want is fine with me. You have great taste, my girl. I already know it'll be beautiful. You just tell me when it's time to pay and I'll be right there."

Trina laughed. "Okay, Mimi."

As Willie sat there watching them, she noticed Ethan rest his hand briefly on the small of Roxie's back. He moved it almost as quickly as it had come to rest, but Roxie hadn't said anything to him. Maybe he thought it was too soon for that sort of public display of affection. Or maybe he realized Willie was watching.

She'd have to find a subtle way to let him know she approved. She did, too. She worried that if things went wrong, it could affect their working relationship, but they were adults. Hopefully, they'd handle it with that same sort of attitude.

Of course, if things continued to go well, then more to the benefit.

Willie's stomach started to vibrate, and she realized it was her phone in her fanny pack. She put her cup down, shoved the last bite of cookie in her mouth, and dug her phone out from in between the travel pack of tissues and the little bottle of jasmine-scented hand sanitizer.

It wasn't a number she recognized, but she answered anyway. She was a businesswoman now. She had to take calls. "Hello?"

"Is this Wilhelmina Pasternak?"

"Yes. Who's this?"

"This is Ernest Lasalle, attorney at law. I represent Zane Klausen, who I believe you know."

Willie frowned. "Can't say that I—oh, Zippy's son."

"Yes, ma'am, that's correct."

Willie straightened. Calls from lawyers were rarely good news. Especially when that lawyer was representing the son of the man she'd just inherited millions of dollars from. "What's this about?"

"My client believes you may have been privy to the creation process of two tricks his father invented during the time you were married, specifically, The Vanishing Waterfall and Electra's Revenge."

The lawyer could have linked any combination of words and it would have made as much sense as those did. Willie frowned as he went on.

"Zane is a magician himself, you see. You may have heard of him. He goes by the stage name of

Zane Steele, Illusionist. He's about to launch his own show."

"Good for him. His father would be proud. Can't say that I've heard of him, but I haven't been out to Vegas since Zippy and I split up."

"Be that as it may, Zane would like for you to sign an NDA concerning—"

"An indie what?"

"An NDA. A non-disclosure agreement."

"I see." She really didn't. "Go on."

"He'd like you to sign this NDA stating that you will not reveal the secrets of those tricks, share information about how they're done, or what creates the illusions involved or, furthermore, disclose the mechanics of how they work. He'd like for you to disavow all knowledge of them."

She already had no idea what he was talking about. But a new idea occurred to her. "Zane was pretty well taken care of when his father passed, wasn't he?"

"If this is about money—"

"It's not, so keep your britches on. But he's fixed all right, isn't he?" She hated to think that she'd got the bulk of Zippy's estate.

"He's very well off, yes."

"Do you know how much I got?"

The lawyer cleared his throat softly. "I do, yes."

"Did Zane get more?"

"He did. But that's all I can say."

"That's all right. That's all I wanted to know."

"So you don't want payment in exchange for signing the NDA?"

"Don't be silly. I was that boy's stepmother, even if it was in name only. I don't want money from him." She grinned. "But I would like two tickets to his show. Good seats. I'm old. I can't see if I'm too far back."

The lawyer exhaled. "I can make that happen. You realize that show won't be live for another month or so."

"That's fine. My social calendar's pretty full this month anyway. So you get me those tickets and send that indie thing and I'll sign it."

"Thank you, Ms. Pasternak. I'll have that overnighted to you."

"Great. You tell Zane I look forward to seeing him on stage." After the lawyer confirmed her mailing address, she hung up, smiling.

Vegas might not be Puerto Rico but would still be a nice trip. And who didn't love a little magic?

Chapter Five

*S*ix hundred thousand dollars. Just thinking about the amount made it easier to breathe. Claire sipped the water Danny had brought her while she waited for him to get his laptop and come back to the table.

"Here we go," he said as he returned. He put the laptop down first then sat beside her.

He tapped a few keys, ran his finger over the touchpad, then brought up the spreadsheet he'd been telling her about. "This shows our initial outlay and where that money will be going. It's not a small amount, as you can see, but we talked to the bank last year. It should be no problem to secure the financing."

"Well, I want to be a part of it. As much as I can be with the money I'm about to get. Obviously, I can't invest all of it, because I need something to live on until I start taking a salary but there has to be some amount I can put in."

"You can put in whatever you feel comfortable with, but you don't really need to supply that much cash. Actually, if you have that money in the bank, we could easily add you to the loan application. If you're comfortable with that. It would mean you'd really and truly be one of the owners. But it would also mean you'd be on the hook for any debts."

Was this really something she wanted to do? Yes. Even if it was a lot of responsibility. She nodded. "I want to be as much of a partner in this as I can be. As much as you'll let me. It's your business. Your idea. I know that. Just like I know it wouldn't be happening without you and your dad."

He smiled. "That might be true, but I fully believe your ideas, your recipes, and your skills are what's going to make this place succeed. If you want to be a part of this, then I want to make that happen. It only seems fair."

"So all I'd have to do is put the money in the bank?"

"Basically, yes. You'll have to fill out all of the loan paperwork, too, which is more than you could possibly believe, but it's a small price to pay for letting the bank do the heavy financial lifting."

"Okay," she said softly. "I want to do this."

"Then we'll make it happen. How soon will you have the money?"

"I'm not actually sure. Soon, I hope." She should have asked Kinnerman that. She made a mental note to call him again when she got home. "Thank you for letting me be a part of this."

He laughed. "You don't have to thank me. It wouldn't be happening if you hadn't made me believe it was possible. Are you working on anything new?"

She smiled. "I'm about to. What's your favorite cookie?"

"That's a tough one, because you know I have a sweet tooth and I pretty much like them all. But if I really had to pick one, I'd go with the classic sugar cookie. You can't go wrong with that. Not when it's made right."

"And that's the trick," Claire said. "When you have such a simple cookie as that, everything has to be perfect in order for it to be better than just okay."

He tilted his head like he was trying to see her better. "What are you working on?"

She laughed. "I'm not telling you yet. I want to see if I can make it happen first. But you'll be one of the first to know, I promise. Will you be home the rest of the day?"

"No, sorry. I have to stop by the new bakery to talk to Ethan about the fit out and then I'm off to the store to help out there for a while."

"The fit out?"

He nodded. "Basically what it needs to look like inside. We're using the same colors as the Mrs. Butter's stores of black, white, and yellow, but adding bright pink. You okay with that?"

"Sounds great."

"Good. I'll show you the mockup for the sign we received from our regular sign people when I get home tonight, which should be by five or six. My dad is going to that play tonight with Willie and your mom."

"Right," Claire said. "I heard something about that."

Danny's smile went slightly mysterious. "Means I'll be home alone. You want to come over and have dinner? We could sit out by the firepit. Maybe take a walk on the beach."

"I'd love to. What are you making?" A night with him sounded perfect, no matter what they did.

"Nothing." He chuckled. "I plan on picking something up on the way home. How do you feel about Indian? Or Chinese? Or is there something else you'd prefer?"

"I like them both, but I'd love some butter chicken. I haven't had that in quite a while." Bryan had never really liked Indian cuisine, so it was a rare occasion when she got to enjoy it.

His brows lifted. "Yeah? I didn't think you'd go for Indian. I am pleasantly surprised. And clearly, I need to stop assuming I know what you're going to like and not like. Butter chicken it is. I'll be sure to get some naan, too."

She let out a soft, happy moan. "I love naan. I shouldn't have the carbs, but boy, is it delicious."

"Does that mean you don't want it?"

She snorted. "No, I do. But we'd better go for that walk on the beach. I'll have to burn it off."

"You got it."

She got up. "I'll see you tonight then. Possibly with dessert."

He stood, putting them face to face. "I'm looking forward to it." He leaned in and kissed her. "I am so glad you came into my life. For all sorts of reasons."

She could only smile as her cheeks warmed. "Me, too, you. See you tonight."

"Tonight." He walked with her to the door, opening it for her. "Hey, do you have enough popcorn, or do you need me to bring you some more?"

She thought a moment. She'd be using up more of it today. "I'll take a medium bag each of regular and kettle."

"You got it."

"Thanks." She wiggled her fingers at him. "Bye."

She went straight back to her kitchen and started pulling ingredients. She set out two sticks of butter to come to room temperature, then went to her bedroom to change into a T-shirt she wouldn't mind getting spilled on.

Baking wasn't always the cleanest of activities, even with an apron.

She used her standard sugar cookie recipe, which was the best one she knew and the same one she used for decorated cookies at Christmas. But she planned on making two variations: one with crushed kettle corn mixed in, and a second with a buttered popcorn-infused icing.

She had no clue if either one would work, but that was the whole point of experimenting.

After tying on an apron, she set the oven temperature and got to work. She had to infuse the milk that would go into the icing first so that it would have time to cool. She had doubts about how much flavor she'd be able to impart to such a small amount of milk, but she could only try.

She started by creaming the sugar and butter together. Doing that right was key. Then she added in the flour. As she was getting ready to fold in the popcorn, which she'd smashed up a bit to get smaller pieces, a new idea came to her.

She divided the dough into two portions, then went back to the pantry and dug around. She found what she was looking for. Toffee bits. She was hoping they'd give a caramel flavor to one batch of cookies. Combined with the popcorn, it should make the cookie taste like caramel corn.

The island where she was working was slowly becoming a scene of organized chaos, but she plowed on, happily working through the mess. She'd get everything cleaned up as soon as the cookies went into the oven.

That took about twenty minutes. And made her realize that if she needed anything from the house in Landry, it was the rest of her baking supplies.

There was no denying it. She was going to have to go back there. And soon.

Chapter Six

Kat's outfit of the green top with the tan pantsuit looked better than she'd anticipated, which pleased her. She'd take every opportunity to gather some extra confidence. She borrowed her grandmother's chunky gold necklace again, like she had to go job hunting the first time, wearing it with the same small gold hoops.

Her nicest shoes were sandals and even though they seemed awfully casual, this was Florida. Sandals were pretty standard. And her toes looked good, thanks to the recent pedicure she'd had.

If Future Florida didn't hire her because she wore open-toed shoes to the interview, that was on them, not her.

Although she really, *really* wanted this job and she hoped her shoe selection wouldn't carry that much weight.

She said goodbye to her mom, who was preoccupied in the kitchen, which smelled amazing, and went down to her car.

She got in, turned on the engine, cranked the AC and immediately decided to take her jacket off until she got to the office. She hopped out and took it off. No sense in sweating in it or getting it creased. She laid it carefully on the backseat, wishing she'd brought a hanger.

As she got back behind the wheel and put her seatbelt on, her phone buzzed. She checked the screen, praying Future Florida hadn't changed their mind.

But then she saw the message sender and smiled. Alex had texted.

Good luck! You're going to get it. I know you are. Text me later, k?

I will, she sent back. *And I hope you're right.*

She leaned her head back against the head rest, letting the cool air coming out of the vents blow over her. What would she do if she didn't get this job? She'd have to find something. But she couldn't think like that. Not today.

She threw the car into reverse, backed up and turned around, making herself focus on positive thoughts the whole drive there.

Somehow the trip to the Future Florida office was both too long and too short. She glanced at herself in the visor mirror to make sure she hadn't suddenly ended up with something in her teeth, then got out, put her jacket back on and walked confidently to the door.

She stepped inside with a smile on her face that she hoped hid the nerves coursing through her.

The woman behind the reception desk glanced up. "Hello. Can I help you?"

"Kat Thompson. I have an interview?"

The woman looked at her computer and nodded. "Just a moment. I'll let them know you're here." She picked up a phone, pressed a button, and said, "Kat Thompson has arrived." Then she nodded. "Will do."

She hung up and got to her feet. "If you'll follow me."

Kat did just that, walking with the woman through the door in the wall behind her desk. It led to a cool, dark corridor and then a conference room with a long wooden table and leather desk chairs.

A man and woman were seated there, but they got up as the receptionist and Kat came in. They both smiled at her.

The man nodded at the receptionist. "Thank you, Marlene."

Marlene left. Kat stayed by the door.

The man gestured to the woman beside him. "This is Molly Hargrove and I'm Tom Phillips. We're on the board of Future Florida and we're very excited to meet you, Kat."

Kat reminded herself to breathe. "Nice to meet you both as well."

He pointed to one of the empty chairs. "Won't you have a seat?"

"Thanks." She took a chair on the opposite side of the table from him. Molly was seated at the head. They both sat down.

Molly opened the folder in front of her. "You have an impressive resume and a skill set that interests us. What made you look at Future Florida for job opportunities?"

Kat had already decided she wasn't going to try to give them the answers she thought they wanted. She was going to speak from the heart and tell the truth. That was how she planned to live her life going forward, so she might as well start now. "There's been a lot of change in my life recently."

Tom shifted in his chair. "Can you elaborate on that?"

"Sure," Kat said. "My father passed away unexpectedly."

"I'm very sorry," Molly said.

Tom nodded. "That had to be hard."

"It was and thank you. But what was harder was what happened afterwards." She studied the table's wood grain as she gathered her thoughts. Then she looked up again. "My mom and I found out that my father had a second family. A second wife. A second daughter. It was...quite a surprise."

Tom and Molly showed their own shock in their raised brows and widened eyes. Molly swallowed. "I can't imagine."

"It's definitely been interesting." Kat let out a soft laugh that didn't hold much humor. "There have been some other things that happened." She thought about Ray and his cheating. And about Alex and the crew at the fire station. "But all of those things combined gave me a lot to think about concerning my life, what I was doing with it, and who I want to be."

She glanced away for a moment before making eye contact again. "I realized I want to be someone different. I want to do something different with my life. I want to help people. Not in the way I help people now as an actuary, but really help people. I want to make a difference. Someone at another charity organization told me about Future Florida and it sounded like the perfect kind of place."

Tom and Molly smiled. Tom spoke. "We do specialize in helping people."

"And in so many different ways," Kat said. "Reading up on the foundation's history has only solidified my desire to be a part of it. In whatever way I can be."

She leaned forward. "What you guys do here is amazing. It's life-changing stuff. You give people the chance to overcome the biggest obstacles in their lives, obstacles they might never overcome otherwise. Who wouldn't want to be a part of that?"

Still smiling, Tom and Molly looked at each other. Molly tapped her pen on the table. "We would certainly agree with that statement." She looked at Kat's resume again. "Have you already left your current job?"

"Not officially, no. I'm on compassionate leave right now, but I'm prepared to put in my notice immediately. It's been a good job and I like the people I work with well enough, but it's not where my heart is. Not anymore."

Tom's eyes narrowed. "You live in Landry, though, don't you?"

"I did. I'm in the process of relocating here to Diamond Beach with my mom. It's all part of us getting a fresh start. And housing isn't an issue, as my father left me half of the family beach house."

"Half?" Tom asked. "Who got the other half?"

"My half-sister," Kat answered. "Which is pretty appropriate." She smiled. "Thankfully, Trina and I are getting along pretty well. I was an only child all my life. It's sort of nice to discover that's no longer the case."

She realized how much she meant those words as she was speaking them. Trina had really given Kat some new ways of looking at things.

Molly spoke next. "It would be two weeks before you could start then? Or longer?"

"Actually, it would be sooner. I have enough vacation days built up that I won't need to return to work at all. I'll need a little time to finish the move, but certainly not two weeks."

"Good to know," Molly said.

They asked her a few more questions, about her strengths and weaknesses, those sorts of things, then seemed to be nearing the end of the interview.

Tom flattened his hands on the table. "Before we wrap up, do you have any questions for us?"

"What sort of jobs do you have available?" Kat

asked. That was something that hadn't come up yet. "And as much as I hate to bring up money, what kind of salaries are you offering? I need to know that I'll be able to pay my bills. You know how it is."

Molly nodded. "Of course. Reasonable questions. Although I'm not sure we're ready to answer the one about the job just yet, as there are several vacancies we're trying to fill. Salaries would, of course, be appropriate for the position. We are a non-profit, obviously, but we also understand the need to, as you said, pay bills. And we like to think we're competitive. We don't want to hire someone, get them trained, and then lose them a few months later to a better offer. We do our best to take care of our team members in such a way that we retain them for a long time."

Tom leaned his arms on the table. "Give us a little time to confer with the rest of the board and we'll be in touch."

Kat had gone from feeling like things were going well to being completely unsure where she stood. Maybe she shouldn't have brought up the money. Maybe that had been the totally wrong thing to say.

But it was kind of an important part of the decision. At least to her.

All she could do was nod, hold her smile in place, and pretend her mood hadn't dropped like a stone in a pond. Somehow, she'd screwed up. "Okay. Sounds good. I look forward to hearing from you."

Chapter Seven

$\mathcal{A}$s Willie and Trina finished up at the counter, Roxie and Ethan stood a little ways back, talking. "Are you headed to the shopping center after this?" she asked him.

Ethan nodded. "I am. Lots to do. Need to make sure the crew is staying on schedule with the salon. I have a second, smaller crew working on the two middle units, just getting them cleaned up and presentable. Plus, I'm meeting with Danny at the bakery to go over a few things so we can get them moving forward, too."

"Wow, you're busy."

He smiled. "It's the only way to be. Also, the faster we work, the sooner everything can be open and operational, and the sooner tenants will be paying rent."

"True." She couldn't argue that. Not when she

wanted the place to be a huge success. Not just Trina's salon, but the whole shopping center. She didn't want her mother sinking her money into a business that ended up failing, for all of their sakes. But Roxie was starting to feel the itch of inactivity.

She needed something to do. "Is there anything I could do to help?"

He shook his head slowly, like he was thinking. "Just make sure all the selections are made for the salon. We still need sinks and faucets. The back room is going to need a sturdy washer and dryer. Then there's all the other stuff you need for a salon. Chairs. Mats for the stylists to stand on. I'm sure Trina knows. But it should be picked out and ordered pretty soon. You never know how long it'll take to get some of those things in. Oh, signage, too."

"We're working on a lot of that already," she said. "But I'll make sure it all gets done." Wasn't really the answer she'd been looking for. She'd wanted something more physical to do. But she supposed it would have to do for now.

"I'd ask if you want to have dinner tonight, but my evening is already spoken for."

"So is mine. I'm going with my mom to see a play at the seniors center tonight."

He laughed. "*Arsenic and Old Lace*?"

"Yeah. How did you know?"

"Because my mother is playing Martha Brewster, one of the old ladies."

Roxie grinned. "So you'll be there? Maybe we can sit together."

"Please, let's," he said. "I really don't want to be there alone."

"Then it's a date."

Willie and Trina approached. Willie waved the yellow duplicate receipt. "All ordered."

"Good," Roxie said. "Because we have a lot more to order."

Trina nodded. "I know. I've been thinking about that and doing a lot of looking online. I've got all kinds of lists made."

"Well, let's finalize some of those decisions today."

Ethan smiled knowingly. "Roxie's right. The sooner you can get things ordered, the better. There's plenty of room in the salon to store anything that comes in." He glanced at Willie. "Did they say when the light fixtures would be in?"

She nodded and looked at the receipt, but Trina answered. "Two to three days, maybe sooner depending on what's in the warehouse. How soon do you think the back room will be done? I found a commercial washer and dryer that should work but I want to get measurements to be sure."

"I can make sure it's done sooner than anything else. We're going to need a laundry sink in there, as well. I've already ordered a shelving unit." Ethan glanced at the time on his phone. "I need to get over to the center anyway. Why don't you guys head over there, too, then you can see the progress that's been made and get your measurements."

Trina sighed. "I didn't think to bring a tape measure."

"Don't worry," Ethan said. "I have one in my truck."

"All right," Roxie said. "To the center we go."

She drove again, staying right behind Ethan's truck. "Ethan's going to be at the play tonight. His mom is in it. She's one of the old ladies who's poisoning people."

"People get poisoned?" Trina looked surprised.

Willie laughed. "It's got 'arsenic' in the title, my girl. What did you think they were going to do with that?"

"I don't know," Trina said. "I guess I should have watched the movie."

"You should anyway," Willie said.

Roxie nodded. "Cary Grant is in it, which should be all the recommendation you need."

"Ah, yes." Willie sighed. "He was really something, wasn't he? I think Miguel looks like Cary Grant a little. If Cary Grant had been from Puerto Rico."

Trina giggled. "Didn't you say that about one of your husbands?"

"What can I say?" Willie shrugged. "I have a type."

Roxie parked next to Ethan, and they all walked toward the salon.

He opened the door for them, gave a nod to the men working inside, then handed Trina his tape measure. "I have to meet Danny at the bakery, but I shouldn't be too long. I'll come back when I'm through."

"Thanks," Roxie said.

She headed in with her mom and daughter. "Sure looks a lot cleaner in here. And brighter."

"The white paint helps a lot," Willie said. "Where is the pink paint going?"

Trina scrunched her mouth to one side. "I was thinking on both of these walls." She pointed to the sides of the salon where the mirrors and chairs would be. "But now I'm thinking maybe the white is better. Maybe I'll keep the bright pink in the shampoo area and let this front part stay more neutral. That would probably be classier."

"Maybe." Roxie nodded. "You know what else I just realized? We need a reception desk and chairs for people who are waiting. A coffee table in the center. Some shelving units for the retail products, too." She blew out a breath. "We have so much to do."

"Ma," Trina said. "I've got this. I've looked at all of that online already. I just need to make some final decisions."

"Really?" Roxie laughed. "You're so much more on top of this than I realized. I should have given you more credit."

"It's okay," Trina said. "None of us have ever done anything like this before. It's good that you're thinking about that stuff. You never know what I might forget."

"True." But Roxie didn't change her mind about what she'd said. Trina was definitely handling this better than Roxie had expected her to, but then, this had been Trina's dream for a while. She should have known her daughter would be capable of getting it done.

A lot of people underestimated Trina because

she was happy and bubbly. For some reason, people equated that with being not so bright. But that was a dumb move itself. Happiness didn't mean a low IQ. If anything, being happy probably made you smarter.

Maybe not Roxie, but Trina? For sure.

Trina tipped her head toward the back room. "Come on. You want to help me measure? Mimi, you can jot the measurements down, okay?"

"You got it." Willie dug in her fanny pack and produced a little notebook and a pen. "Ready."

With a little chuckle, Roxie followed her daughter to help. She would be very happy to work here, even if all she did was sit at reception and take care of clients. Trina was going to be a woman to be reckoned with, Roxie could feel it in her bones.

They got their measurements done, talked more about the wallpaper and paint choice, then studied the ceiling where the new lights would go. Which was when they realized they wanted one more lighting fixture: a sparkly chandelier for the reception area.

About that time, Ethan returned. "How's it going? Did you get what you need?"

Trina handed the tape measure back to him. "The washer and dryer will fit. I'll order them this afternoon. But we're going to need another light." She pointed toward the front. "For reception. We'll go back to the lighting store and add one to the order."

"Okay," Ethan said. "I got a call from the paint store. Everything will be delivered tomorrow. I'm going to have the guys cover the floor, but just so you know, before you open, I'll have this floor cleaned and polished. It'll look like brand new."

Trina smiled. "I can't wait."

"Do you want to go over with me where you want the wallpaper?" Ethan asked. "Same with the paint. I need to know what colors are going where."

"Here's what I was thinking," Trina started as she walked with Ethan toward the back of the shop.

Roxie stayed where she was, smiling as she watched her daughter work. It was a proud moment, seeing her daughter take charge. So sure of herself. Like she'd been opening salons all her life.

Ethan glanced back and caught Roxie's eye. He smiled like he knew what she was thinking and feeling. Maybe he did. He had a daughter of his own.

Roxie felt certain she'd never forget this day. The day she knew that no matter what else happened in life, her child was going to be okay.

Chapter Eight

Margo listened as Conrad read back the last few paragraphs. He had such a nice speaking voice and when he read, he seemed to know exactly where to put the emphasis and inflection in the words. Of course, it probably helped that he'd co-written those words. She nodded. "It reads well. And I think it flows nicely. I like that a lot."

"So do I. We've earned a break, don't you think? A little snack, maybe? At least a fresh pot of coffee and some cake. I picked up a nice apple crumb from Publix on my shopping trip last night."

She smiled. "Writing this book with you is going to make me fat."

He looked over her figure. "More of you wouldn't bother me in the slightest."

"Conrad!" But she laughed and shook her head.

He could be incorrigible sometimes. Still charming, even if he was a little naughty.

He grinned, obviously pleased with himself. "Come on. Just a small piece."

"All right." She was a little peckish. They'd ordered in salads for lunch from the pizza place in town and they'd been delicious, but salad, even with chicken on it, only went so far. "But we should talk through the next few chapters while we have our break."

He got up. "You're quite the taskmaster."

"One of us has to keep this project on track."

He saluted her, eyes glittering with amusement. "Yes, ma'am." Then he snorted. "How about that. I might actually like being bossed around by a woman. At least if that woman is you."

She pursed her lips. "That's going to make things a lot easier."

He laughed out loud. "I guess it will." He started for the kitchen. "Coffee and cake and brainstorming, coming up."

She followed him and took over the coffee making while he got the cake out, along with some cups and plates. "I have a little news to share with you."

"Oh? What's that?"

She glanced over at him. He was getting a knife out of the drawer. "I've decided to sell my place in Landry and buy something here."

He stopped what he was doing to look at her. "You mean that?"

She nodded. "I do. I'm staying. We all are and I want to be near my family."

"I'm not trying to influence your decision, but there's about to be a house for sale in this neighborhood."

She smiled. "That actually does sound like you're trying to influence my decision, but I don't mind. I like this neighborhood. And being close to you would be a bonus. I'm not ready to buy just yet, though. I have to sell my place first."

"This house isn't up for sale yet. The owners are Sal and Mirna Clarke and I know for a fact that they're planning to move to Georgia soon to be near their daughter and grandkids. It's a nice house. Nothing too big, maybe twelve hundred square feet. But it has three bedrooms, two baths, two-car garage, nice landscaping. Small pool but big enough to swim laps in. Might need a little updating here or there, but if you talked to them and did a deal without a realtor, they might give you a better price."

Margo pushed the button to get the coffee

brewing. "That's an interesting thought. I'm just in the very early stages of all of this. I don't even have my car here. I have to take care of moving everything, although I really have no place to put it."

She considered that. "I suppose I might have to get a storage unit for a couple months."

"Do you have a lot of things?"

"I have a houseful. Not a tremendous amount that I'm attached to, but I have a few pieces that are dear to me. And honestly, it makes no sense to buy new at my age. For financial reasons as well as practical ones."

"Right, I get that. But you don't have to do all that alone, you know. I can help."

"That's a lot to ask, Conrad."

He shook his head. "No, it isn't. What kind of boyfriend would I be if I didn't lend a hand on something like that?"

She couldn't help but smile. "Is that what you are? My boyfriend?"

He straightened ever so slightly. "Well, aren't I?"

"I don't know." She hadn't expected this conversation. "Are you? Do you want to be?"

"Haven't I made that clear?" His brow furrowed. "I like you a lot, Margo. You already know that. I can't see myself with anyone else. And if you're moving here, then I see great things ahead for us."

"I haven't been anyone's girlfriend in a very long time." Her heart beat just a little faster at the idea.

"So you're out of practice then? Good to know." His eyes narrowed like he was taking that into consideration. "I suppose I can give you a couple weeks' probationary period, see how you do."

She sharpened her look. The rascal. "A probationary period? I should go home right now, except I didn't drive."

He chuckled and came closer, taking her in his arms. "I do enjoy when you get your back up. Why is that so sexy?"

"You're terrible." She did her best not to smile as she drifted into his embrace.

"I really am. I need a good woman in my life to straighten me out, don't you think?"

"You do." She nodded but he kissed her right in the middle of it. She hadn't gotten used to the kissing. It still felt fresh and new and set all sorts of things alight in her.

When he broke away, he touched her cheek. "What do you think about going over to see the Clarkes and their house? I could call them."

"I wouldn't want to impose."

"I'll set it up for tomorrow then. How's that?"

She'd be a fool not to. Getting a deal on a house in this market would be something. And being near Conrad was a bonus she hadn't expected. "All right. Tomorrow. But please let them know I'm not quite ready to buy. That I have to sell my own place and figure all of the moving logistics out."

"I will."

Behind her, the coffeemaker sputtered out a few more drops. She patted his chest. "Coffee is ready. We should get our cake and get back to work."

"We should. We have that book signing coming up after all."

She rolled her eyes as she turned to get the carafe. *Girlfriend.* She repeated the word in her mind a few times. Was that what she was now? It sounded so strange. She'd been someone's wife for a good portion of her life. She'd been a widow for about as long.

"Girlfriend" wasn't a label she'd ever thought she'd wear again. It felt like something that belonged on a younger person. Someone with more years left.

But she was going to wear it all the same, because if Conrad the former Marine could be her boyfriend, then she could return the favor and be his girlfriend.

They took their coffee and cake to the kitchen table and used their break to talk about the next chapter of the book, the red herring they were setting up, and how they saw it playing out based on the clues they'd laid.

With every word, Margo's confidence that they'd finish the book grew. She knew there was still a possibility that it might not happen, but they were both determined. And that meant a great deal.

Not only that, but the more she talked with Conrad, the more time she spent with him, the more she was convinced there wasn't anything he couldn't do.

After all, he'd gotten her back into the world. Gotten her to write a book. And now she was going to move to a different city, in part because of her daughter and granddaughter, but she'd be lying if she said Conrad hadn't influenced that decision.

Finishing the book with him ought to be a piece of cake.

Chapter Nine

*I*f Trina had laid down for more than two minutes, she would have fallen asleep. As it was, she was thinking about crashing on the couch right where she was. Making decisions, big decisions like the ones she'd been making all day, was exhausting. She still had things to print out and file in her binder, but she didn't have a printer.

They really needed to sort out some stuff if they were staying here in Diamond Beach. There were things back at the house in Port St. Rosa that she needed. Although their printer wasn't so hot. It didn't work more often than it did.

She sighed, her brain aching from all the hard thinking she'd done. There was so much to remember. Good thing she had her lists and her binder.

"What's wrong?" her grandmother asked from

her chair. She was paging through a gossip magazine. "You sound like something's wrong."

Trina shook her head. "Everything's great. Just a little worn out, is all. If we didn't have that play tonight, I'd probably take a nap."

Her grandmother looked at the time. "You still could. A little one."

Trina laughed. "I'm afraid if I lay down, I won't get back up until it's time to go to bed for real." Then she held up a finger. "But we do need to have a little chat about what we're doing."

"In what way?"

"In the way that we're staying here. How are we going to get our stuff moved? Are we selling the other house? Ma's car is still back in Port St. Rosa. She's going to need that."

Her mother was currently at the pool, swimming laps before it was time to get ready for the play.

"Right," Mimi said. "Those are all good questions. Is there much you need or want from the house? Besides your clothing and such."

Trina thought about that. "I don't know. A lot of our stuff is kind of worn. Most of it was secondhand to begin with. So maybe not. Other than the stuff you mentioned, my clothes and shoes and accessories. There are a few things. The photo albums. A couple of keepsakes. But there's a lot I could leave behind, too."

Her bed in that house was a twin that she'd slept on since she was maybe eight or nine. Her bed here was so much nicer it wasn't even a competition.

"Then it shouldn't be too hard to sort out," Mimi said. "Maybe your mom and I can go back and take care of that while you stay here and deal with getting the salon open."

"But then I won't have a car."

"Your car will stay here. I'll rent us one and we'll drop it off when we get there. We'll have your mom's, like you said."

"Yeah, I suppose that would work. But there is something else I need."

"What's that, sweetness?"

"A printer. I know everything's supposed to be paperless and all that, but I like having paper copies of things. It's easier to keep straight. At least to me it is."

Mimi nodded. "I agree with you. I'm the same way. Where can we get a printer? Is there a place in town?"

"There's a Walmart. We can get one there."

Her grandmother dug around in her fanny pack and pulled out a credit card. "Here. Go get whatever you need. And pick me up a bag of Twizzlers, will you? I want them for the play tonight."

Trina smiled as she took the card. "You don't think they'll give me any grief about this not being my card?"

Her grandmother frowned. "If you go through the self-checkout lane, you could be an albino gorilla and they wouldn't say boo."

"I suppose that's true." Trina got up and went into the bedroom to grab her purse. She came back to the living room. "I'll check in with Ma before I go and make sure there's nothing else we need."

"Good girl."

Trina took the steps down to the ground floor and walked over to the pool. Her mom was just getting out. "Hey, I'm headed to Walmart to get Twizzlers for Mimi and a printer so I can print out some of the salon stuff."

"Don't forget a cable," her mother said.

Trina nodded. "I'm going to get a wireless one. You need anything? Or do we need anything for the house?"

Roxie grabbed her towel and started to dry off. "We could use eggs. If you feel like getting them."

"Sure, I'll pick some up. It'll be a quick trip, because then I have to get ready for the play, although I'm not dressing up too much." Trina glanced down at what she had on. "Probably not much fancier than this."

Her mother nodded. "Same. Although now that I know Ethan's going to be there, I want to look nice. Hey, have you talked to Miles lately?"

"I texted with him a bit at lunch."

"Did you invite him to the play?"

"No, he's on shift tonight. I told him how things were going and that we're staying here and all that." She smiled. "He was happy we're staying."

Her mom smiled, too. "I bet he is. His girlfriend is about to be a major businesswoman."

"Ma, I don't know about all that."

Her mom walked over. "Trina, you are going to be the best, most sought-after hair stylist in this town. Your shop is going to be the number one place to get your hair done. People will be on a waiting list to see you. Mark my words. You have what it takes."

Even though her mom was still wet from the pool, Trina hugged her. "Thanks, Ma. That means a lot to me."

Her mom hugged her back, laughing. "You're going to get all wet!"

Trina shrugged as she let her mom go. "It's Walmart. No one's going to care."

"True. See you when you get back. I'm going up to shower."

"See you later." Trina was true to her word and made the shopping trip as quick as possible, which wasn't hard to do, since she was only getting a few things. One last-minute item was a three-hole punch, but that was going to help her stay organized, so she considered it a business expense, too.

Buying the printer was a little harder. She had to look at what they had, then make a decision as to which one would best serve her needs without costing an arm and a leg. At least she didn't need color. That might save her some money.

In the end, she picked the third from the cheapest, which had color anyway. She also got a cable, since it was an option and she knew the wireless connection could get disconnected pretty easily. She'd hooked up their last printer, so she figured she'd be able to manage this one, too. She snagged a large bag of Twizzlers, a carton of eggs, and a Peppermint Patty for herself as a treat.

It had been a long, intense day. A little mint and chocolate would be just the thing. But then she saw a box of Junior Mints and grabbed them. Those she could take with her to the play. The Peppermint

Patty she'd stick in the fridge for the next long, intense day.

She went through self-checkout and, just like Mimi had predicted, there wasn't a single bit of fuss over using her grandmother's card. That bothered Trina a little. It meant there were shady people out there probably getting away with stuff they shouldn't.

But then, that was part of life, wasn't it? An unfortunate part, but a part all the same. She carried her things out to the car and headed home.

She took the elevator up, which was sort of lazy, but her arms were full. Back in the house, her mom was now sitting with her grandmother in the living room. Roxie was in her robe, hair wrapped up in a towel. Mimi was in her light blue track suit that had a rhinestone zipper. Her eyeshadow was light blue to match.

"I'm back," Trina announced.

"That was quick," her mom said. "You need help with anything?"

"Nope. I'm going to set up this printer, print a few things out so I can keep myself organized, then get ready for the play."

"You've got time," Mimi said. "In fact, we should

all have a little something to eat before we go. Some cheese and crackers, maybe?"

"Sounds good," Roxie said. "I'll put a plate together." She got up and went into the kitchen, which was a good bit smaller than the one upstairs, but it served their purposes. And while the kitchen was smaller, the living room area was bigger, with a big, comfy sofa and nice side chairs and a long, low coffee table that they often used as their dining table. Dinner and a movie was a big thing for them.

They had a much bigger enclosed deck, too, which also made a great place to eat. Perfect views of the beach and water were easy to see from the outdoor dining area or the seating area.

Trina got her printer set up in the corner of the living room using the box as a stand. She had it operational after the second try. That seemed like some kind of record to her. Printers were notoriously tricky. At least she thought so.

She carefully went through all the purchases they'd made today and printed out the invoices, making a note of the costs, then punching holes in each one and filing them in the proper section of her binder.

When she'd done the last one, she added up the

expenses. She blinked at the amount the calculator app on her phone was showing.

Was that right?

She went back through the invoices and totaled them up again. The number was the same. And just as hard to believe. The fact that it didn't include the printer or the hole punch only made it worse.

Her mom came over with a plate of cheese, some sliced summer sausage, grapes, and another plate of crackers. "Here you go. Who wants what to drink?"

Trina looked at her grandmother. "Mimi?"

Her grandmother was sticking a piece of cheddar on a Ritz. "What's that, sweetness?"

Trina swallowed. "We spent a lot of money today."

"I'm sure we did. We ordered a bunch of lights, paint, wallpaper, six client chairs, some shelving units...something else, right?"

Trina nodded. "A washer and dryer, three new sinks, work mats, and six mirrors." Beautiful, baroque gilt mirrors that would add the nicest touch of glamor at each workstation. They should, too, for what they cost. Maybe they'd been too much of a splurge. Trina sucked in air.

Her grandmother's brows bent. "What's wrong? You look a little green around the gills."

"We spent almost twenty-three thousand dollars."

Her grandmother nodded. "Sounds about right."

"Don't you think that's...a lot?"

Her grandmother took a bite of the cheese and cracker, then shook her head as she chewed. After a moment, she spoke. "You're opening a new salon. It needs to be nice. It needs to look like money so women don't have any trouble spending money there. We're going to spend more, too. We haven't even started on product, yet."

Trina took a breath and looked at her laptop. That was true. Maybe she'd look for a less expensive line than what she'd been considering.

"Nope," Mimi said.

She looked at her grandmother again. "Nope what?"

"Whatever you're thinking about cheaping out on, don't. You buy exactly what you want, you hear me?"

"But Mimi—"

"I mean it, Katrina."

Trina smiled. Her grandmother only used her full name when she meant serious business, which wasn't often. "Okay, Mimi. Whatever you say."

Chapter Ten

*J*ules strummed the last few notes of the outro. As the sound died away, she finally looked at her tablet again, where her agent, Billy Grimm, was her audience of one via video chat. "And that's *Dixie's Got Her Boots On*."

Billy, who was sometimes called Wild Bill because of his long salt-and-pepper goatee and bushy eyebrows, sat staring through the screen, eyes narrowed behind his oval wire-rimmed glasses. "I've never heard you do anything like that."

She nodded, a twinge of trepidation creeping into her belly. "I know, I know. It's really different for me." She glanced down at the strings of her guitar. "Maybe I should just sell the song."

"You will not."

She looked up again.

"It might not be something you've done before but that doesn't mean you can't do it now. And now is exactly the right time." He pointed at her through the screen. "There's a place in the market for this. It's new and fresh but it's exactly what's starting to rise up in country at the moment."

Jules smiled. "That's what my son said. I guess I should be listening to more current music, because that was news to me."

"It's flipping brilliant is what it is." He grinned, his mustache hiding most of his upper lip, and rubbed his hands together. "Jules, this is going to be big for you. I mean *big*. How soon can you cut a demo?"

"You want to release this as a single?"

He nodded. "I do. We'll still put it on the album, of course, but we need to get this out soon. Create some buzz and get people talking. That alone will raise the sales of your catalog. So how soon can you get it recorded?"

In Landry, she had a recording studio in her house. Here, she had nothing. She stalled for time. "I'm still polishing. And I still need to put the backups together. This is really new, Billy. You're only the second person to have heard it."

"Well, do whatever you need to do but get it

done. You're sitting on something that could potentially be a career-changer."

"You really believe in it that much?" He hadn't been this keen about her work in a while. Always complimentary, but this was new.

"I do. But that's because of how much I believe in you. You've always been good, Jules. Solid as they come. But you've never had the kind of breakout you deserve." He tapped the desk in front of him. "This is that song."

A shiver went through her, a good one. Billy had never been wrong before. She nodded. "I'll see what I can do to get it recorded."

"Good. Then you get it to me, and we'll get it released. I hope you're working on the rest of the songs for this album, because I'd like to get that out as soon as we can, too."

She had a few ideas for other songs, but nothing she'd gotten serious about. Obviously, the time to do that was now. "I'm...working." Not as much as she should be, but that would change today.

"That's what I want to hear. Keep in touch, now."

"I will. Thanks, Billy. Bye." She tapped the screen to end the call and sat back.

Cash had gone to the beach for a little while and taken Toby with him. She'd promised to come down as soon as the call was over. Cash would want to be in the water, and he couldn't do that while he was watching Toby.

She left her guitar on the couch and went down the outside steps to the second floor, so she could change into shorts and a tank top, her mind swirling with all she needed to do. Not just the songs she needed to write, but how she was going to get a demo made without going back to Landry. Which she just might have to do.

"Hey there," Claire said as Jules came through the sliders. "How's it going?"

Jules nodded, not sure how to answer that. "It's... going. I have a lot to do. All good, though." She smiled to underline that point. "What are you up to?"

"Baking."

Jules rolled her eyes. "Yeah, obviously." She laughed. "What are you baking?"

"Something new. Come try one. You can be my guinea pig. I asked Kat but she said she wasn't feeling up to it."

"Kat's home? How did her interview go?" Jules asked as she came over.

Claire shook her head and lowered her voice. "I

don't think it went well. She looked upset and went straight to her room."

Jules glanced over. The door was shut. "Poor kid."

"I know," Claire said. She pointed at the cookies. "Come on, try one."

"I don't know if being your guinea pig is a good thing or a bad thing,"

"Neither do I," Claire admitted. "I haven't even tried them yet. I've been letting them cool."

Jules looked over the racks of cookies. Some were drizzled with icing, some weren't. Some had darker bits in them, too, but otherwise they didn't look all that strange. Except for the white chunks in them. "What is that? White chocolate?"

Claire shook her head. "Popcorn."

Jules glanced at her sister. "You put popcorn in cookies?"

"Just try one." Claire picked up one of the cookies without icing. "Come on—we'll do it together."

Jules took one of the same kind. "I'm game." She bit into it, not sure what to expect, but was instantly and pleasantly surprised. "Hey," she said around a mouthful of cookie. "This is good. Tastes like...I don't know what it tastes like, but I like it. Salty and sweet is always good in my book."

"Thanks," Claire said. She was smiling as she chewed. "It really is pretty good. It's a sugar cookie with pieces of kettle corn in it. Let's try an iced one."

She picked one of those up and broke it in half, handing one piece out to Jules.

They both tasted it and, again, Jules nodded. "This one has a much more intense popcorn flavor."

"It's the icing," Claire said. "It's infused with popcorn."

"I don't even know how you do that."

Claire broke one of the cookies with the dark bits in half next, also giving one piece to Jules. "Same as the first cookie but with toffee bits."

Jules tried it as Claire took a bite. Jules's brows went up. "Hey, this tastes like caramel corn."

"Perfect." Claire took a second small bite. "That's exactly what I was going for."

"These are obviously for the bakery."

"They are. I'm going to share them with Danny tonight."

"He's going to love them." Jules popped the last bit of cookie into her mouth. "Speaking of tonight, shouldn't Mom be getting home soon? I thought she was going to that play with Willie and Roxie tonight."

"She is, but she might be going straight there from Conrad's. I'm not sure."

Jules snorted. "Mom with a boyfriend. Who would have thought it?"

Claire nodded. "I know, right?"

"Well, I need to change and get down to the beach. Cash is there watching Toby."

"You change, I'll bag up a few cookies for him to taste."

"Okay." Jules went into the bedroom and put on shorts and a tank top and grabbed her sunglasses and a beach towel. She made sure she had her phone in her pocket, then went back to the kitchen, got the cookies from Claire, and went straight to the beach.

It wasn't hard to find Cash, since he had Toby with him. Cash had him off the leash and was throwing a stick for him to chase, which he was doing to the best of his little legs' ability. Even at top speed, Toby wasn't that fast. Especially not on sand.

Jules grinned as she walked up to them. She crouched down as Toby came running toward her. "Are you having a good time, baby?"

Cash came over, bringing the leash. "I think I've worn him out."

"I'm all right with that. He needs the exercise." She took the leash and clipped it back onto Toby's collar. "Thanks for helping with him."

"No problem. How did the call with Billy go?"

She straightened and exhaled. "He liked it, a lot. He repeated a lot of the same things you said. He was very enthusiastic. The only problem is he wants me to cut a demo and get it to him for immediate release."

Cash squinted. "Why is that a problem?"

"Because I don't have a studio here, honey."

"There has to be one in town. And if anyone would know, it's Jesse."

"Yeah, you're probably right. I need to call him."

"Why haven't you already? I thought you liked him."

"I do."

"But what?"

She sighed. "But I don't know. I guess...I guess I've been trying to do this too much on my own. I've been self-reliant for a long time. But it's more than that. I do like him." She liked him a lot. "I don't want him to think I'm taking advantage of our new friendship for my own purposes."

Cash laughed. "Mom, the guy is crazy about you. He would love to help you. He's not going to think you're taking advantage of him, I swear. Especially if you debut your song at the Dolphin Club. That would be a pretty big deal for him."

She thought about that. "Yeah, I suppose it would be."

"So you'll call him?"

"I will." Wasn't like she had a choice anyway, unless she wanted to go back to Landry. "Oh." She held out the bag of cookies. "Aunt Claire sent these for you. She wants to know what you think of them."

"Cool. They'll be perfect for when I come out of the water." He put them with his flipflops and towel, then grabbed the skim board. "Thanks! See you back at the house."

"Okay." She looked down at Toby. "Come on, little man. We have a call to make."

Chapter Eleven

illie added a second spritz of Jean Nate, touched up her lipstick, then went out to wait by the elevator for Roxie and Trina. "Hurry up, you two. Miguel said the car is only five minutes away."

Trina and Roxie came out of their rooms at the same time. Both of them looked lovely. Roxie was adjusting her bra strap. "Hold your horses, Ma."

Willie rested her hands on her fanny pack, which was fuller than usual, thanks to the bag of Twizzlers and the flask she was smuggling.

Trina turned the light off in her bedroom. "I'm ready. Do we have the tickets?"

"We pick them up there," Willie said. "They're under my name." She pushed the call button for the elevator. It opened right away. She got on, then

Trina, then Roxie, who put her hand on the doors to keep them from closing.

"What's wrong?" Willie asked.

Roxie shook her head. "I feel like I'm forgetting something."

"You have your phone?" Trina asked.

"Yeah." Roxie took her hand off and the doors shut. "It's not like we're going out of town. I'm sure whatever it is, I'll be fine."

Trina smiled. "You look nice, Ma. Excited to see Ethan?"

Roxie nodded. "I am. I like him an awful lot."

"I feel the same way about Miles," Trina said. "We're going to hang out tomorrow, since he's off. We're going to the beach and he's going to teach me how to surf."

"How fun," Willie said.

The elevator reached the first floor and the doors opened again.

Trina got out first, turning around to face her mom and grandmother. "Unless you think I should stick around, in case I'm needed for something at the salon?"

Willie waved her hand as she got off. "Go and enjoy your day. Nothing's going to happen that your mother and I can't handle."

"She's right," Roxie said. "A day off will do you good. And it's not like you're going to be gone all day."

"Well, we might get dinner after."

"Even so," Roxie said. "It'll be fine. Oh, I know what I forgot. I left my lip gloss on the bathroom counter. Too late now."

Miguel was standing at the end of the driveway next to a big silver SUV. He was in tan pants and a tropical shirt. He waved at them. "*Buenas noches,* ladies!"

Willie grinned. Miguel had the sexiest accent. "Hiya, Miguel." She kissed him on the cheek. "Thank you so much for getting us a car."

"You are welcome." He opened the door for her. "Your chariot awaits, my lady."

"I'll sit up front," Trina said, already opening the front passenger door.

Willie stared up into the SUV. "Miguel, that's a big step. I'm not sure I can get up there with my hip."

Willie leaned in and said something to the driver, who then hopped out, opened the very back of the SUV and came around to their side.

He was holding a folding step stool. He put it down in front of Willie, then offered her his hand. "How's that?"

Willie nodded. "Much better." With the driver's help, and Miguel's, she climbed in.

Miguel used the step stool, too. Roxie came around and got in next to Willie on the other side. The driver shut their door, put the stool away, and got back behind the wheel.

As he pulled away, Willie leaned in toward Miguel. "How are you this evening?"

He grinned at her. "I am in the company of the most beautiful women in my neighborhood. I am very happy."

Trina turned around to see them, smiling. "Thank you for providing us with transportation, Mr. Rojas."

"Call me Miguel, please." He took Willie's hand. "Your *abuela* makes me feel young. First names are fine."

Roxie nodded. "Yes, thank you. It's a real treat to be taken care of like this."

Miguel looked proud. "We will have a good evening."

When they arrived at the seniors center, the driver came around with the step stool again and helped them out.

They all walked inside then followed Willie up to the desk that had a big sign hanging over it that read

Tickets. Willie put her hands on the counter. "You're holding some tickets for Willie Pasternak?"

The young woman working there nodded. "I'll get those for you, Ms. Pasternak." She went through an alphabetical file and produced them a moment later. "Here you are. Enjoy the show. There's a concession stand just to the left, bathrooms are on both sides, and here are programs for all of you as well."

"Thank you." Willie walked off to one side, so they'd be out of the way, and distributed the tickets. "Here's one for everyone. I'm sitting next to Miguel. Roxie, you and Trina can figure out which one of you wants to sit next to me."

"I'll sit by you, Mimi," Trina said. "Ma's already got a seatmate."

Willie looked up to see Ethan standing beside Roxie. "Hello, there. I heard your mother is one of the actors?"

He nodded, looking somewhere in the middle of nervous and unsure. "She is. Not sure what to expect. I hope she does all right."

"Should we get our seats?" Miguel asked. "Or see what the concession stand has to offer?"

"Concessions," Willie said. She doubted they'd have alcohol, but if they did, maybe she'd get a little drink. Otherwise, she had the flask of rum in her fanny pack. Rum, she'd found, went better with Twizzlers than gin. "See you in there."

She and Miguel walked over to the concession stand and got in line.

Miguel looked around. "There are more people here than I thought there'd be."

"Same." Willie had figured a play at the seniors center would be no big deal, but there was an impressive crowd, all things considered. "Would you ever live in a place like this?"

Miguel studied a few of the activities posters on the walls. "I would hope not. I'm sure some people would find it a good life, but I like being with my family. Why? Are you thinking about something you haven't told me?"

She laughed. "No. Just curious. I like being with my family, too."

"Have you given any more thought to what we talked about earlier?" He smiled. "My, uh, question?"

"You mean your proposal?"

He nodded.

"Oh, I've thought about it. But with Trina getting half the house, there's really no need. Although it was the sweetest thing. It really was. To think you'd do that for me..." She put her hand on his arm. "You're a real peach, Miguel."

He put his hand on his heart. "I would not see anything bad happen to you, Willie."

"And I appreciate that."

They moved up in line to where they could see the menu.

"No alcohol," Willie said. "As I suspected."

"They probably don't have a liquor license," Miguel said. Then he leaned in. "But do not worry. I have a small bottle of rum with me. We will get cola and fix them ourselves."

She giggled. "I have a flask of rum in my fanny pack."

His grin went ear to ear. "You are my kind of woman, Willie."

Trina caught up with them as they got to the front. "Will you get me a bottle of water?" She fished a few dollars from her purse.

"Put that away," Willie said. "I'll get your water. You want a snack, too?"

"No, the water is plenty. I was going to bring my Junior Mints, but I ate them already."

Willie saw her granddaughter's eyes linger on the Sour Patch Kids. "Then go in and find our seats so all we have to do is find you."

"Okay, Mimi. Thanks." Trina headed in.

"Such a good girl," Willie said. When they reached the counter, she ordered two Cokes, a bottle of water, and a bag of Sour Patch kids. She insisted on paying when Miguel attempted to put money down. "You got the car. This is on me."

Then they went inside the auditorium. Trina spotted them and waved, making it easy for them to locate their seats.

They settled in. Miguel, Willie, then Trina. Willie handed her the water and the candy. "Here you go."

"Mimi, you didn't have to get me these."

"So you don't want them?"

Trina laughed. "No, I do. Thank you."

"You're welcome."

Roxie showed up with Ethan just as Miguel was adding rum to their sodas. Roxie sat next to Trina and Ethan beside her.

Willie leaned to see him better. "How did you end up with a seat next to us? Don't tell me that's the seat you already had?"

He shook his head and smiled. "I know people." Then he laughed. "I found out the seat next to her was empty, so I swapped my ticket."

Trina looked around. "Where's Margo?"

Willie looked around, too. Margo had ended up

getting her own ticket, so she would have had to pick it up herself.

"I'm right here," a voice came from nearby. Margo was inching through the row of seats ahead of them. "This is my friend, Conrad. Conrad, this is Miguel, Willie, Trina, Roxie, and..." She shook her head. "I'm sorry, I don't know you."

"Ethan." He stood and shook Conrad's hand. "Nice to meet you."

"You, too," Conrad said. He waved at the rest of them. "Nice to meet all of you."

The lights dimmed once, silently announcing the show was about to begin. Everyone took their seats and the lights dimmed again, but this time they stayed dark.

Miguel handed Willie her drink back. She could smell the subtle sweetness of the rum. She took the cup, then lifted it. "Here's to murder and mayhem."

He touched his cup to hers, grinning like a schoolboy who'd just gotten away with something. "And rum."

Chapter Twelve

Claire packed up a container with a selection of the three kinds of popcorn cookies, but still had a lot left over. She'd made too many and she certainly wasn't going to eat them. She was doing her best to cut back on carbs. Maybe Cash would help. That boy had a metabolism to be envied.

She put the remaining cookies into two of the aluminum tins she had left over, then went to get ready for her evening with Danny.

Doing so only reminded her that her wardrobe was sad and colorless. Once again, she thought about how much she wanted to change it. Well, the insurance money was on its way. She could use some of that to buy some new clothes. It had been a long time. And she was in desperate need of an update.

Especially now that Trina had given her such great new hair.

She went with a simple black flowered sundress and sandals, but grabbed a little sweater, because she knew even if they sat by the fire, the evening might still be a little cool.

She did her makeup, fluffed up her hair a bit, then made sure she had everything she needed in her purse.

Her phone buzzed with a text from Danny. *Ten minutes or so before I'm home.*

Perfect, she responded.

She went to check on Kat, knocking softly on her daughter's door. "Honey? You okay?"

There was no answer. Claire knocked louder. "Kat? You in there?"

"Hang on." Kat came to the door wrapped in a towel. "Sorry, I was in the shower."

"Oh. Are you going out?"

She nodded. "Yeah, over to see Alex at the fire station."

Claire was glad about that. "You seemed upset when you got home. What happened? Did the interview not go well?"

"I don't really know. I thought it did, but then it

sort of didn't. I don't know what happened, except I asked what the salary would be."

Claire hoped that was just Kat being overly critical of herself. "Well, maybe it's not as bad as you think. They probably have a lot of other people to interview."

"Mom, they wouldn't even tell me what the job was. It could have been the janitor for all I know."

"Really?" That was odd. "Then maybe you don't want to work there."

"Yeah. But I kind of do."

"You'll find something. Look, with the insurance money coming, we're no longer in panic mode. The bakery will be up and running soon and all kinds of good things are going to happen for us. You'll see."

Kat smiled. "I know. And I'm okay. I was just a little down when I got back. Alex will cheer me up."

Claire nodded. "Danny does the same thing for me."

"Hey, you don't have any treats I could take to the fire station, do you? Those popcorn crispy bars were a huge hit."

"As a matter of fact, I have some popcorn cookies you can take."

Kat made a face. "Popcorn cookies? Is that a thing?"

"It is now." Claire laughed. "Your aunt and your cousin liked them. Take a tin of them and see what the guys at the fire station think. I'll leave it on the island for you. The other tray on the breakfast bar will be for Cash."

"Okay, thanks."

"Have fun tonight."

Kat nodded. "You, too."

With a smile, Claire went back to the island and redistributed the cookies so that one tin had more. She put the tin with the lesser amount of cookies on the breakfast bar, hoping Cash might find it while she was out.

Then she grabbed her purse, the cookies for Danny, and went down in the elevator to the ground floor. She walked across the small yard to Danny's house, arriving as he was getting out of his car.

"Perfect timing," he said.

"Do you need help?" she asked. "I've got one free hand."

"No, thanks, I've got it." He took a brown paper shopping bag from the floor behind his seat, and they walked up the steps together.

As he dug for his keys, she could smell the butter chicken. "I'm hungry and that food is only making me hungrier."

New Day At The Beach House

"Same here. It's been a long day. I'm glad to be home, glad to be about to eat, and very glad to be with you." He unlocked the door and pushed it open. "After you."

She walked in.

"What's in the container?"

"My new experiment. Which will also be dessert."

"No way," he said. "I can't wait that long. Let me see."

"You have the patience of a child at Christmas."

He laughed, setting his shopping bag on the counter. "When it comes to the bakery, that's true. If I could snap my fingers and have it ready tomorrow, I would. I can't wait to get it open."

"Same here, trust me." She took the lid off the container and showed him what was inside. "Popcorn cookies."

"Okay, those look very interesting."

"And those sound like the words of a man who doesn't think they're a very good idea."

He grinned. "I swear I wasn't thinking that. But I may have some doubts."

She put the container down in front of him. "Then try one. There's your basic popcorn sugar cookie, the same cookie with a popcorn-infused glaze, and the same cookie minus the glaze but with toffee bits."

Hesitantly, he reached in and took one of the basic sugar cookies. He took a bite. He started nodding as he chewed. "This is a lot better than I thought it would be." He took a second bite. "It's actually pretty good. Anyone who likes popcorn—and sugar cookies—would probably love this."

She tipped her head, smiling coyly. "Don't you like both of those things?"

"I do. And I'm impressed with what you've come up with. These are really perfect for the bakery. Do you ever bake anything that doesn't work?"

"Sure, but I've been doing it long enough that I've become a pretty good judge of what will work. Try the other two."

He did as she asked. But it was the toffee chip cookie he held up. "Okay, this is something special. It tastes like caramel corn in a cookie."

She smiled as he confirmed what Jules had already noticed. "That's what I was going for."

"Claire, you've hit this out of the park. People are going to go nuts for these."

"Speaking of nuts, there are, of course, many variations I can do on those. Chocolate, peanut butter, nuts—you name it."

He nodded as he unpacked the shopping bag. "I love all of it. I think we can do some test batches, too. See what customers like the most."

"Maybe we could do a free cookie on your birthday kind of thing? Or a frequent shopper card with a free cookie for every twelve purchased? I was thinking about making the cookies big. Like this." She held her hands about five inches apart. "What do you think?"

He got plates down. "I think you're the creative director and whatever you want to try is fine with me." He smiled as he looked at the cookies in the container again. "I am so glad you're part of this team. I meant it when I said you were making this possible."

His words warmed her up inside. "I've never been so happy about anything in my life. Outside of having Kat, that is. This whole thing has just filled me with a joy I didn't know I was capable of feeling. Thank you for that."

"We make a great team."

"Yes, we do."

"You want to eat out by the firepit?"

She nodded. "I would love that."

"Then let me get a tray to take everything down on. We need drinks, too. There's bottled water in the fridge, ginger beer, and maybe some sodas."

She went toward the fridge. "What do you want?"

"Ginger beer. Perfect thing for Indian food."

"All right, I'll have one, too." It wasn't a low-carb drink, but it was kind of celebratory, and that was the mood she was in.

Danny loaded everything onto the bamboo tray he'd pulled out of a cabinet, then she added the bottles of ginger beer to it as well. She went ahead of him to open the sliders onto his back deck, waiting until he'd come through to close them again.

She followed him down the steps to the firepit. He set the tray on the little table between their two chairs, then got the fire started.

"This is nice," she said. "I've been looking forward to this all day. I need a firepit at my place."

"I know a place," Danny said.

She smiled. "I bet you do. I think, if it's okay with everyone else, that I'd like to make some improvements to the ground floor. At least a screen like you have, so the parking area is separate from the living area."

"I can help with that, you know."

"I know," she said. "But you're about to be even

busier. We both are. And now that I'm getting that insurance money, I can afford to hire someone."

"True."

They tucked into their food. She realized she was spending money that had yet to arrive, but the check would come and when it did, she was obviously going to be careful with it. There were a few things, however, like some new clothing and some improvements to the house, that were long overdue.

And those things weren't going to make a dent in six hundred thousand dollars.

Chapter Thirteen

Kat arrived at the fire station with a new sense of peace about the interview. No, it hadn't turned out the way she'd expected, but she'd probably set her bar too high. She could only chalk it up as a learning experience and move on.

She parked, grabbed the tin of cookies, and headed in through the open garage bay doors and past the firetrucks and ambulances. She went straight to the breakroom where she knew Alex and the guys would be.

"Hey," one of them called out. "The treat fairy has arrived."

Alex turned and smiled when he saw her. "You brought more popcorn bars?"

She shook her head. "Nope. Something different this time."

He came over and gave her a quick kiss. "The guys are going to start liking you more than me."

She laughed. "You haven't seen what I brought yet."

"Well, we're just about to eat. Tonight is taco night. You're hungry, right?"

She nodded. "I am." She hadn't been earlier, but being around Alex was already making her feel better.

"Great, because I set a place for you."

Her smile felt like a permanent expression around him. He was so kind and considerate. "Thanks. I'll take these in to Larry."

"He'll probably rope you into helping."

"I don't care. I'm happy to pitch in." She waved at Miles, who waved back, then headed into the kitchen.

Alex came with her, announcing her to the man who did all the cooking. "Larry, our guest has arrived, and she did not come empty-handed."

Larry stood at the stove. He glanced over his shoulder. "Kat! So nice to see you. Are you eating tacos with us tonight?"

"I am."

"Outstanding. What kind of dessert did you bring us this evening?"

Kat put the tin down on the long counter. "A new creation of my mom's. Something she's trying out for the bakery. Popcorn cookies."

Larry's brows lifted. "Is that right? Well, those crispy bars of her were amazing, so I'm going to give her the benefit of the doubt on this one."

Kat didn't blame him. She wasn't so sure what they were going to taste like, either. "What can I do to help?"

"Start setting up the taco bar. It's make-your-own, so we do it buffet style. Alex will show you; he knows the drill."

"I do," Alex said.

Working together, they quickly got things set up, arranging it all on the counter. Taco shells, tortillas, and all the fixings anyone could possibly want. There was beef, chicken, and beans to start with, then chopped onions, chopped tomatoes, three kinds of salsa, shredded lettuce, cheese, sour cream, black olives, and hot sauce.

On the table went two big bowls each of yellow rice and refried beans, and one large bowl of guacamole. There were also a couple of smaller bowls of tortilla chips, a plate of lime wedges, and several pitchers of ice water.

Kat was amazed by the spread. If she hadn't been

hungry before, seeing all of that food would have definitely got her appetite working. The firefighters ate well.

Before long, Larry rang the bell and the crew shuffled in. They stood around instead of taking their seats, all of them bowing their heads as the chaplain said grace for the meal. Then they hustled down the line with an efficiency that seemed appropriate for men used to responding quickly.

Kat and Alex got in line, too. Once her tacos were fixed, she and Alex went to the table, where they took seats next to each other. Miles sat on the other side of her.

"How are you, Kat?"

"Good. You?"

He smiled. "Good. Wondering how Trina's enjoying the play."

Frank, the fire chief, gave Kat a nod and a smile from the head of the table. "Nice to have you with us again, Kat."

She was surprised the man had remembered her name. "Thank you for letting me join you again."

The mood around the table was the same as it had been the first time Kat and Trina had been at the station for a meal. Lots of joking and storytelling.

The tacos were great. Kat had made two, one

chicken and one beef. But the plates around her were piled high. These guys were big eaters.

Alex had four on his plate and was more than halfway through. "Hey, Miles and Trina are going surfing tomorrow. You want to join them?"

Kat hesitated. "I don't know how to surf."

Alex grinned. "Neither does Trina."

She looked at Miles. "Are you going to teach her?"

Miles nodded. "That's the plan. You should come. I haven't been doing it as long as Alex, but it's not that hard."

"Not that hard?" She snorted. "Are you kidding? It looks impossible."

"Nah," Alex said. "You'll get the hang of it in no time, I bet. I promise to give you all my best tips and tricks."

"Okay." It wasn't like she was starting a new job. And it was something that she and Alex might be able to share—if she could even do it. Plus, he taught kids how to surf. He was bound to be patient. "I will."

"Great. Trina has the details about when and where. Afterwards, we'll grab some dinner at Coconuts. Have you been there?"

"I don't think so."

"Really low-key place with great burgers and great fish tacos. Although you might not want tacos again." Alex grinned. "I could eat them every day."

Several guys got up and went back for seconds. Kat probably could have had a third, but she decided not to. She wanted to save room for one of her mom's cookies, no matter how questionable they might be.

As dinner wound down, Larry caught her eye. "You want to bring that tin over? I think we're ready for something sweet."

She nodded. "Sure." She got up to get it and pulled the foil off the top as she came back to the table. "My mom sent another contribution. A new experiment. Popcorn cookies."

A couple of curious looks greeted her words, but that didn't stop them all from digging in. The tin got passed around and the cookies quickly disappeared.

"Does your mom want to know what we think of these, too?" one guy asked.

Kat nodded. "I'm sure she would."

"They're weird," said another guy. "But really good. Like, surprisingly good."

Even Frank, the chief, took one. "Can't go too wrong with a sugar cookie," he said. "But these are not bad at all. If you left that tin in front of me, I'd definitely have a few more. Tell your mom she's got another winner on her hands and give her our thanks." He reached for a second. "We are more than willing to taste-test anything she's got. You can tell her that, too."

Kat laughed. "Okay, I will. But you might be sorry. No telling what she'll come up with next."

After dinner, they all helped clean up, making short work of the chores. Then they went back out to the lounge. Tonight wasn't only taco night, but also, apparently, movie night. The movie was *The Dark Knight*.

Kat settled onto one of the couches with Alex and as the lights got turned down, she prayed there'd be no emergency taking him away from her this evening. Being with him, even with all the other guys around, was just what she'd needed. She couldn't have cared less if it was Batman or the Muppets on the screen.

Halfway through the movie, her phone vibrated. She checked the screen and saw an email had come in from Future Florida. She put her phone away. She already knew it was going to be a "thanks but no thanks" response and that could wait until later.

Right now, she just wanted to forget about that and enjoy the moment.

The moment only lasted a few minutes more, though. The siren in the station went off.

The chief came in. "Truck One and the bus." Kat knew that meant the ambulance. "Three-car accident on Palmetto."

"That's me," Alex said. He kissed her cheek. "I'll text when I can."

"Okay." She got up but stayed out of the way as half the station filed out, Miles among them. She gave the guys a few minutes, then said goodbye to the rest of the crew and headed home.

She was parked at the beach house before she remembered the email from Future Florida. She pulled her phone out and decided to take a look before she went inside. Better to get it over with out here.

She opened up her inbox and tapped the email to read it.

She stared at the words in front of her. They were offering her the position of data scientist, a job that entailed combing through their mountains of gathered information to help them decide all kinds of things, from how to better fundraise to where they should be investing to even who they should be helping.

She would be compiling data and helping them

make important decisions. It was a big deal. Far bigger than what she'd thought she'd end up doing.

Not only that, but the salary was almost double what she was making now. And if that wasn't enough, they were also offering her a small, five-figure starting bonus if she agreed to sign a three-year contract.

All things considered, it was a very good deal. She grinned. One she was absolutely going to take.

Chapter Fourteen

*E*than had been holding Roxie's hand ever since intermission and she loved it. The play wasn't bad, either. Funnier than she'd expected, and his mom was surprisingly good. Roxie had no complaints about the evening, which was also kind of surprising.

Truth be told, she hadn't anticipated a night at the seniors center being anything special, but it was turning out to be a great time.

When the play ended, she and Ethan joined the rest of the audience in a standing ovation. Ethan's mom, Judy, looked thrilled as she lined up with the rest of the cast members and took a bow.

He leaned in to whisper in Roxie's ear. "I have to run out to my truck. Be right back. Don't go anywhere."

"Okay." She wasn't sure what was going on, but she didn't move.

He returned a couple of minutes later, holding a bouquet of multicolored roses. "For my mom."

Roxie smiled. "That is so sweet."

"I'm going to wait out front for her."

"I'll wait with you. If that's all right." She wasn't sure Ethan was ready to introduce her to his mom and she didn't want to push it if he wasn't.

"That would be great. I'd love for her to meet you."

"Okay." Roxie let Trina know what was going on.

Trina nodded. "I'll tell Mimi where you're going. We'll see you out there. But I think she wants to hit the bathroom first."

"No problem."

In front of them, Margo and her date, Conrad, turned around. Margo was all smiles. "That was fantastic, wasn't it?"

Roxie nodded. "It was. Ethan's mom was Martha Brewster."

Conrad looked surprised. "Was she? Outstanding performance."

"It was," Margo said. "You must be proud."

"Thanks. I am," Ethan said. He held up the flowers. "I brought these for her no matter how the play went, but now I'm extra glad I have them."

He and Roxie made their way out through the throng and waited off to one side. Very soon, the cast came out, still in their costumes and makeup.

Ethan gave his mom a big hug. "You were so good." He handed her the flowers.

"Thank you, sweetheart." His mom looked at Roxie.

Ethan quickly introduced them. "Mom, this is Roxie Thompson. I'm remodeling the old strip mall for her and her mom. They bought it. Her daughter is opening a beauty shop there. Roxie, this is my mom, Judy."

"Isn't that nice," Judy said. "And you came to the play! That was so kind of you."

Roxie shook her hand. "Actually, my mom and I were planning to see the play before I'd even met your son. And he's right, you were great in that role. I haven't laughed like that in a while."

"You are so sweet." Judy looked at her son. "Are you two dating?"

Roxie snorted. Mothers certainly liked to be direct.

Ethan nodded. "We are, Mom."

"Well, good for you," Judy said.

More people came over to congratulate the cast on their performance, so Ethan and Roxie said goodbye and went to find her family.

Trina waved at them as they approached. "Mimi and Miguel are both in the bathroom. I think there's a line in the ladies. I also think Mimi's a little tipsy."

"Tipsy?" Roxie frowned. "There was no alcohol."

Trina shrugged. "She and Miguel both snuck some in."

Roxie rolled her eyes. Nothing her mother did really surprised her anymore.

"Hey," Ethan said. "Do you guys want to go to the diner for something to eat? I don't know about you all, but I didn't have dinner and I'm starving. Plus, they have great pie."

Trina nodded. "I'd be okay with that. Might help Mimi to get some food in her, too."

Miguel came out and Trina told him what Ethan had just suggested. He nodded. "That sounds nice. I like pie."

"Should we invite Margo and Conrad?" Roxie asked. This whole thing had been Willie's attempt at getting Margo back out into the world, but Margo seemed to be doing just fine with that on her own. All the same, it would be rude not to invite them.

"We should." Trina looked around. "They're over by the bulletin board. I can run over and ask."

"Or just tell them where we're going," Roxie said. "They can meet us there."

"Okay." Trina went off on that errand.

"I can't believe the turnout," Roxie said to Ethan.

He nodded. "Diamond Beach is a big tourist area, but a small town at heart. People like to support each other."

"That's nice," Roxie said.

Willie came out, still wiping her hands on a paper towel with exaggerated effort. "That took forever."

"We're going to the diner to get something to eat," Roxie said. "You okay with that? Or do you need to go home?"

Willie gave her daughter a look. "I could use a little something to soak up all that rum."

Roxie's eyes narrowed and she decided to give her mother a little grief. "Where did that rum come from, Ma? There was no bar."

Willie just giggled. "Miguel brought some, too, you know."

Roxie shook her head.

Trina came back. "Okay, they're in and Conrad's going to give me a ride to the diner. That way, if you,

Mimi, and Miguel can all go with Ethan, we won't need to get an Uber."

Ethan said, "Sure, that's no problem. There's more than enough room in the backseat."

"Cool," Trina said. "See you over there. You do mean Digger's Diner, right?"

"Right," Ethan said.

Fifteen minutes later, they were all at Digger's, where they ended up in the big corner booth that was meant for eight.

Trina, Ethan, and Roxie scooted in to take the seats that were hardest to get to. Margo, Conrad, Willie, and Miguel filled in the rest.

"Ethan," Margo said. "Why didn't you invite your mom? We could have had the star of the show here."

He smiled. "I texted her, but she had plans with the rest of the cast already."

Their server, Sara, brought them menus and glasses of water, but Roxie had already decided she was getting pie. That would be her dinner and her dessert.

Ethan seemed to be on the same page. "What kind of pie do you have today?"

Sara flipped to a page in her notebook. "Tonight, we have mile-high strawberry, coconut cream, blueberry custard, chocolate silk, cherry crumb, apple raisin, and, of course, key lime. They can all be served à la mode, as well."

"Wow," Roxie said. "That's a lot to choose from."

"It is," Ethan agreed. He looked at Sara. "Thanks. I think we're going to need a minute."

"Sure. Take your time."

As the server left, Ethan glanced at Roxie. "Are you thinking about getting pie?"

"I am. But I don't have a clue which one."

He smiled. "They're all good. All the ones I've had, anyway. I might try the blueberry custard, since I like both of those things and haven't tried that one yet."

"It does sound good, but I was thinking about the apple raisin with a scoop of vanilla ice cream." She laughed. "If I'm going to be eating something naughty, I'm going all the way."

"I applaud your thinking." He pushed his menu away. Then he put one hand under the table so he could hold her hand again.

She smiled and stared at her menu. She couldn't remember when she'd had such a fun evening.

Sara came back and took their orders. Everyone got pie except for Margo, who got a chicken salad sandwich, and Willie, who got a cheeseburger.

When the food arrived, everything looked so

good. Roxie eyed Ethan's pie, which was a layer of custard topped with a layer of blueberry pie filling.

He pushed his plate toward her. "Go on. I know you want to try it."

She stuck her fork in and took a small taste. "You can try mine, if you want."

"Definitely." He helped himself to hers.

The blueberry custard was really nice. A little tart from the berries, but creamy and sweet from the custard. It wasn't a combination she would have thought of, but she liked it a lot. She ate some of her own next.

It was everything she'd hoped for. Because she'd ordered it à la mode, her slice had been warmed up first. To her, it sort of tasted like a baked apple. There was brown sugar and cinnamon mixed in with the apples and raisins and the ice cream just made it all come together.

Ethan cleaned his fork off. "That is good."

"So is yours."

He nodded. "You can't beat Digger's for pie." He looked around the table. "How's everyone's food?"

Lots of nods and happy confirmations answered him. Trina, who'd gotten the mile-high strawberry, barely looked like she'd made a dent in her slice.

He nudged Roxie's leg with his. "Maybe we

should come back here by ourselves sometime, huh?"

She nodded, about as happy as could be. "I'd like that."

But then, she would have gone anywhere with him.

Chapter Fifteen

Margo thought it was very generous of Conrad to take not only her home, but Trina, too. With Ethan driving Roxie, Willie, and Miguel, it meant they didn't have to get one of those Uber rides. Margo would have gladly pitched in for that, but the two men insisted that it was no big deal for them to drive.

Margo certainly didn't mind. It was a kind gesture. She just wasn't sure how comfortable she felt about the prospect of Conrad kissing her good-night in front of such a crowd. Public displays of affection were, to her mind, a little tasteless and something that should be reserved for one's own private time.

It hadn't escaped her that Roxie and Ethan had been holding hands at the diner. Granted, Margo and Conrad had held hands during the play, but it had been dark in the auditorium, and she was sure no one else had seen them.

During the drive home, she kept the conversation on two topics: the play and the diner. She didn't want to discuss the book in front of Trina. It wasn't her or her family's business what Margo was doing.

At last, Conrad pulled into the driveway. He stayed to one side so that Ethan could pull alongside his vehicle.

"Thanks so much," Trina said. "It was really nice to meet you, Conrad."

"You, too, Trina. Best of luck with the salon."

"Thanks." She hopped out, leaving Margo and Conrad alone.

He reached over and took her hand. "I had a great time. Thanks for inviting me."

"It was a lovely evening. Tomorrow morning around ten?"

He nodded. Then he leaned in and gave her a quick kiss. "You bet. And eleven to look at the house."

"Right." The idea of looking at the house made her a little nervous, but change made a lot of people feel that way. "Good night, then."

She got out and went toward the elevator. Trina held the doors open, but Willie and Roxie were both still a ways off. Willie had a grip on Roxie's arm and looking less than stable.

Trina stepped out but kept her hand on the doors. "Go on up. You have two floors to go. I'll wait for my mom and Mimi."

"Thank you." Margo stepped in and pushed the button for the second floor as Trina took her hand away.

She'd had a nice time. Better than expected. But she would have preferred to spend the evening with Conrad alone. She supposed that was just who she was. She was never really going to be a people person.

Nothing wrong with that. Not everyone needed to be gregarious. Conrad was more than enough for both of them. And, goodness gracious, he knew everyone in town. Or they knew him.

Margo stepped off as the doors opened on the second floor.

She'd lost track of how many people had come up to him at the seniors center. She'd just nodded and smiled and made no real attempt to remember the names of anyone he'd introduced her to. What was the point? There were too many of them.

At least, she thought, if they ever did do a book

signing, it would be well-attended, so that was something.

She went into the bedroom to change and get ready for bed. Jules was already in there, slouched against her pillows on her bed, her knees pulled up to rest her notebook on. Toby was at the foot of the bed. But Jules was dressed in jeans and a T-shirt and didn't look like she was turning in anytime soon. Not while wearing a full face of makeup.

"Hey, Mom. How was it?"

"It was well done for an amateur production. I enjoyed it. We went to Digger's Diner afterwards."

"How nice."

Margo sat on her own bed to take her sandals off. "What are you working on?"

"Song ideas." Jules sat up and put her notebook down. "I talked to Billy today. He wants me to get him a demo of my new song as soon as possible. Jesse was the only one I could think of that might be able to help me, so I'm actually headed over to see him shortly. He's been swamped all day, but he said he'd have time to sit down with me around nine."

"That's so late."

Jules smiled. "Not in the music world, it isn't."

"I suppose not. Are you taking Cash with you?"

Jules nodded. "He should be down any minute."

"And Claire is...?"

"Still at Danny's. But Kat just came home. She has some news, but I'll let her tell you herself. Did you try the new cookies Claire made?"

"No." Margo had some very small regrets about getting the chicken salad sandwich at the diner. Everyone's pie had looked so good, but she'd had cake at Conrad's earlier and she only allowed herself a certain amount of sugar in a day.

"Well, you should try one. Even if it's just a little piece. Claire's really done something new and interesting."

Margo nodded. "Maybe I'll have one with a cup of tea." She wished she'd invited Conrad up. They could have watched a forensics show together. Although maybe Kat would be interested.

The sound of the sliders opening was followed by Cash's voice calling out, "Mom, I'm ready. I've got your guitar."

Jules got up. "Coming." She grabbed her purse off the dresser. "See you later, Mom. Kat's already promised to take Toby out for his bedtime pee."

"Okay. Have a good night."

"Thanks."

As Jules and Cash left, Margo slipped into a pair

of lounging pajamas, then went to Kat's room and knocked. "Kat? I heard you have news."

Kat opened the door with a big smile on her face. "I do. Future Florida offered me a job. A really good one."

"Oh, sweetheart, that is the best news. I'm so happy for you." She hugged her granddaughter. "That is just fantastic."

Kat nodded. "I am thrilled. I really thought I'd blown it, but I guess I didn't. I mean, obviously."

"Well, clearly they know what a catch you are."

Kat's grin was enormous. "How was your night? You went to the play, right?"

"We did and we had a lovely time. I was thinking I might watch a show or two. Maybe have a cup of tea and one of these cookies your mom made. Care to join me?"

"Yeah, totally. Those cookies are really good. The guys at the fire station loved them."

"You went to the fire station?"

They walked out to the kitchen together.

"Just to see Alex. I ended up eating with them. They had tacos. And tonight was movie night, but about halfway through the movie, they got called out to an accident, so I came home."

"Hard job, being a first responder." Margo put

the kettle on. A first responder would make a very interesting main character. In a different book. She stored the idea away for later.

"It is. They're such a nice group of guys. I'm so glad I've gotten to spend some time with them."

"How are you and Alex getting on?"

Kat smiled as she got the tin of cookies from the other counter and set them on the island. "We're doing just fine. We're going surfing tomorrow with Trina and Miles. The boys are supposed to teach us. Not sure how that's going to go, but it should be fun regardless. Afterwards, we're going to a place called Coconuts for dinner."

Margo got out two cups and put a tea bag in each one. "I was going to tell you to be safe, but I don't think you can be safer than with a firefighter and a paramedic."

Kat laughed. "No, probably not. How's Conrad?"

It was Margo's turn to smile. "He's well. I've never met a man who knows so many people in town. Or is known by so many. I bet he spoke with eighty percent of the people who came to see the play tonight."

"Wow. Maybe he should run for mayor."

"Oh, no," Margo said. "He's got too much on his plate already."

"Right, the book. How's that coming along?"

"Surprisingly well. I'm happy with it." Margo didn't mention she was going to look at a house tomorrow. It was far too early. The house might not be for her at all. No point in getting anyone excited about it. Including herself.

The kettle whistled, so they fixed their tea and took a plate of cookies over to the living room area.

Margo found a good show, *Hot Cold Cases*, and they settled in to watch. She tried one of the cookies, the smallest one. It was drizzled with a little icing. Too sweet for her taste, but very good all the same.

She was blessed to have two talented daughters, and now with Kat and this new job, Margo's pride knew no bounds.

She glanced over at Kat, who was glued to the show. Margo smiled. This was just as good as being with Conrad. Different. But just as good.

Chapter Sixteen

*J*esse was waiting for Jules and Cash when they came through the doors at the Dolphin Club.

"Hi," Jules said. "Thanks for making time for me."

He made a face. "Like I wouldn't?" He bent and kissed her cheek. "Anytime." Then he shook Cash's hand. "I'd ask if you've made it to the beach yet, but you look like you got some sun."

"Yeah," Cash said. "I've been getting some time in on the skim board."

"Cool." Jesse put his hands on his hips. "Ready to talk business?"

Jules nodded. "Very."

"Come on back."

They walked with him to his office, the noise of the club ebbing and flowing as they passed different areas. It was quiet in his office, though. He closed the door after they came in. "So, you need to record a demo."

Jules and Cash sat on the couch. "That's right," she said. "What did you mean by, 'We can handle that'?" That was all he'd told her on the phone, other than asking her to come by later when he'd be free.

Jesse sat in his desk chair. "We have a studio here. It's nothing special, but it'll get the job done. It hasn't been used much." He laughed in a self-deprecating way. "I had such big dreams when I remodeled this place. I thought we'd be doing all sorts of things here and I wanted to be ready for them."

"But you didn't?" Cash asked.

"Not the way I thought we would." Jesse smiled. "We've done a few recordings in there. Nothing big, though. But it's operational and it should do the trick."

Jules let out a sigh of relief. "That's fantastic. But that's not all I need."

"No?" Jesse looked on with interest. "What else?"

"I need some studio musicians. I'd love a drummer, a bass guitarist, and a fiddle player, but anything would be better than just me. I've already talked Cash into playing rhythm."

Jessed looked at him. "Yeah? Cool. I love that."

Cash shook his head. "I haven't learned the song yet, but I'm going to do my best."

Jesse's brow furrowed. "What song is this, by the way?"

"My new one," Jules answered.

"Have I heard it?"

She put her hand on her guitar case. "No one has, until today. I played it for Cash, who then persuaded me to play it for my agent and that's why I need a demo. He wants to get it out there as soon as possible."

"As a single?"

She nodded. "Yes. But it would be on my new album, too."

Jesse leaned back in his chair, steepling his fingers and looking very curious. "Do I get to hear this new song?"

She laughed. "I had a feeling you'd ask, that's why I brought my guitar. In case I had to convince you."

"Hey, when it comes to Julia Bloom, I don't need convincing. But I would definitely love to hear it."

Cash grinned. "And you'll only be the third person to have done so."

Jesse looked tickled by that. "Which is pretty epic, I have to say."

"It's the best thing she's ever done," Cash said.

"Thanks, kiddo." Jules shot him a look as she got her guitar out. "No pressure or anything."

"Well, it is, Mom. Even Billy said it was that good."

Jesse's brows lifted. "Now I *really* want to hear it."

Jules put her fingers on the strings, adjusted her grip on the guitar slightly, then began to play.

Jesse sat mesmerized through the whole song, during which Cash kept rhythm with his hands against his leg. She was a lot more comfortable playing and singing this time, having already gotten so much great feedback from her son and agent and she felt like that confidence came out in the song.

She really did love the tune and the words had come together so well. For the first time since writing it, she really gave herself over to the music, putting herself in the place of the woman whose story she was telling.

She finished with a flourish and when she was through, Jesse just shook his head. "That was everything I'd hoped for and more. The day you release that song, your life is going to change."

"It's going to blow up," Cash said. "I just know it."

Jesse wiggled his finger in Cash's direction. "He's right."

Jules grinned. "I hope you're both right."

Jesse got up, walked to the door, then walked back, clearly in thinking mode. "You don't just need a demo. You need a video for this."

"That would be great, but I don't know about *need*," Jules said. She put her guitar back in its case. Videos were a lot of fun. She'd done a couple. But they cost money and they didn't always make that money back.

Cash nodded wildly. "Yes. That is exactly what you need. It would go viral. The right video, anyway."

Jules patted the air like she was trying to push a lid down onto a boiling pot. "Okay, the two of you need to come back to earth. I need a demo first. Let's get back to that for a second, all right? Nothing happens until that's done."

"Right." Jesse returned to his chair. "I can get you the musicians. That shouldn't be a problem. I'll make the calls tomorrow." He looked at Cash. "Can you come in around one, maybe help me for a bit? At least with the scheduling?"

"Sure," Cash said. "Whatever you need."

"Thanks," Jesse said. "Of course, Jules, you can come in, too, if you want. You can play around in the studio. Have a look at the setup. Get comfortable in there. Cash and I can work on scheduling the musicians. I know a slide guitarist. In fact, she plays a resonator. She's got a real down-home, bluesy style. Not sure if Rita's in town but if she is, I'd highly recommend her."

Jules loved a slide guitar. "That would be perfect." She could feel her excitement kicking up. "Do you think you could get a fiddle player?"

He nodded. "Bobby Perkins plays fiddle and he's in the house band that's on stage right now. I can get the rest of the musicians from there, too. How about some backup vocals?"

Cash nodded and looked at her. "For the chorus and maybe on the bridge, Mom. We could at least try it."

Jules exhaled. This was becoming bigger than she'd imagined it could be in such a short time.

"Listen, if money is an issue," Jesse started.

She shook her head. "It's not. I can afford to pay them. I just didn't expect this to come together this fast or this completely." She smiled. "But I'm glad about it. I want this demo to be as good as it can be."

Jesse smiled right back. "We've got our work cut out for us, no question about that, but we will make this happen. And when it's done, it's going to be amazing."

"Thank you."

He laughed and shook his head. "Thank *you*. I have wanted to do something like this since I fell in love with music and to do it for Julia Bloom? On a song like this? I can't tell you what a privilege and an honor it is. I am truly excited."

"So am I," Jules said. She meant it, too. She'd gone from having her doubts to feeling that bubbly excitement that came with knowing she had a good thing on her hands.

And this was shaping up to be maybe the most exhilarating thing she'd ever done musically. Having Cash and Jesse along for the ride was only going to make it more fun.

Jesse rubbed his hands together. "All right, I know we have a ton of work to do but there's not too much more that we can get done tonight, other than I can show you the studio. But before we do that, why don't we celebrate?"

Cash was clearly on board. "Sandbar sundaes?"

Jules laughed. "I'll stick with a glass of champagne, if that's what you were offering."

"Anything you want," Jesse said. "Sandbar sundaes included." He picked up the house phone and ordered a bottle of champagne and a sundae for Cash.

When he hung up, Jules cleared her throat softly. She'd made her decision. How could she not with all Jesse was doing for her? "There's one more thing."

"What's that?" Jesse asked. "Did we forget something?"

"No, it's not like that. It's just, I was thinking—I'd like to debut the song here. Live. What do you think?"

A slow smile spread across his face. "I think that's the second-best thing I've heard all night."

She frowned. "Second-best?"

He nodded, eyes lit up and filled with amusement. "The first best was you singing *Dixie's Got Her Boots On*."

Chapter Seventeen

Trina slept hard. The day—and night— had worn her out. Eating a big old piece of pie for dinner probably hadn't helped, no matter how delicious it was, because within an hour of getting home from the play, she'd crashed hard.

But sleep was good and necessary, and she didn't mind it one bit. Now that she was awake, however, she wanted coffee. She'd need it, because she had a few things she wanted to get done before she and Kat went to meet Miles and Alex for their day of surfing. Which sounded so fun she could barely stand it.

Trina pulled on her robe, putting her phone in the pocket, and went out to the kitchen. There were no lights on and no signs of life, proof that both her mother and grandmother were still asleep.

They'd probably crashed just as hard as she had.

They'd shared the same sort of day. And, of course, Mimi had overindulged slightly.

She'd want coffee for sure, so Trina quietly got a pot of coffee going, then slipped outside to sit on the deck and watch the day arrive. The sun was up but just barely, leaving a few strands of pink in the sky. Looked like it was going to be a beautiful day.

Just right for spending time at the beach and in the water. Her tan might actually turn into something after today.

She checked her phone. There was a message from Miles. *Missed you last night. Looking forward to today.*

Smiling, she texted him back. *Same here.*

She was about to go and check on the coffee when her mom came out with a cup. She put her phone on the cushion beside her. "Morning, Ma."

"Morning, Trina. How did you sleep?"

"Like it was an Olympic sport, and I was the gold-medal winner."

Her mom laughed. "Good for you. I slept pretty hard, too. And based on how much rum I think your grandmother had, I wouldn't look for her for another couple of hours."

Trina snickered. "Mimi and Miguel sure are something together."

"They are," her mom said, coming to sit by her on the sofa. "It's like they revert to being teenagers. But I say good for her. Good for both of them. We should all be that lucky to find companionship like that at their ages." She lifted her cup to her mouth. "At any age, really."

"I agree. Although you and Ethan aren't doing too badly."

Her mom smiled and took a sip of coffee. "No, we're not."

Trina got up. "Going to get coffee. I'll be right back."

"Take your time." Her mom leaned back and put her feet on the table. "I don't plan on leaving this spot for a while."

Trina went in and got her coffee. It smelled so good. It was exactly what she needed. Well, this cup and maybe two or three more.

She rejoined her mom. The sun was strong and bright now, the remnants of pink in the sky gone. "What are your plans for the day?"

Her mom shook her head. "Not sure. Is there anything you need me to do?"

"We're getting low on groceries."

"I can handle that. Anything I can do for the salon?"

Trina sipped her coffee and thought about the list in her head. She wished she had her binder in front of her, but she remembered quite a few of the items on it. "I need to talk to the sign people. I need to figure out what products I'm going to use as well as offer for sale. I need to buy towels, and I need to order tools."

"Tools?"

"You know, blow dryers, curling irons, flat irons, brushes, combs, Barbicide..."

"Right," her mom said. "Can I help with that, though? Seems like something you'd want to pick out yourself."

"It is. I'm going to try to do some of it this morning before Kat and I leave to meet up with Miles and Alex."

"Well, I'm happy to help if there's something you think I can do."

Trina nodded. "Do you think I should get white towels? Or black towels?"

"Not hot pink?"

Trina laughed softly. "I think there's too much chance they'll bleed color when washed. And not everyone will be flattered by that much pink close to their face. I think something neutral is better."

"Then white," her mom said without hesitation. "Black will fade, and you can bleach the white ones."

Trina smiled. "Good point. Could you order those for me? If I send you the supplier's link?"

"Sure. How many?"

"Four dozen should be enough to start with."

"I can definitely get that done for you. Won't you need a fridge and a coffeemaker for the breakroom, too?"

"We will. Good thinking. You want to handle that?"

Her mom glanced over. "You trust me to get them?"

"Sure. The fridge doesn't have to be anything fancy. Just something to hold drinks and people's lunches. Although an ice maker would be nice. You might want to check with Ethan about the size, too. The coffeemaker really only needs to be sturdy."

"You want a Keurig?"

"I don't know." Trina made a face. "Then you have to stock all those little cups and make sure you have the kinds people like. I think it's easier just to have the standard one-pot kind."

"You know they make the kind that do both. Big pots as well as the little cups. If you got one of those, you could offer more variety. I can take care of buying it for you."

"Yeah? That would be perfect. Thank you. I'll check those things off my list. Email me the confirmations when you get them, too, okay? I'm trying to keep track of everything."

"I will."

They sat in silence just drinking their coffee and watching people on the beach. Lots of walkers. Some people with dogs. A few with small children who were already claiming their spot for the day. One man had a kite.

"What time do you have to leave?"

"About quarter to two," Trina said.

"You have lots of time to get stuff done then."

Trina nodded. "I do. It just gets a little overwhelming when I think about how much there remains to be done."

"Yeah, I get that. It's a lot. But you're doing a great job."

"Thanks." Trina smiled. It was always nice to hear that from her mom.

"You want some breakfast? I was thinking about making some protein pancakes. They're low-carb and better for you. Not sure how they'll taste, since it's a new recipe."

"I'm game to try them. Do you think you can make them without waking Mimi up?"

"I'll shut her door, but I don't think anything will wake her up until she's good and ready."

Trina giggled. "Oh, Mimi."

"You can say that again." Her mom stood up to go inside.

Trina got up, too. "I'll come in with you. I could use another cup of coffee."

"Same here."

They went in and refilled their coffee cups. Trina hovered nearby as her mom pulled everything together to make pancakes.

Her mom shot her a look. "Don't you have work to do?"

Trina shrugged. "I was going to help with breakfast."

"Nope. I can do that. You work on your to-do list." Her mom winked at her. "If you're going to be a boss, you have to learn how to delegate."

Trina rolled her eyes good-naturedly. "Right. Okay. I'll get my laptop and bring it out here."

"I'll be right here, fixing your breakfast, Ms. Thompson."

Laughing, Trina went off to her room to get her laptop, her binder, notebook, and a pen so she could jot down any notes she needed to. When she returned, her mom was already mixing ingredients in a big mixing bowl with a handle and spout.

She set up on the sofa and went to work, pulling up the websites that offered beauty tools to salons. She might not be able to talk to the sign people just yet, but the internet was twenty-four-seven. She could at least get the tools ordered.

She went through the various types she'd need for the shop, ordering six of each, and putting them all in her shopping cart. She repeated that on each website so that she could compare what she was spending.

They were all within fifty bucks of each other, but then she did a quick search, found a coupon code for one of the sites that would get her free shipping and twenty percent off. That sealed the deal. She put in her grandmother's credit card info and hit the Order button.

Just as she was printing out the emailed receipt, there was a knock at the front door. No one ever knocked at the front door. Not unless they'd ordered pizza.

She and her mom both looked in that direction. Trina got up. "I'll get it. You're busy."

"Thanks. I hope they didn't wake your grandmother."

Trina nodded and went out to see who it was. A man in a red and yellow uniform stood there with several large envelopes in his hands. "Are you Wilhelmina Pasternak, Roxanne Thompson, or Claire Thompson? I need a signature from the last two but not the first."

"None of the above," Trina said. "But Wilhelmina is my grandmother. She's still asleep. And I can get Roxanne for you. Claire is up one floor."

He handed her one of the envelopes. "I'll wait for Roxanne."

She went back to the kitchen. "Ma, it's for you and you have to sign." She put the other envelope on the counter. "That's for Mimi."

"Okay." Her mom wiped her hands on a towel and came out. Trina trailed behind, watching as her mother scrawled her signature across the little hand-held machine the man took off his belt, then he handed her the envelope.

They went back to the kitchen.

"What do you think it is?"

Her mom shook her head. "I hope it's the insurance check. Although I have no clue why your grandmother got an envelope, too." She went around to the other side of the counter and flipped the pancakes on the griddle before opening it.

She pulled out a sheet of paper and a long check. She nodded. "That's what it is."

The check was in two parts, the top half folded over the actual check. Her mom unfolded it, looked at the check, and frowned. "This isn't right."

"Why not?"

"It's supposed to be six hundred thousand." She turned the check around so Trina could see it. "It's only for half that."

Chapter Eighteen

Claire was just back from her walk with Kat, who'd already gone to take a shower, and was about to make coffee when a man appeared at the sliding doors on the back deck. That was highly unusual. He was in a delivery uniform, so he seemed all right. She went to check on what he wanted.

"Can I help you?" she asked through the glass.

"Claire Thompson?" He held up a large envelope. "I need a signature. The women downstairs said I could find you here."

The insurance check. It had to be. Claire opened the door, nodding. "That's me."

She signed his little machine, thanked him, and took the check. She started back to the kitchen but before she could open the envelope, Roxie was standing at the edge of the kitchen, obviously having just come up the steps that connected the two floors.

Roxie looked upset. She had a piece of paper in her hand. "We were supposed to get equal shares."

Claire shook her head. "What are you talking about? I haven't even had coffee yet."

"The check. The insurance. Somehow you got more than me."

"What?" Claire ripped off the little tab to open the envelope and pulled out the papers inside. She looked at the number on the check. A pit opened up in her stomach. That was *not* the right number. She shook her head again. "I don't know what you got, but I did not get six hundred thousand as expected."

"You didn't?"

"No." She stared at the figure on the check. Just because she hadn't had coffee didn't mean she was reading it wrong. It definitely said three hundred thousand. She felt sick. Yes, it was still a good amount and a lot of money, but it was half what she'd been expecting.

How was this going to impact her involvement in the bakery? She'd already started making so many plans.

"So? How much did you get?"

Claire frowned. "That's kind of a personal question."

Roxie rolled her eyes. "I got three hundred. Does

that help?"

Claire heaved out a breath. "That's how much I got, too."

"You did?"

Claire showed Roxie the check. Seeing the number for herself seemed to take a little of the heat out of her.

"I'm sorry I assumed you got more than me." Roxie frowned. "That son of a—we were supposed to get equal shares, weren't we? Half and half is six hundred. Apiece."

"It should be." Claire tried to remembered what Charles Kinnerman had told them about the life insurance money. "Something isn't right."

"Yeah, I'll say. Maybe they already took taxes out but there's no way it would be half."

"No, it wouldn't be. And I don't think they could have taken out any other expenses. I'll call Kinnerman as soon as his office opens. Maybe you should, too, so he knows we both got the wrong amount."

"Couldn't hurt." Roxie let out a deep sigh. "This isn't as big a deal for me as I suspect it is for you. I'm sorry. For both of us. But especially for you."

"Thanks." Claire definitely hadn't been expecting that. "But I'm sure we'll get it cleared up and have the correct amounts soon." She had to believe that, because otherwise, she was going to have a small breakdown.

Roxie moved toward the stairs. "Maybe we can compare notes later on what he tells us?"

Claire nodded. "Yes. Let's do that."

"All right. Sorry to barge in on you."

"It's fine. I probably would have done the same if I'd opened mine first." Claire glanced at the check again as Roxie went back downstairs. How could the insurance company have gotten it so wrong?

She put the check back in the envelope and put that on her nightstand for safekeeping, then went back to make coffee.

Kat came out of her room dressed in shorts and a T-shirt. "Coffee smells good."

Claire just nodded as she pulled up Kinnerman's number on her phone.

"Are you okay? You look...not like yourself."

"The life insurance check came. It's half the amount it's supposed to be."

Kat's brows bent. "Probably just a clerical error."

Claire shook her head. "Roxie got the same wrong amount, too."

Kat leaned her hip against the counter. "That would be a strange coincidence."

"Which means it's probably not."

"Have you called the attorney yet?"

Claire looked at the time. "No, but his office should be open by now. I'll go into the bedroom. Help yourself to coffee. I won't be long."

Kat just nodded as Claire went to her room.

She sat on the bed as she tapped the button to call.

Kinnerman's receptionist answered and Claire asked to speak to him. The woman put her through.

"Good morning, Claire."

"Good morning, Charles. Roxanne and I got the insurance checks this morning. Neither one is for the right amount."

"How do you know that?"

Claire closed her eyes and tried not to say anything she'd regret. "Bryan had one point two million in insurance. Which means we should have gotten six hundred thousand apiece. We didn't. We each got three hundred thousand."

"That's the correct amount."

She barked out an angry laugh. "Charles, I can do basic math. Three hundred is not half of one point two million."

There was a moment of silence, then he cleared his throat. "There were...other beneficiaries."

"Other beneficiaries? Like who?"

"I'm not able to share that information with you."

A little anger unfurled in her belly. "I was his wife. Of course you can share it with me."

"Not according to the stipulations laid out in Bryan's will."

"You never said anything about this when you read his will."

"Because it didn't pertain to you." He sighed. "I'm sorry, Claire, but I can't say anything further."

"Thanks, you've been absolutely useless." She hung up, immediately missing the days when phones had actual receivers that could be slammed down to make a point.

She strode back out to the kitchen. Kat was sitting at the breakfast bar, drinking her coffee, and scrolling through her phone. "I have to go downstairs for a minute. Don't wait on me to eat if you are."

"I can wait. I'd rather have breakfast together." Kat looked up. "Why do you look angrier than you did before you made the phone call?"

"Because I am. I'll explain when I get back."

"Okay," Kat said. There was concern in her eyes.

Claire stomped down the steps. "Roxie?"

Roxie met her as she reached the bottom. "Not so loud, my mother's still asleep."

"Sorry," Claire said. "I called him."

Roxie tipped her head toward the living room. "Come in and tell me."

Claire followed her back. Trina was at the breakfast bar, a plate of thin pancakes in front of her. There was plate next to her, too, the chair still pulled away from the counter.

"I've interrupted your breakfast," Claire said. "I can come back."

"No way," Roxie said. "You want a pancake? I made extra."

"No, thank you. That's kind of you. Kat's waiting on me upstairs." Claire sighed. "All Kinnerman would tell me is that there were other beneficiaries and that Bryan's will had specified that they shouldn't be disclosed."

"Other beneficiaries?" Roxie frowned. "Do you think he left money to Charles? To cover all the costs of the legal stuff?"

"He could have." Claire thought about that. "But there's no way what Charles has done would have cost six hundred thousand dollars. And Charles said *beneficiaries*. Plural. That means Bryan left money to several people."

Trina nodded. "At least two more."

Roxie looked as unhappy as Claire felt. "Do you think we should contact the insurance company directly?"

Claire shook her head. "We could try, I guess. But everything's going through Kinnerman. I don't think they'll tell us anything."

"I'll call anyway. See what I can find out. Can't hurt."

"I suppose not." Claire's anger turned inward and became the kind of cutting ache that made her feel like she might cry. "He had to know we'd need that money. How could he leave it to anyone else?"

Roxie nodded, sympathy filling her gaze. "I don't get it, either. I loved the man, still do, but I can honestly say I hate him a little bit right now. At least we have our houses to sell."

Claire sniffed and nodded. "You know, the good thing about us both staying here is splitting the expenses."

"That's definitely a silver lining," Roxie said. "I'm sorry about all this."

Claire took a deep breath. "I am, too. We should be on the same side. Not against each other. We're living in the same house. And probably will be for some time."

"Probably."

Claire put her hand out. "Can we call a truce? Do our best to be nice to each other?"

Roxie smiled, hesitated, then pulled Claire into a hug. "You bet."

Claire hugged her back and, for a moment, they embraced, each seeming to understand exactly what the other was feeling.

Then Roxie let her go. "You need anything, you let me know. I should be around most of the day."

Claire nodded. "Same here. Although I have to run to the store. Today I'm going to start working on some of the family recipes that Danny gave me."

"Oh, nice," Roxie said. "I hope that bakery is a huge success. And not just because my mom owns the shopping center. I really do want you and Danny to make a go of it. He's a nice guy and you deserve the break."

Claire couldn't agree more. "Thanks."

"Listen," Roxie said. "I have to go to the store, too. If you want to save some gas, we could go in one car."

"Okay." Claire nodded. "I'd like that."

Claire wasn't sure if she would or not, but becoming friends had to start somewhere.

Chapter Nineteen

Willie blinked and squinted as light filtered through the blinds and into her eyes. She usually loved the sun, but feeling the way she did this morning, it was a horrible thing to wake up to.

With a soft groan that had more to do with her throbbing head than her aging body, she staggered into the bathroom, did what she had to do, then leaned on the sink and took a look at herself in the mirror. She shook her head at the reflection staring back at her. "Maybe you should lay off the rum, Wilhelmina."

She heard soft voices coming from the other room, and she smelled coffee. And something that might have been pancakes or French toast. Either would have been acceptable, because that was what she needed. Fortification. She tugged on her chenille robe and went to see what her girls were up to.

They were at the breakfast bar, finishing up whatever they'd made for breakfast.

"Was that French toast?" Willie asked.

"Nope," Roxie said. "Protein pancakes."

Willie's lip curled. Those sounded healthy.

Trina looked over. "Mimi!"

Willie winced. "Not so loud, my girl. My head's not having it." She went directly to her chair, knowing her girls would take care of her in her time of need. "Rum is the devil's drink," she muttered, eyes closed.

Soft laughter answered her.

Willie peeked at them. "I might be old but I'm not deaf."

"Sorry, Mimi," Trina whispered. "What can I get you?"

"Coffee, lots of sugar and creamer. Toast with jam. Some regular pancakes would be nice, too. I need carbs. And Aspirin."

"You're dehydrated. You need water and an IV," Roxie said. "But I don't have the ability to do that for you here. No equipment."

Willie waved her away. "I don't need an IV, but I probably am dehydrated."

"Of course you are. That's what overindulging does to you."

Trina came over with a large plastic tumbler of ice water. She set it on the little table next to Willie's chair. "Here you go. I'll be right back with the Aspirin. Then I'll make you some toast."

"Thank you, honey." Willie sipped the water. It was nice and cold. Maybe she'd live after all.

"I'll make the toast," Roxie said.

Willie exhaled and drank a little more water.

"I can whip you up some more pancakes if you like. We finished what I made."

"I would like that very much," Willie said. "Thank you. But none of that protein nonsense."

"Yes, Ma."

She kept her eyes closed, listening to her daughter whip up fresh batter.

"Here you go, Mimi."

Willie opened her eyes a slit to see Trina standing over her, hand out, two small white pills on her palm. Willie took them and downed them with a big gulp of water.

Trina came and sat next to her on the end of the couch, as close as she could be. "What else can I do for you?"

"Your mother's making me pancakes."

"And toast," Roxie called out.

"I think I'll be all right." Willie lifted her hand. "No, wait. I left my phone by the bed. Can you—"

"Be right back," Trina said, hopping up again.

The pop of the toaster releasing two slices of bread was a happy sound, Willie thought, but still a little loud.

"Raspberry jam?" Roxie asked.

"Please," Willie answered. "Buttered first."

"I know how to make toast," Roxie snapped back. Then she sighed. "Sorry, Ma. Got some less than stellar news this morning."

Willie shifted slightly and opened her eyes as much as she dared. "I'm sorry. What happened?"

"The insurance check came and it's for half what I thought it would be. Claire got the same amount, because we compared notes. Claire called the attorney and get this—" Roxie poured circles of batter onto the griddle. "Apparently, Bryan had *other beneficiaries*."

"What in the Sam Hill is that supposed to mean?"

"No idea. But he thought enough of them to give them a share of his life insurance."

Willie grunted. "Scummy low-life. Who could be more important than the two women who gave birth to his daughters?" Bryan was a bigger loser in death than he'd been in life, and that was saying something.

"My thoughts exactly." Roxie came over with a plate bearing two crisp pieces of toasted bread generously slathered with jewel-toned jam. In her other hand was a cup of coffee, light with cream.

Willie had never seen anything look so good. She picked up the first slice of toast and took a big bite. It only took a few chews for the sugar and the carbs to kick in. That was exactly what the doctor ordered. She had a sip of coffee, then gathered her thoughts. "Could the lawyer, Kinnerman, be one of the beneficiaries?"

Roxie shrugged. "Claire and I talked about that. I don't think we'll ever really find out. It's all being kept secret by the stipulations put in Bryan's will."

"If we could get a copy of that, we'd know," Willie said. She wondered if such a thing was possible. Maybe. But she wouldn't know where to start to look or which courthouse to contact.

"Oh, that reminds me." Roxie got up and came back with an envelope. "This came for you."

Willie took the envelope but put it next to the chair. "Just some paperwork I have to sign for Zippy's attorney."

Trina came back, hands empty. "Mimi, your phone isn't by the bed. It's not on the nightstand or the floor, because I checked."

Willie groaned. "I could have sworn I put it there. If I lost that thing..."

"We'll call the seniors center this morning," Roxie said. She was back in the kitchen, flipping pancakes. "I'm sure someone would have turned it in if they found it."

"Hmph." Willie wasn't so sure. "You really think any of those senile old people would even remember finding a phone?"

Roxie came back with a plate of pancakes glistening with butter and syrup, just the way Willie liked them. "I know you're hungover, but that's no reason to be cranky."

Willie gave her daughter a look. "That's every reason to be cranky."

Trina put her hands on her hips. "Does that mean you're mad at Miguel for bringing the rum?"

Willie shook her head. "We both brought rum. If I'm mad at him, I have to be mad at myself. I just overdid it, is all. I should have eaten something more substantial than cheese and crackers before we went to the play. That would have helped." She smiled at both of them. "I'm allowed to indulge once in a while, you know. But I'm already starting to feel better."

"Good," Trina said. She returned to her spot on the couch. "Now, I have to get some more work done before I leave."

"Leave?" Willie frowned. "Where are you going?"

"Surfing with Miles, remember? And Kat and Alex, too."

Willie nodded as it came back to her. "Anything you need your Ma and I to do today? For the salon, I mean?"

Roxie came over with another cup of coffee for herself. "I already have my assignment. I'm buying towels. Then I'm going grocery shopping. Or maybe I'm buying towels after that. Depends when Trina gets me the links."

"I still need estimates for the sign, as well," Trina said. "They were supposed to have them to me already."

"I'll call them for you," Roxie said.

Willie cut into her pancakes and forked up a bite. "I can help, too."

"Mimi, you help every time you pay for something. You just rest and feel better," Trina said.

Roxie pulled her phone out. "Danny Rojas just texted. He said his father has your phone, Ma. Not sure how that happened, but he's on his way to bring it over. Miguel is apparently still in bed."

Willie exhaled in relief. "I'm so glad it's not lost. It would have been a major pain to replace that thing." Poor Miguel. Was he feeling as bad as she was? At least she knew Danny would take care of him.

Trina didn't look up from her computer as she typed something on the keyboard. "It is. I'm glad it wasn't lost."

Willie nodded, but she was too busy eating pancakes to engage in any further conversation.

Chapter Twenty

While her mom had been downstairs, Kat had taken Toby out for a quick pee. Now Toby was snoozing on the couch while she and her mom were working on fixing breakfast for the rest of the house. Eggs, bacon, toast, fruit, and a side of home fries, the last three mostly so that Cash would leave a little food for the rest of them. Kat and her mom wouldn't eat the potatoes, the bread, or much of the fruit.

They'd both decided to avoid carbs when they could, although Kat was really doing it to support her mom. She didn't feel like she needed to lose weight.

She might think differently after spending the day in a bathing suit around Alex, though.

Kat had just put bacon on the griddle and was slicing up a melon when her grandmother came out of the bedroom, already showered and dressed for the day. "Morning, Kat."

"Morning, Grandma. How are you doing?"

"Good, dear. How are you?"

Kat smiled. "Happy. Excited about the new job. After breakfast and before I head off to go surfing, I'm turning in my two-week notice."

"Good for you." Her grandmother went straight to the coffee.

"I won't have to wait two weeks, though. I have enough vacation time built up that I won't actually have to go back to work."

"Even better." Her grandmother glanced at Kat's mom, who was beating eggs in a bowl with a little cream and looking less than pleased, which Kat understood. "Morning, Claire."

"Morning, Mom."

Margo fixed her coffee, then sipped some of it before going to stand by her daughter. "Did someone die overnight that I'm unaware of?"

Claire shook her head. "No. But Bryan's life insurance check came this morning. It was only half as much as I was expecting it was going to be. Same for Roxie. According to the attorney, some of the money went to other beneficiaries, and we have no idea who that might be."

Kat watched her grandmother's face go from surprise to anger. "He has a lot of nerve doing what he did and then not leaving you your fair share."

Claire shrugged. "I guess it's easy to be a big man when you know you're not going to be around to deal with the consequences." She tipped the eggs into a large pan that already had a good amount of butter melted in it and gave them a stir. After that, she flipped the slices of bacon over. "And what's done is done. It's not like I or Roxie can do anything about it."

Margo scowled into her coffee. "It bears repeating that it's a good thing he's dead."

The bedroom door opened and Aunt Jules shuffled out in her robe, sleepy-eyed but smiling. "Morning, family. Please tell me there's coffee and a lot of it."

"There is," Kat said. She put the last slice of melon on the plate and moved on to making toast. "You look happy. I take it you had a good night with Jesse?"

Aunt Jules yawned before she answered. "I did. That man is amazing. He's going to make it possible for me to record the demo that my agent wants. He's getting musicians together for me and everything. If not for him and the Dolphin Club, I'd be headed back to Landry."

"Speaking of," Kat said, now that most of her family was all in one spot. "What are we going to do about getting ourselves moved out of there and permanently into here?"

Her mom sighed. "That's going to take a lot of work."

Kat shook her head. "I don't think it will. Not if we agree that most of the furniture could be sold or donated. It's not like we have room for it here anyway." The toast popped up. She took it out and started a new batch. Thankfully, their toaster held four slices, so one more round and that would be it.

Her mom seemed to think about that. "That's mostly true. But that dresser in the guest room belonged to my grandmother. I'd like to keep that."

"I should think so," Margo said.

Kat's mom stirred the eggs before she looked over. "If you want it back, you can always take it. There's room for it in my bedroom here in the corner."

Margo nodded. "Good. But what about the buffet in the dining room?"

Claire sighed as she looked around the space.

"It's an antique, too. I'd hate to get rid of it, although I'm not sure where I'd put it."

"Okay," Kat said. She spread butter on the toast she'd already made. "So there are a few things like that we need to hang on to. If you could make a list of what you want to keep and what's okay to donate, I can sort through the house in a couple of days. I already talked to Alex. He's willing to come with me and help. Maybe Cash can come with us, too."

"For sure," Aunt Jules said. "I know he'll do it. So long as it's not the day we'll be in the studio recording."

Her mom glanced over. "That's very kind of both of them. But how will you bring everything back?"

"Rent a truck," Kat said. "Plus, we can put stuff in my car and yours."

"It's still a lot of work," her mom said. "Are you sure you want to tackle it?"

"Yes. And I'm going to have time to do it before I start at Future Florida. With the signing bonus they're giving me, I can pay for the truck, too. Cash can drive it back, Alex can drive my car, and I can drive yours." She needed to get the jam out of the fridge and put it on the table.

"It would be good to have my car," her mom admitted. She stirred the eggs again, then added a little salt. "But what if I forget to list something that's important to me? I'd hate to lose a memento just because I didn't come along."

"So come," Kat said. "Ride with us, then you can sort through things and drive your own car back. You could do it all in a day easily, if that's what you wanted." The final batch of toast popped up. She added it to the plate and went to work buttering it.

"A day would be good. I'll just have to let Danny know I'll be away."

"Plus," Kat said. "Donating all that stuff to charity would give you a nice write-off come tax time. Then the house will be empty and ready to go up for sale."

"Which I really want," her mom said. "We'll figure out a day to do it." She looked at her sister. "What day will you and Cash be in the studio?"

"Not sure yet, but I'll tell you as soon as I hear from Jesse."

"Claire?" a male voice called up from downstairs.

Her mom walked over to the top of the steps. "Danny? What are you doing down there?"

Footsteps followed and his voice got closer. "Willie's phone ended up in my dad's pocket last night. I was just returning it to her."

Danny appeared on the landing. He waved. "Morning, all."

Everyone waved and said good morning back.

Kat wasn't surprised that her mom was smiling again.

Claire looked up at him. "Do you want to stay for breakfast?"

"Thanks, but I can't. My dad was just getting up and about to slice some chorizo for an omelet when I left. I just wanted to say hi."

"Okay," Claire said. "I guess I'll talk to you later, then."

He nodded. "For sure. Bye."

He went back down the steps.

As he left, the elevator opened and Cash came out, hair still tousled from sleep. Toby hopped down off the couch to greet him. "Smells good in here."

"You're just in time to set the table," Kat said. She took the plate of toast over, then returned for the jam and butter.

"Okay." He came over and got plates.

Her mom was putting the eggs and bacon on a big platter.

"Hey," Kat said to her cousin. "Would you be willing to help me one day with moving stuff out of the Landry house? Not everything. Just the stuff we want to keep and bring back here. Alex is going to help, but an extra set of hands would be great. Plus, I might need someone to drive my car back. I haven't fully worked out the details yet."

Cash nodded. "As long as I'm not helping my mom in the studio, sure. I have to go over to the Dolphin Club today, actually." He put plates on the table, one at each spot. "Mom, are you coming with me?"

"Since I've already had a look at the studio, I think I'm going to stay here and work on new music."

"Okay," Cash said. "Then can I use your car to go over there?"

"Of course." Aunt Jules got up to refill her coffee.

Cash looked at Kat again. "Once I know what the recording schedule is going to be like, I can tell you what days I'm available."

Kat smiled. "Thanks, Cash. So, are you working at the Dolphin Club now?"

He'd returned to the kitchen for utensils. "I mean, sort of. Besides my mom's stuff, I'm helping Jesse put the open mic night together." He shrugged. "That's work. Did you get that job you interviewed for?"

Kat grinned. "I did."

"Dude, that is awesome." He put his fist out.

"Thanks." She bumped hers against his, then carried the plate of melon slices to the table. "All right, fam. Get your coffee or juice or whatever and let's eat."

Toby let out a woof, making Kat laugh. "Not you, little man."

"He might need breakfast, too," Aunt Jules said. "I'll check his bowl."

While her aunt did that, Kat got herself more coffee. She knew her mom wasn't happy about the insurance money, but Kat wasn't really bothered. Not with this new job on the horizon. And her mom had the bakery to look forward to.

Things might have been bumpy for a while, but she felt like that was all behind them. She hoped, anyway.

They deserved an easy path from here on out, didn't they?

Chapter Twenty-one

After cleaning up the breakfast mess and loading the dishwasher, Roxie went to get her shower. Trina was still working on the computer in the living room and Roxie's mom had fallen asleep in her chair with some game show on the television.

Trina said the sound didn't bother her, so Roxie let them be. She went into her room, but before she started the shower, she did some squats, some lunges, then moved on to pushups and triceps dips off of a chair. She finished with some leg lifts and crunches.

This afternoon, she hoped to swim some laps again. Being here at the beach made her want to work on her fitness even more than before.

If she was really going to be working at the salon,

she wanted to look her best. Kind of important in a beauty shop.

She'd even been thinking about changing the color of her hair. Not completely. But maybe she'd lighten it up to a strawberry blond instead of it being such a bold red. Might be fun for the summer.

She'd see what Trina thought. She trusted her daughter's opinion on things like that. She turned on the shower, then went to pick out her clothes while the water got hot. She went with white denim shorts and a blue gingham top. Not nearly as bright or sparkly as her standard stuff, but she was going grocery shopping with Claire.

Not exactly a dressy occasion. But she'd be wearing her white crystal flipflops, so she wouldn't be completely boring. Maybe her cherry earrings, too. Those were super cute. And if she really felt like glamming up, she'd tie a scarf in her hair, pinup-girl style.

Happy with that, she got in the shower and, since she had time, did a full exfoliation and shaved all the areas.

When she got out, she moisturized, plucked a few stray brow hairs, then wrapped up in her robe and did her face. Nothing too much. No lashes. Again, the grocery store wasn't a nightclub, and she didn't want looks from Claire because the woman thought she'd overdressed.

As Roxie filled in her brows, she thought about their earlier conversation. Could they really be friends?

Roxie thought it was possible on her end, but she wasn't so sure about Claire. That was a woman who had been deeply hurt. What Bryan had done was awful, no doubt about that, and he deserved all of their bad thoughts and feelings, but Claire seemed very much like she held Roxie accountable, too. Or at least she had seemed that way.

Only time would convince Claire that Roxie was just as innocent in all of this as she was. Until then, Roxie would do her best to keep the peace and be nice. She much preferred having Claire as a friend than a foe.

Although, Claire had skin in the game now that she and Danny were renting a spot from Willie. Claire ought to be as sweet as pie to the daughter of her new landlady. Didn't mean Roxie thought she should be fake about it.

But being nice wouldn't hurt anything. And it could actually help.

Willie wasn't about to do anything against Danny. Not with her being involved with his dad.

Roxie stood back to look at her brows and make sure they were even. Funny how things worked out, wasn't it?

Satisfied with her brows, she lined her eyes, added lots of mascara, then used her cream blush to make her cheeks look healthy.

With the sun she'd been getting, she had the start of a nice tan. She didn't want too much. Had to protect the skin. But a little color made her feel like a million bucks. Did wonders for the legs, too.

She finished her makeup and got dressed, deciding on the hair scarf after all. It was too cute not to. Then she texted Claire to see when she'd be ready before going back to the living room.

Willie was snoring softly. Roxie kept her voice down as she spoke to Trina. "Are you ready for me to order those towels?"

Trina smiled. "You look great, Ma. I love that outfit. I love the whole look."

"Thanks." Roxie did a quick pose, pinup style. "Now, what about those towels?

Trina laughed. "I already took care of it. I found the ones I liked and just put the order in. I appreciate you being willing to help."

"I can still call the sign people."

"They emailed me right before you went into

shower. They showed me three mockups. You want to see them? I haven't decided yet."

"I'd love to." Roxie came around the coffee table and sat by her daughter.

Trina pulled up the email and then clicked on a link. That took her to a page that had three versions of the new salon sign.

Roxie leaned in. "They look so real. Like they're really on the building already."

Trina nodded. "It's the software they use. Which one do you like?"

Roxie shook her head. "They all look nice. Which one do you like?"

"I don't want to tell you yet. I'm afraid I'll influence you."

Roxie bit her lip and studied the different designs. Finally, she pointed at the one in the middle. It had a silhouette of a woman with beautiful flowing hair, then "A Cut Above" next to it in a nice font. "I like that one best."

Trina grinned. "So do I. I want to show Mimi, too, but I don't think I should wake her."

Roxie leaned back. "Ma. Ma, wake up. Trina needs to show you something."

Trina snorted. "I could have done that."

Willie came to with a start. "What is it? What's

happening?"

Trina answered her. "I just wanted to show you the new salon sign, Mimi."

Willie put her hand on her chest. "Nearly gave me a heart attack."

Roxie rolled her eyes. "Are you still hungover?"

Willie shot her a look. "I was feeling better, until I was so rudely awoken."

"Sorry," Roxie said. "But I didn't think you'd want to miss this."

Trina turned the laptop so her grandmother could see the screen better. "We like the middle one the best. What do you think?"

Willie peered at the screen, then nodded. "I think it's beautiful. And classy. Get it ordered."

"Okay," Trina said.

Roxie's phone buzzed. She looked at it. Claire was ready. She sent a quick message back. *Meet you at the car.*

Then she nudged Trina. "I need your keys so I can go to the store."

"Oh, right. They're in my purse. You want me to get them?"

"I don't mind. I'm going that way anyway." She kissed Trina on the cheek. "You have fun surfing in case I'm not back by the time you leave. Be careful, which I know you will be, but still. Don't get hurt."

"I'll do my best."

Roxie got up and kissed her mom on the cheek, too. "Try to stay out of trouble while I'm gone, all right? We'll go to the pool this afternoon, if you want."

Willie nodded. "I would. Some time in the sun might bake the rest of this rum out of me. Say, can I invite Miguel over?"

"Sure, if you want." Roxie wiggled her fingers at them. "Bye."

She left the living room and went through the reading nook, stopping at Trina's room to extract the keys from her purse. Then she took the stairs down to the ground floor. Claire wasn't there yet, so Roxie walked over to the pool.

The water looked so inviting.

The elevator doors opened and Claire stepped out.

Roxie walked back over. "Ready to go?"

"Yes." Claire nodded but she was checking Roxie out. "You always look so..."

Roxie braced herself.

"Cute," Claire finished. Then she exhaled. "I feel like everyone's mother next to you."

Roxie laughed. "You *are* someone's mother."

"So are you, but you don't look like...this." She indicted herself.

Roxie wasn't sure what to say to that. She did her best. "So you're a little curvier. You could dress differently if you wanted."

"I actually do want." Claire sighed. "I just don't have the money right now. I still wouldn't end up looking like you."

"What do you mean you don't have the money? We just got checks for three hundred thousand dollars. I know it wasn't what we were expecting, but it's still a lot."

"I realize that, but I need to put that money in the bank and keep it there so I can be part of the financing for the bakery. I can't go spending a bunch of it."

Roxie nodded in understanding. "Okay. Do you have any other money you could spend?"

"I have some. But I'm not sure what a hundred bucks or so is going to buy me when it comes to a new wardrobe."

Roxie smiled, an idea forming in her head. "What if I told you it could get you more than you think?"

Claire's brows bent, her expression skeptical. "How?"

"Get in the car. We're making a stop before the grocery store."

"Where?"

"You'll see. Just keep an open mind." Roxie wasn't sure what Claire would think of the amazing place Roxie liked to shop at here in Diamond Beach, but she'd soon find out.

"Okay." Claire took a step toward the car. "Could we also stop at Southcoast Credit Union? I need to set up an account there and deposit my check."

"Sure. I should probably do the same."

They both got in the car. Claire glanced over. "Thanks again for driving."

Roxie shrugged. "Well, Kat is taking Trina to meet the boys for surfing, so it just made sense."

Claire nodded. "It would still be nice to have my car."

"I hear you," Roxie said. "I'd like to have mine, too. We're only going to get busier. We need to figure out how to get our stuff from Port St. Rosa to here."

Claire clipped her seatbelt in. "We're working on that, too. Tell me more about this place you're taking me to shop."

But Roxie just smiled. "You'll see soon enough."

Chapter Twenty-two

It was such a nice day that Margo and Conrad were working on his screened porch. The breeze was lovely, and it was a pleasant change to look at his backyard as opposed to his office walls. Beyond the pool, he had some fruit trees along the back fence and the blossoms smelled so good.

"Earth to Margo. Come in, Margo."

She glanced over and realized she'd been staring out at his landscaping. That wasn't the reason she was distracted, though. They were minutes away from leaving to look at his neighbors' house. "I'm here. Just thinking."

"About the house?"

She nodded. "What else?" She sipped her coffee, but it was only lukewarm now. "I'm sure it won't be right for me but I'm afraid I've already got my hopes up."

He got up from the table they were using as a work area. "So have I. I would love for you to be nearby. The Clarkes' house is walking distance."

"That would be nice. When's the last time you were in their house?"

His eyes narrowed. "It's been a good few years. Which means I don't really know what kind of shape it's in. But anything broken can be fixed. Anything you don't like can be changed." He put his hands up. "And I know that means money, but it doesn't all have to be done overnight, either."

She turned to face him fully. "I understand that, but if it's the main living areas, they will have to be dealt with before I move in. And I don't want to be house poor."

He put his hands on her arms. "I'm sure it'll be fine. I'm not without skills, you know. I can fix things and paint and—"

"You are a very sweet man to offer, but we aren't exactly young anymore. You're potentially talking about a lot of work."

He shrugged. "Painting a room isn't a lot of work. If it takes a little longer than hiring a professional, who cares? You're not about to be homeless."

He was right. She knew that. But it was her nature to focus on the worst-case scenarios. "I guess we'll know soon enough how much work it'll take. And what kind of money they expect to get for this place."

"I promise you, it'll be fair. They understand that not going through a realtor will mean saving on the commission they'd have to pay. That will be factored in."

"Good." She glanced at the time. "Should we go?"

"Let me just make sure I hit Save." He went back to the computer and tapped the keyboard. "All done. Let's go see your new house."

She wasn't so convinced, but she gave him a smile all the same.

They drove, which seemed ridiculous when they arrived two minutes later. Conrad hadn't lied about it being close.

She sat in the car for a second, staring through the window. The house was white brick with a gray roof, gray shutters and a dark blue door. The landscaping was a little overgrown and could use some color, but the yard had two nice big trees in it. Shade in Florida was always a good thing.

"What do you think?" Conrad asked.

"I might want to brighten up that door color. And the landscaping could use a good manicure. Some flowers, too. Maybe window boxes on the house would be nice."

"All very doable. Ready to go in?"

She nodded and they headed for the front door. Conrad rang the bell, but the door was answered so quickly, Margo knew their arrival had been noticed.

The gray-haired woman at the door was petite and round and very smiley. "Hello, Conrad. So nice to see you."

"You, too, Mirna. This is my friend, Margo. The lady I said might be interested in the house."

Mirna stuck her hand out. Her nails and her lipstick were the same shade of coral. "Hi, Margo. Nice to meet you. Welcome to our home." She giggled. "Which might become your home!"

Then she looked behind her. "Sal. *Sal*! Conrad and his girlfriend are here."

Margo sucked in a breath at the use of the word "girlfriend." It really wasn't something she was used to. But the house was what really caught her eye. It was neat and tidy and obviously well-maintained, but definitely dated. The interior had a very *Brady Bunch* kind of feel to it. At least the flooring had been replaced with large neutral tile at some point. But there was still wood paneling on one wall.

An older man came from the other side of the house. "I was trying to find that survey." He smiled at them. He was as thin as Mirna was round, but only a few inches taller. His bushy mustache seemed to suit his kindly face. "Hello, there, Conrad. Young lady."

Margo smiled. "I'm Margo."

"Pleasure to meet you. I'm Sal, in case you hadn't guessed," Sal said. "Come on in. The missus and I will go sit on the lanai so you can wander as you like." He pointed right. "Master bedroom's that way, the other two bedrooms are on the opposite side."

"Thanks," Margo said. She liked the pair of them. They seemed like the sort of people who'd be good neighbors. She had no doubt they'd be missed when they moved.

"Appreciate it, Sal," Conrad said. He looked at Margo as they came in and shut the door behind them. "Master first?"

She nodded and got her phone out so she could take pictures of everything.

They went in. It was a good-sized room with a lot of natural light. To the right were two small walk-in closets that faced each other, making a small hall that led to the bathroom.

The burnished gold carpet that started at the threshold would have to go, as would the foiled wallpaper. She took a couple of photos, then leaned in toward Conrad. "I guess the Seventies was the last time this place was decorated."

"Good guess. My word, it's like a time capsule." Conrad ran his hand over his head. "That's all cosmetic, though. Easy enough to change."

"It is." Margo concentrated on the size and shape of the room, ignoring the garish décor. She did her best to imagine it painted a soothing sea blue with a light driftwood-colored hardwood floor. The sunlight streaming in was good. The room could really be something.

She turned to him. "Let's have a look at the bathroom."

Conrad gestured toward it. "Lead the way."

She groaned softly as she went in. It was a sea of harvest gold. The tub, the sinks, the toilets. She snapped some shots. "I'd have to change all of this. I can't live with this color."

"I'm with you there. But it would be a chance to put your signature on things. Really make it a showplace."

That appealed to her more than he knew. It would be all new and just the way she wanted it.

That was tremendously enticing. But it wouldn't be cheap. Bathrooms and kitchens were the most expensive to redo.

She already understood one thing about this house – a lot depended on how much they were asking. And how much she could get for her place. The difference between those two numbers would determine what changes she could make, because she wasn't comfortable dipping too deeply into her savings.

She was almost afraid to see the kitchen, but there was no point in putting it off. "Kitchen next."

Conrad nodded. "Off we go."

The tile she'd seen when they came in continued into the kitchen, which had miraculously been updated in the last couple of decades. It wasn't new by any means, but it was newer. And the oak cabinets seemed to be in good condition. They'd be cheaper to paint than replace.

The appliances would have to be replaced, but that was all right. These were sort of an off-white. She'd get stainless steel.

She stood back and got a picture of the whole room. Then she ran her hand over the laminate countertop. "Quartz would be a big improvement in here."

"New cabinets, too?" Conrad asked.

"No." She opened a drawer, inspecting the condition of it, then moved on to the upper cabinets and looked at those. "I think they could just be painted or resurfaced. Maybe with a nice light color."

"Color?" He seemed surprised.

She smiled. "Do you think I don't like color?"

He laughed. "I honestly wasn't sure."

"What if I told you I could see these cabinets in a soft buttery yellow with white quartz countertops and a blue and white tile backsplash?"

"Really?" His brows lifted. "That sounds pretty nice, actually. You wouldn't get tired of it?"

"No, I don't think I would. But if I did, I could always have the cabinets painted again."

"And the walls?"

"White."

"You always know what you want, don't you?"

She smiled at him, letting her gaze drift over him. "Yes. I do."

Chapter Twenty-three

*J*ules gave Cash her car keys and sent him to the Dolphin Club early, along with some money to buy himself lunch. Then she texted Jesse to give him a heads up that Cash would be there sooner than expected, but that she was staying home to work on new music.

I hope you don't mind, she added.

Not at all. I can put him to work. Although I'll miss you.

Same. That wasn't a lie, but the truth was, she needed some alone time to think about the rest of her album. One great song wasn't enough.

And she didn't want the rest of them to be throwaways. The pressure was no joke. Especially with the way everyone who'd heard *Dixie's Got Her Boots On* had reacted.

She strummed that tune first, quietly singing

along but without any real effort. She just wanted to get herself back in that same headspace. She thought about the natural progression of what would happen next in Dixie's story.

What would happen if Dixie had really walked into a bar, found her husband cheating on her with another woman, gotten him home, and then shot him.

Jules slowed the song down considerably and changed it to a minor key, giving the song a more plaintive and haunting sound.

Dixie would want to get rid of the evidence.

What was the best way to do that? Jules could only think of one thing. Fire.

She started singing softly, not really sure where things were going just yet. "House on fire, flames climbing higher..."

That wasn't quite it, though. Something about it was too real. She understood what that meant, but knew it wasn't something she'd be able to explain to most people. She smiled. Jesse would probably get it.

She added a bluesy little riff and nodded. That sounded right. "House on fire, flames climbing higher, memories turned to ash..." No. She tried again, thinking through a few phrases. "House on fire, flames climbing higher, dust to dust, ash to ash, with a little bit of luck, this too shall pass."

She smiled. She was getting somewhere. She kept it bluesy as she worked her way forward, stopping every once in a while to jot down the lyrics she liked.

Amazing herself, she had the rough first draft of her next song in less than an hour. Some of the lyrics needed work and the bridge wasn't quite there, but *House On Fire* was good. She was happy with it.

Could she do more? She tried to really sink into the story she was telling, and what the mood of the album would be. A woman empowered? A woman driven to a dark place? The consequences of her actions?

A new thought came to her in the form of a single word. Redemption. Then a title popped into her head. *Last Sunday Sermon.* What if Dixie went to church one more time before turning herself in to the police? What if she went up front at the altar call and prayed not for herself, but for the baby she'd only just realized she was carrying?

"The preacher doesn't know I've got *two* souls to save," Jules sang softly. "How am I ever going to be that brave?"

She grinned. "Oh, that is sad and perfect."

Country music loved tragedy. And what was more tragic than a pregnant woman going to jail because she'd just killed her baby daddy for cheating on her?

Jules felt gleeful. There was no other way to put it, but this was country music gold. She wrote on, strumming a few notes here and there and filling the pages of her notebook with song ideas and little bits of music and lyrics she liked.

It wasn't until her stomach rumbled that she looked at the time. She should break and eat lunch. She was on a roll and she hated to interrupt that kind of flow, but then again, if she got too hungry, that could interrupt her just as easily.

Not only that, but Toby could probably use a break and Jules wasn't sure, but she thought she was the only one home. She put her guitar down and jumped in the elevator. She got off one floor down.

"Toby?" She didn't see him in the living room. She went into the bedroom to find him asleep on the little throw rug between the two beds. "There you are."

He wagged his tail.

"Do you want to go out?"

Reluctantly, he got up.

She laughed. "You don't have to, you know."

With a little doggy sigh, he wandered toward the

living room. She followed him all the way into the laundry room, a sure sign that he wanted to go out, since that's where Jules kept his leash. She clipped it to his collar and took him downstairs.

Once on the ground floor, he jogged toward the patch of grass on the side of the house and peed right away.

She glanced at the pool. The water looked so good. That was the only problem with living in a beautiful place. The desire to play hooky from work and life and all of one's responsibilities was strong.

She could have easily thrown on a suit and spent the rest of the day lounging poolside, reading a good book and soaking up some rays.

But she had an agent who was expecting an album from her, and that album needed songs. At least nine. She'd never released an album with fewer than that, so her fans would expect that many. Less than that and they might not be so happy.

Toby was busy sniffing a new weed that apparently hadn't been there yesterday. Maybe when Cash got back from the Dolphin Club they'd come down for a quick swim.

Jules sank into her thoughts again. What if one of her songs was a cover? She knew what song it would be, too. *Folsom Prison Blues*. She'd have to reach out to the estate of Johnny Cash and see what it would take to procure a mechanical license.

She loved Johnny Cash, not just as a singer and musician, but as a songwriter. There were very few others who compared to his poetry and originality. She admired him so much, she'd named one of her sons after him.

Getting the permission and license would take time and phone calls. Time she'd much rather spend on her songs. Maybe Billy could handle some of that for her. She reached for her phone and realized she'd left it upstairs.

Toby had moved on from the weed to a spot of bird droppings on a rock.

"Okay, Toby, that's enough sniffing for one day. Let's go. Back upstairs and you can have a treat."

That got his ears up. He trotted toward the elevator.

As they went upstairs, a new song idea came to her. One that would be Dixie talking to her unborn child. Her daughter, maybe? Or would a son be more interesting? Jules decided she wouldn't know for sure until she played around with it.

On the second floor, she gave Toby a peanut butter dog cookie, then fixed herself a lunch of a ham and cheese wrap with a side of celery sticks and apple slices. Inspired by Toby, she added a heaping tablespoon of peanut butter to dip them in.

Toby ate his cookie and hopped up on the couch for another nap.

Jules took her plate and a tall glass of ice water upstairs via the elevator. She'd call Billy, then get back to work. If things went well, she might have two more songs mapped out before the end of the day. If she got permission to do the cover of *Folsom Prison Blues*, that would give her five in total.

Four more and she'd be set.

But what if... What if she could come up with a duet that Cash could sing with her? Would he? He had a nice voice, no matter what he thought. She'd heard him sing ever since he was a kid.

It was just a matter of getting him to agree to do it and she wasn't sure he would. Then again, she'd talked him into playing rhythm guitar for her.

Having her son on the album with her would be quite a way to introduce him to the world. Even if he never worked in music again, it would be a memory that would last them both a lifetime.

She walked out of the elevator and set her plate and glass down on the coffee table, then picked up her guitar again.

She was hungry, but the ideas were coming too

fast to ignore and not just about the mother-son duet. Although that would be something amazing if she could pull it off.

She scooped up some peanut butter with one of the apple slices and stuck it in her mouth. As she chewed, she settled her guitar in her lap, then grabbed her pen to jot some notes. There'd be time to eat the rest later.

Chapter Twenty-four

Claire stood on the sidewalk in front of the shop, staring through the large windows. Standing on a plywood platform, a couple of mannequins, one missing a head, the other armless, displayed summer dresses. Behind them was a back-drop of mismatched shower curtains that made seeing much more of the store impossible.

She didn't know what to make of that.

Obviously, the building had once housed some sort of real store. A good-sized one. Maybe a grocery store. Or an old department store. But this? This was Roxie's hidden gem? Her secret to great clothes without spending a lot of money?

Claire looked at the redhead beside her. "You're kidding, right?"

"Not at all." Roxie frowned. "I love Classic Closet.

And if you remember, I did ask you to keep an open mind."

"It's a *thrift* shop. This stuff is secondhand. Other people have *worn* these clothes."

"So what? They're clean. Or they can be cleaned."

Claire's lip curled. "I don't think this is for me."

Roxie cocked one hip out. "Oh, suddenly you have more money to spend?"

"No, but...secondhand clothing?"

"There's nothing wrong with it," Roxie said. "In fact, it's environmentally sound. It's basically recycling."

"Yeah." Claire was unconvinced.

Roxie rolled her eyes. "Look, you can stay out here, but I'm going in."

"To look for what?"

"I have no idea. That's the beauty of this place. I always find something I didn't know I needed." She plucked at her gingham top. "This came from here. I looked up the brand, too. This top was fifty bucks new. I got it for three fifty."

Claire's mouth came open. It was a cute blouse. "For real?" Maybe she was being a little hasty.

Roxie nodded, smiling. She pulled the door open. "Wouldn't hurt to look, right?"

"I suppose not." Claire followed Roxie in.

Once inside, there was almost too much to look at but, thankfully, the racks were divided into areas with signs hanging over them. Men's, women's, kids, household, miscellaneous. There were smaller sections inside those. Shoes were all together, as were pants, tops, accessories, and so on.

Naturally, things were divided by sizes, too. It was a lot more organized than Claire had been able to see through the windows. She'd actually been picturing bins of old things that had to be dug through. This place, while old and somewhat rundown, was clean and tidy.

She was a little embarrassed that she'd thought otherwise. Her mother had always donated to thrift and charity shops, but never patronized them as a customer.

In Claire's mind, thrift stores were for the poor and needy. More of her mother's influence.

And while Claire might not be needy, she wasn't exactly flush, either. Having all that money in the bank was great, but she couldn't touch it. Not until the financing stuff was all taken care of. And even then, she could only really dig into it for household bills and genuine emergencies.

Buying a new wardrobe was neither of those things.

"What sort of stuff are you looking for?" Roxie asked from one rack over. "You said you wanted a new wardrobe, right?"

"I do," Claire answered as she perused the rack in front of her. "But I don't really know what kinds of things I should get, other than I need more color. Everything I have now is so blah." She felt eyes on her, looked over, and realized Roxie was watching her. "What?"

Roxie had a coy expression on her face. "I could put an outfit together for you."

Claire pursed her lips. "I'm sure you could."

"No, I mean it. Something nice. You said yourself that I always look cute."

Claire thought about it. Might be interesting to see what Roxie came up with. And she had nothing to lose. "All right, why not?"

Roxie grinned. "Okay, I'd better go get a cart. This is going to be fun."

Claire wasn't so sure.

Fifteen minutes later, she was standing in front of the dressing rooms with Roxie, who had a whole shopping cart full of clothes. When it came to shopping, the woman was no joke. Claire had barely been able to keep up. Roxie knew brands and what to look for in a thrifted item and whether or not it was worth the money.

Roxie rubbed her hands together. "All right. Outfit number one."

"Number one?" Claire glanced at the cart. She'd thought most of that was stuff Roxie had picked out for herself. "How many did you get me?"

Roxie shrugged one shoulder. "A few. Don't worry about it. I wasn't sure what you'd go for, so I thought a wide selection was better."

Claire nodded. "Let's see it."

Roxie pulled out a tiny white tank top and white capri leggings that looked way too small, along with a teal and navy scarf.

Claire shook her head. "No way."

Roxie made a face. "You don't even know what it is yet."

"Yes, I do, and no."

Roxie rolled her eyes. "First of all, this tank top is shapewear by Yummy Mummy, and it would be forty bucks if new." She glanced at the tag. "As it is, it's priced at six bucks and it's got a blue dot on the tag. All blue dots are half price today."

Yummy Mummy was high-end shapewear. Claire knew, because she had some, bought from Dillard's at full price. "I'm still not wearing something like that by itself."

"Of course not, silly." Roxie lifted the scarf. "This goes over the tank and the leggings."

"A scarf?" Claire crossed her arms. Roxie had so much to learn.

Roxie blew out a breath. "It's not a scarf, it's a tunic." She put the tank and leggings back on the cart and held the top by the shoulders, shaking it out to reveal a slightly shear but flowy tunic that would easily cover Clair down to mid-thigh. It was mostly teal with a navy paisley pattern and a few sequins scattered over the front.

"Oh." It was prettier than Claire had realized. Surprisingly, it didn't look cheap, either. Who was donating all this stuff?

Roxie picked up the rest of the outfit and pushed it toward Claire. "At least try it on. The whole thing would be less than fifteen bucks."

Claire lifted her brows. "For the whole thing?"

Roxie grinned. "I told you."

Claire slipped into the dressing room and pulled the curtain shut. She had a slight out-of-body experience as she shed her clothes and tried to think through how she'd gotten here. Her, Claire Thompson, at a thrift shop, trying on someone else's castoffs.

But Roxie was right. What was wrong with that? Nothing. And while it might feel odd to Claire, she needed to get over herself. She tugged on the leggings.

She wasn't a wealthy woman. She pulled the tank top down, thankful it was so stretchy. She no longer had a man to rely on, although Danny was no slouch in that area, but he wasn't her husband. They were business partners, which required her to be someone he could rely on.

That meant watching her money. Being financially sound. Making smart decisions.

The thrift store seemed pretty smart so far.

She put the tunic on and smoothed it out. The fabric was really nice. Maybe even silk. She wondered how much the top was. She checked the tag. Twelve dollars, but it had a blue dot. Six bucks? For this?

She glanced at her reflection in the mirror. The color was beautiful and really made her face come alive. The drape of the fabric was very forgiving, too, but the tank top and leggings were doing a great job of making the silhouette underneath smooth and trim.

She pulled the curtain back. "What do you think?"

Roxie smiled. "I think you just found outfit number one."

"Yeah? You think it looks all right? Not too young for me?"

"It does make you look younger. But not like you're trying too hard." Roxie nodded in appreciation. "If you don't buy it, I will."

Claire smiled. "I'm getting it." She held out her hand. "Next outfit."

Roxie stayed with her for the next twenty minutes, giving her opinion on everything Claire tried. There were two outfits Roxie didn't like, giving Claire some confidence that the woman was being straight with her.

She ended up with three complete outfits, two tops, a cute pair of floral Bermuda shorts that she never would have tried on her own, two sundresses, and a small raffia handbag.

Roxie picked up a new top and a pair of sunglasses.

Claire spent just under the hundred dollars she'd wanted to. She was very happy.

And she had Roxie to thank.

Chapter Twenty-five

*H*aving never been surfing, Trina wasn't sure what to bring other than sunscreen and a towel. Kat, on the other hand, had a whole beach bag. Trina pointed at it as they walked toward the car. "What are you bringing? You're making me think I forgot something."

"Probably too much," Kat said. "I brought a change of clothes, since we're going out to eat afterwards."

"Oh." Trina was wearing shorts and a T-shirt over her bikini. She'd just figured she'd put them back on after she dried off. "Should I have brought clothes, too?"

Kat shrugged and unlocked the car. "Up to you. You want to run back up and get something?"

Trina stood there, trying to decide. She could

grab a bag and throw a sundress in it. Maybe a little makeup bag. A hair tie. "I'll be right back. I'll hurry."

"Okay," Kat said. "I'll get the AC going."

Trina ignored the elevator and took the stairs, using her key to get in the front door.

Willie peered at her from the living room. "Change your mind?"

"No, just forgot some stuff." Trina got her beach bag and tossed in her sparkly black flipflops along with a black tank-style sundress that had pink and red flowers on it. She added a red hair clip, then dug through the rest of her accessories.

Into a smaller bag she put some jewelry: big red hoop earrings and two matching bracelets. Into a cosmetics bag, she put the bare essentials: mascara, eyeliner and a hot pink lipstick, which could double as a cream blush. She tossed in a bronze eyeshadow stick, too, just for good measure.

She started out of the room, then realized if she wasn't wearing her bikini anymore, she'd need underwear. That went in the bag. Finally, she headed for the door. "Bye, Mimi."

"Bye, honey."

Trina hustled down the steps and jumped in the car. "Okay, sorry."

"No problem." Kat got the car moving and they

were off to meet the boys. "Are you nervous about learning to surf?"

"Nah. Are you? I think it'll be fun."

"I'm not great at sports. I just don't want to make a fool of myself, you know?"

Trina nodded. "I don't think Alex expects you to be great at it on your first attempt."

"Yeah, probably not." Kat smiled.

A few minutes later, they pulled into the parking lot at Carlton Fiske park, the same place they'd come for the sandcastle building contest. The boys were already there, unloading surfboards from Alex's truck and Miles's SUV.

The girls got out, grabbed their stuff, and went to meet them.

Trina leaned up and gave Miles a kiss on the cheek. "Hiya."

"Hi." He smiled. "Ready to catch some waves?"

"I hope so."

He glanced over at Alex, then said, "We have something for you guys."

"Yeah?" Kat said. "You mean a surfboard?"

Alex shook his head and took a plastic shopping bag out of his car. "Something else. We got you each a rash guard."

Trina didn't love the sound of that. "Surfing gives you a rash?"

Miles snorted. "It can. From laying on the waxed surface of the board. But the shirts are good for sun protection, too."

"You put wax on the boards?" There was so much Trina didn't know about surfing.

Miles nodded. "To help you grip the board when you're standing up. Otherwise, the deck is super slick. That's the part you stand on."

"The deck," Trina repeated. She felt cooler already from learning some of the terms.

Alex pulled the rash guards out of the bag. A blue one for Kat and a pink one for Trina. "I think we got the right sizes. They're meant to fit snug. The last thing you want is a lot of loose fabric tugging you down."

He handed them to the girls. Trina put her bag down and pulled the long-sleeved shirt over her head. It had the logo of the surf shop on the front. Chauncey's. She smiled. "How do I look?"

Miles nodded appreciatively. "Like a real surfer girl."

Kat had her rash guard on, too. Alex gave her a thumbs-up. "All right, let's get down to the beach and get this lesson underway."

Miles carried both of the boards he'd brought. Alex did the same. They found a nice open spot on the beach and put their stuff down.

The guys put the boards down, too, setting them all parallel to each other and flat on the sand.

Alex rubbed his hands together. "Okay, first things first." He went through some of the words they'd need to know, explaining terms like how the front of the board was the nose and the sides were the rails. Then he pointed out the fins, which were on the underside of the board, and the leash, which was connected to the top of the board and would be used to keep the board attached to them by a Velcro ankle strap.

Next, he talked about the waves. "The shoulder of the wave is where it hasn't broken. You always paddle toward that part when you're surfing."

Trina nodded. "Paddle toward the shoulder."

He went over a few other parts of the wave before pointing at Miles. "Rules."

Miles stepped up. "Basic surfing etiquette, especially for newbies like you guys, is don't cut in on other people's waves. Now, this beach gets a lot of newbies, so there won't be too many hardcore regulars here, but when there are, you defer to them."

Kat put her hands on her hips. "Aren't you guys hardcore regulars?"

Alex laughed. "Yeah, we are. And you'll get cut some slack, since you're with us and you're chicks, but you still shouldn't cut in on a wave someone else is already riding. Don't sit in the way of anyone already riding a wave, either. Move as best you can. Some of the gray bellies will go mental on you."

"Gray bellies?"

Miles grinned. "The old-timers. Gray bellies are another surfer term for sharks, which is what we call the old-timers, since they've been in the water so long."

Trina giggled. "Good to know."

Kat didn't look so amused. "Are there actually going to be sharks?"

"Always a chance," Alex said. "But also pretty rare. Even more rare when you're in a group. If you were alone, your odds might go up."

Kat made a face. "I am never surfing alone."

Miles nodded. "Most of us don't. It's just safer with company, for a lot of reasons."

"Okay," Alex said. "Other things you need to know. Don't ever let go of your board. Look at the nose. How pointed it is. Under the pressure of the water, that thing can become a missile. It's hard and got some weight to it and the last thing anyone wants is to get rammed."

Trina grimaced. "But that's why we have the leash, right?"

"Yes, but leashes can break," Alex said. "Doesn't happen a lot, but it's not unheard of."

Miles continued. "The ocean is a powerful thing. Do your best to hang on to your board. Not just because of the people around you, but also because surfboards float. A wave can't push you to the bottom if you've got hold of your board."

Trina glanced over at Kat. She looked a little unsure. Trina shot her a smile. "We're going to be just fine."

Kat smiled back but it was tight. "I know."

Alex looked at Miles. "I think they're ready for pop-ups."

"Definitely." Miles nodded. "Let's get you guys doing some pop-ups so you're comfortable," he said. "Then we'll hit the water."

Trina had no idea what pop-ups were, but she was ready to go.

Chapter Twenty-six

Kat glanced down the lineup several yards away where Trina and Miles were on their boards. Trina was smiling and laughing and looked like she was having a ball.

Kat wasn't. Not exactly. She knew she was getting wound up in her own imagination too much, but she couldn't help but wonder if every little thing that touched her foot wasn't something with a lot of teeth and sandpaper skin. She was thankful that Alex was close by on his board, but she kept hearing the theme song to *Jaws*.

"Hey," Alex said. "You okay?"

He'd noticed, so there was no denying it. She took a deep breath. "I'm not as comfortable in the water as I thought I'd be."

He reached out to take her hand. "If you don't

want to do this, you don't have to. I'm not going to like you any less."

She laughed. "That's good to know." Then she shook her head. "I do want to do this. The whole shark thing just kind of got into my head."

"They're really not all out to eat you, you know. They're actually pretty beautiful creatures. Kind of misunderstood, too. They're killed by humans in far greater numbers than they kill us."

She felt a tiny pang of sympathy for the creatures, even though she was still afraid of meeting one. "Have you ever seen one? When you were out here, I mean."

He nodded. "Sure. Dolphins, too. Occasionally a sea turtle. All kinds of cool fish. That's one of the things I love about being out here, is being surrounded by that kind of nature. It's pretty epic."

She loved how he looked at things. "I guess it is pretty epic."

"Also, I have no doubt that a shark would go for me before it would go for you." Alex grinned. "I am much tastier."

She snorted. "Oh, is that right?"

"Heck, yes. Who wants a skinny girl for dinner when they could have a tasty hunk of muscle like me?"

Laughter bubbled up inside her, taking away a lot of her fear. Didn't hurt that Alex thought she was skinny, either.

He glanced over his shoulder at a rising swell coming toward them. "All right, let's paddle. We're getting this one."

She went flat on her board as he did the same, cupping her hands and using them to push through the water.

As they began to separate, Alex called after her, "Just do everything like you did it on the beach."

She nodded, knowing he probably couldn't see her, but focusing on what he'd taught her, trying to match the speed of the wave with her paddling. She felt the board lift. The wave was under her. She gave an extra hard push, her heart thumping with adrenaline.

Pop up, hands in the center, curl your toes, land with bent knees. She did all of those things as they went through her head, pushing up with her front foot and planting her feet, knees bent.

She was going to fall over any second, she could feel it, but then she got her arms out and her core engaged and, for a few impossible seconds, she was up, gliding almost airborne on the crest of the wave, the world beneath her feet, the breeze blowing her hair back, the salt spray dancing over her skin.

She was flying. Arms out, she turned to look for Alex and lost her balance. As she started to go down, she grabbed the rails of the board. The wave washed over her, and she came off the board, but she was in close enough to plant her feet on sand now. She walked toward the beach a little more, stopping when the water was just below her knees to get her bearings.

She picked her board up, holding it under her arm. She spotted Alex. He was still on the wave.

He rode it all the way in, then jumped off, grabbed his board, and sloshed through the water toward her. "You did it, baby! You did it! You got up on your first wave. That's freaking amazing!"

He kissed her on the mouth, right there in the middle of the water.

She was laughing and crying, happy tears that completely surprised her. She nodded. "I can't believe I did it."

"I am so proud of you," he said. "You conquered your fear. A lot of people would never have made it into the water, but you not only made it, you rode a wave. You are a rock star. How did you like it?"

She sniffed, grinning ear to ear. "It was the coolest thing I've ever done. I felt like I was flying."

He nodded. "It's like nothing else. Until you've experienced it, you can't really understand what it feels like to soar like that."

She licked her lips, tasting salt. "I want to do it again."

He smiled. "Yeah?"

She nodded. Maybe there *were* sharks out there, but she didn't care quite so much anymore.

They spent two more hours in the water. Kat got up three more times, although the second time she went down just as fast. Trina managed to get to her feet twice but once only made it to her knees. The boys got up every time they caught a wave.

On her last attempt, Kat didn't have the strength to push up and realized she was wiped out, no surf pun intended. Her arms and legs felt like jelly. She waved at Alex and pointed toward the beach. He nodded, so she went in.

He followed a few minutes after her. "You okay?"

"I'm great, I'm just beat." She wanted to sit, but she'd be covered in sand if she did that. "I've got nothing left."

"You did really good today. You lasted longer than I thought you would." He glanced back. "Miles and Trina are on their way in, too. I think we're all ready to call it a day and get something to eat. Sound good?"

"Sounds perfect. Any chance we could shower?"

He nodded. "We can use the facilities at the firehouse, if that's all right with you guys. There's a women's locker room, too, even though we don't currently have any women on the crew. We used to, but Jill moved to Texas because of her husband's job. Anyway, you'd have it to yourselves and there's towels and everything."

"Works for me."

Trina and Miles walked up to join them, boards under their arms. Trina looked as tired as Kat felt.

"Man," she said. "That was fun but exhausting."

Miles laughed. "Surfing burns a lot of calories, which is why we're going to Coconuts and eating everything on the menu."

Trina shook her head. "I don't know about everything, but I am definitely getting dessert."

"You know what?" Kat said. "So am I. After we shower. I need to get this salt off me."

Alex nodded. "All we have to do is load up the boards, then we're off."

While the boys took care of the boards, Kat and Trina pulled off their rash guards, and dried themselves as much as possible. Kat explained about going to the firehouse to clean up and change.

"Cool," Trina said. "A shower would be the best right now. You did pretty good out there today."

"So did you," Kat said. "I want to do it again. Do you?"

Trina nodded. "Yeah, I'm game. I'm kind of surprised you do, though."

Kat lifted her chin, smiling as she said words she'd never imagined would come out of her mouth. "What can I say? I think I might be a surfer girl now."

Chapter Twenty-seven

*W*illie snoozed a little on the poolside lounge chair. The sun and the warmth lulled her to sleep without her even trying. The beautiful day, the distant rhythm of the waves, and being out by the pool made the nap even better.

It helped, too, that Willie's hangover was finally gone. She was never drinking that much again on a mostly-empty stomach. Well, not that much rum, anyway. She was old enough to know better and too old to be that foolish.

If she'd been the kind of woman who got embarrassed, last night would have done it. Thankfully, she was too old for those sorts of regrets, too. She chose to live her life without caring what other people thought.

The sound of splashing water made Willie open her eyes.

Roxie was swimming laps, something Willie should probably do, but she was too comfortable to move. She checked the time on her phone. She'd invited Miguel over and he should be here any moment. Wouldn't do to get her hair wet, not with how nice it looked right now. Trina had fixed it up for her a bit before she'd left to go surfing.

"Hola!" Miguel called out.

She lifted her sunglasses and saw him coming through the side yard. She smiled. What a nice sight to see. "Hello, there."

He was in swim trunks with an unbuttoned tropical shirt, sunglasses, a straw fedora, and had a towel draped over his arm. On his feet, he wore tobacco-brown wide-strap leather sandals.

The man, Willie thought, looked like a movie star in everything. She patted the chaise next to her.

He unfurled his towel over the chair and sat, kicking off his sandals to cross his ankles as he reclined. "You look lovely, as always." He patted her hand. "How are you?"

Willie went with straight-up honesty. She blew out a breath. "For most of the day, I was feeling the effects of all that rum last night."

He nodded in sympathy. "Aye yai yai, so was I. We overdid it, I think. I am sorry about that."

She shook her head. "Nothing to be sorry for. We had fun."

"Too much fun," Miguel said.

"Eh, it's only too much fun if someone ends up with a tattoo they don't remember or needing bail money." Although now that she thought about it, she hadn't really looked all of herself over yet today. It was possible she'd come home with ink, but she didn't think Miguel would have let her do that alone. "We didn't get tattoos, did we?"

"No." He laughed. "You are some kind of woman, Willie." He looked at her. "You're feeling better now?"

"Oh, yes. I'm good. Been staying hydrated. You?"

"I am better, too. Looking forward to a good dinner, though." He patted his stomach. "I made breakfast for Danny but didn't eat much of it myself. My appetite is coming back now, thankfully."

"I have to have carbs when I'm hungover. Roxie made me pancakes for breakfast, and we're ordering pizza for dinner. Well, I am. Roxie will probably get a salad. The place we order from does a nice one with Italian meats and cheeses on it."

He nodded. "That sounds good. Danny is making *pollo guisado* for us this evening. That's chicken stew. Very delicious. Claire and Ivelisse, my granddaughter, are coming over, too. We have a lot to talk about with the bakery, so it's a business dinner."

"I'm sure you're all very busy with that," Willie said.

"We are." He looked around. "Where is your granddaughter?"

"She's out with Kat and the two young men they've gotten to know. The boys took them surfing today. They're going out to eat somewhere after."

"And the rest of your house?"

"Claire is here, but I don't know what she's doing. Jules and her son were down just a few minutes ago for a quick swim, but then they went back in to work on some music. He was working at the Dolphin Club today. We should go sometime. You love music."

"I do. She's a singer, right?"

Willie nodded. "She is. I looked her up on the internet. She's a pretty good one, too."

"Life is funny," Miguel said. "You never know who you're going to meet, do you?"

She shook her head. "You really don't."

"You should come over later, after our business is done. Meet my granddaughter."

Willie smiled. "Yeah?"

"Yes," Miguel said. "I've already told her about you."

Willie was touched. If Miguel wanted her to meet his granddaughter, he was obviously serious about how he felt about her. Sure, he'd already asked her to marry him, but that was when he thought she might end up without a place to live.

"I'd love to meet her," Willie said. Roxie was getting out of the water. "What time?"

"I'll text you after we finish our dinner. You can come for dessert, if you like. Ivelisse is bringing a *tres leches* cake from the Latin grocery store. That means three milks. It's one of my favorites."

"Okay, sounds good." Willie lifted her finger as her daughter joined them. "But I'm not drinking anything tonight."

He made a face. "Don't even talk about it." He sat up a little straighter. "What do you say we get in that water? It looks so nice."

Roxie grabbed her towel and wrapped it around herself before she sat down on the other side of Willie. "You should, Ma. It's beautiful."

"I will, but I don't want to get my hair wet."

Roxie didn't lay down. Instead, she turned to see her mother better. "Do you want me to get you a pool noodle from the storage closet? There's a ton of them in there. You can just float around and not have to worry about going under."

A noodle would definitely keep her head above water. And require minimal effort on her part. Willie nodded. "That would be perfect. Thank you, honey."

"Sure." Roxie looked at Miguel. "You want one, too?"

"That's very kind of you. Yes, I will take one."

Roxie slipped on her flipflops and went back under the house. She returned with two fat foam noodles, a purple one and a green one. She held the purple one out to her mother. "Here. It almost matches your lavender hair."

Willie laughed. "Thanks."

She and Miguel stripped down to their suits, grabbed the noodles, and headed for the pool steps. The water was just cool enough to be refreshing without being too much of a shock to the system. They both went right in, tucking the noodles under their arms and floating off toward the deep end.

Willie enjoyed letting her feet dangle. It was like being weightless and she relished the feeling. In some ways, it made her feel like a kid again.

Miguel had his noodle tucked under his arms. He reached out to hold onto the ends of her noodle, putting them face to face. "This is very nice."

"It is," Willie agreed. "Why don't we do this more often?"

"I don't know," Miguel said. "But I have a pool at my house, too. And there's hardly ever anyone in it."

Willie giggled. "You mean, so we could be alone? Whatever do you have planned?"

He shrugged as best he could without losing his noodle, his eyes twinkling. "Such things are best when they just happen, don't you agree?"

Willie grinned. She loved spontaneity. "Oh, definitely. Does that mean you're inviting me over for a private pool date?"

He nodded. "You're welcome anytime. But with a little notice, I can make you some lunch, too."

"That sounds like a great way to spend the afternoon. Maybe tomorrow?"

Miguel smiled. "Why not? There's a very good chance Danny will go out to one of the shops, or maybe the new location. I'll text you."

Willie kicked her feet, closing the distance between her and Miguel even more. "And maybe by tomorrow, one little pina colada will be just the thing."

He leaned in and gave her a quick kiss before laughing softly. "I thought you were worried about getting a tattoo you won't remember."

"You'll make sure that doesn't happen, won't you?"

He nodded solemnly. "I promise."

"Good. But if I do end up with a tattoo, just make sure it's someplace no one else can see it."

Chapter Twenty-eight

Margo paced the length of Conrad's office. The lanai was too warm this afternoon, even with the fans on, for them to work comfortably out there, so they'd come back to his office and the air conditioning.

But her mind was not on the book. Instead, it was on what she'd done. She couldn't believe she'd said yes to buying the Clarkes' house. Now it was hard to think of anything else and Conrad had obviously noticed, because he kept giving her a certain look. Eyes narrowed but still shining with that knowing gleam, mouth tightly closed, his nose in the air like he could practically smell what she was thinking about.

Finally, he sighed. "You're doubting your decision."

She exhaled and sat down next to him. Pacing

was getting her nowhere and they hadn't added any new words to the book in the last ten minutes. "I'm not doubting it, exactly. The Clarkes gave me a great price. I'd be a fool not to buy that house. Even with the work it needs. It's just...it's a big decision."

The largest one she'd ever made on her own.

"It is. You're right. But you can always walk away."

She shook her head. "No. I don't want to." The house, despite its outdated décor, was about as perfect as a house could get. About ten minutes from the beach house, walking distance to Conrad's. And in a safe community with good schools, which would be great for resale when that day came for her daughters, who'd inherit the house. Not far from the police or fire station. "I just need time to settle into the idea."

"You have a month."

"I can't take a whole month to decide if I'm going to buy the house or not. I already told them yes!" She got up and started pacing again. "Besides that, I need to get my own house sold. And my things moved out. Which means I also need to figure out where those things are going to go."

She groaned softly. There was so much to do. It felt overwhelming.

He spun his chair to face her. "All you need is a storage unit for a month or two. You said so yourself. I'd offer you my garage but I don't think I can fit an entire household in there."

"That's nice of you, but I'm sure you're right. I need to bring most of my furnishings, too, since I'll have a lot of space to fill." Should she be buying a condo instead? That probably made more sense. Condos had very little maintenance. Just a fee that took care of it all.

She shook her head. "I'll have to find a lawn service and a pool service, too." She pinched the bridge of her nose.

"Maybe you should go home and talk to your family about it. Their reassurances might make you feel better. Or are you afraid to tell them?"

She stopped pacing to stand by the window, looking out. The mature trees in this neighborhood were another great feature. "I'm not afraid. I told them I'd be looking for my own place. My daughters and granddaughter don't need me living with them. Not that they act like they'd mind, but they need their own space." And she was rather looking forward to being so close to Conrad.

"Then what's bothering you? Is it the work that

needs to be done at the house? Because I promise I'll help you in whatever way I can."

She sat back down again. "I know you will, and I appreciate that. I think it's just..." She thought about what was really bothering her and the truth came to her, but it was difficult to say out loud.

"What is it?" Conrad asked softly.

"It's everything that needs to be done. It's starting to feel overwhelming. And...I've never done this without a man. My house in Landry was purchased with my second husband. My house before that was purchased with my first. Now I'm buying a place all on my own and it's daunting. Maybe it's more than I can handle. I'm not a young woman anymore, Conrad."

"No, you're not." Conrad nodded. "But you are a very *capable* woman."

"I appreciate that you think so but what if I make a mistake? What if I forget to do something?"

"What kind of mistake could you make that would be so terrible? What could you forget that couldn't still get done?" He smiled kindly. "And just FYI, you're not alone in this, you know."

He really was the sweetest man. "I understand that, Conrad, but I can't expect you to hold my hand. We aren't married. You have your own things to take care of. Your own life and responsibilities. I cannot dump all of this on you."

He winked at her. "Not that I'm not willing to help—I am, very much so, as I've said—but I meant that you have two grown daughters. Why not ask them to help you? I bet they would love to be needed in that way. Love to know that you value their input."

Margo exhaled a gentle breath. "I can't ask them. They're busy with their own lives. Jules has an album to write and record and Claire is in the midst of developing recipes for the new bakery she's helping to open. They already have so much on their plates."

"Margo." He shot her another of those looks. "Your daughters aren't the kind of women who will be too busy for their mother. You raised them better than that."

"True." She couldn't argue that. Her girls were remarkable women. She wanted to think he was right, that they'd have time. That they'd want to be involved. But would they really? They were very busy. And the idea of them turning her down...it hurt just to think about. "But I don't want their own endeavors to suffer because of me."

"You need to give them credit that they'll have

enough discernment to know just how much they can help."

She nodded, still unconvinced.

He glanced at the computer screen. "Maybe we should call it a day. We could head off to the Home Depot and have a look around at all the things you could put into your new house. Flooring, tile, carpet, appliances. Would that bring your excitement back?"

He was such a dear man. She smiled. "I am still very much excited, I promise you. I've just allowed myself to do too much thinking. To focus too much on all the things that could go wrong. And that's what's got me so overwhelmed. It's just so hard not to think that way."

"I suppose when you've lost two husbands, thinking about what could go wrong comes naturally to you."

A faint pang of grief went through her, muscle memory because she'd experienced so much of it in her life that her body knew exactly what it felt like at any given time. She nodded. "It's hard not to."

"I bet. So what do you say about that trip to Home Depot? The distraction might be just the thing to help you see the light at the end of the tunnel."

"You are so good to me." She cupped his face in her hands. "So kind and patient. Thank you." She kissed him. "I think a visit to the Home Depot sounds wonderful."

"Get your purse. I'll get the AC started in the car."

Twenty minutes later, they were staring at flooring selections in the cavernous warehouse of Home Depot, the familiar orange signs announcing each section of the store.

She was happy to be here. Happy to focus on the end result as opposed to the work required to get there. "There is so much to look at."

Conrad grimaced. "Does that mean you feel even more overwhelmed?"

Margo laughed. "Heavens, no. I can eliminate half of these without a second glance. When it comes to knowing how I want the house to look, I have no issues with making decisions. I've seen three possible options for the master bedroom already." She pointed at them. "They're all variations of the same idea. And the bathroom makeover will be just as easy. So will paint colors."

"That's fantastic." He narrowed his eyes. "You should use that same decisiveness to talk to your daughters about helping."

She held his gaze for a moment, knowing he was right. "I will. Tonight. I promise. But first, maybe we could get an early dinner and you could help me talk through that discussion a little more? Or have you had enough of me for one day?"

He laughed and took her hand. "Margo, you're about to live down the street from me and I'm still not sure I'm going to get enough of you. I think I can handle dinner."

Margo just smiled, flattered as all get out. An impulsive thought flitted through her mind with all the hope and promise of spring's first butterfly. There was every chance she was eventually going to end up marrying Conrad.

And she was more than okay with that.

Chapter Twenty-nine

Jules shook her head, amazed at her son, who'd just scrawled out a new verse for one of the songs she was working on, *Man of the World*. The song would be a mother's prayer for her son and it would be her and Cash's duet. She read it over again. "That's perfect."

Cash glanced at her, clearly skeptical. "You really think so? Or are you just saying that because you're my mom?"

"I think it's both. I'm saying it because it really is good, but I'm also saying it because I'm impressed that I gave birth to such a talented child."

He laughed. "I'm not a child anymore, Mom."

"No, you're not. But you'll aways be my baby."

He rolled his eyes even as he was smiling. "I know."

"Listen, I don't know about you, but today has

been a long day. We've both accomplished a lot. What do you say we pick this up again tomorrow? I'm sure you want to get to the beach or something."

He shrugged. "Are you sure?"

"Yes. My brain is starting to feel a little mushy. Why? Do you want to work more?"

He shook his head. "No, I'm good. I should probably get a shower."

She narrowed her eyes. Knowing her son as she did, she had to ask. "You don't usually shower this late unless you have a good reason to. And you definitely don't shower before going to the beach."

"I'm not going to the beach." His mouth bent in a funny smile, and he looked away. "I might have a date."

"What? How? Where would you have met anyone?" But she knew before he answered.

"Her name's Sierra and I met her at the club today. She's really sweet. She's one of the backup singers Jesse wants to use but she's also a server at the club. That's why she's there. To be close to the music side of things."

Jules nodded. "How old is she?"

"Twenty-six. Plays piano. Has a really good voice, too." He put up his hands, fingers splayed. "I know what you're going to say, that she might only have said yes to me because she's trying to sing backup for you, but she's cute and I'm a guy and—"

"Nope. All I was going to say was go have fun." That wasn't entirely true. She'd been thinking the same thing he'd put into words but she couldn't very well say anything now that he had. "You're old enough to decide who you want to go out with. And old enough to figure out a person's true intentions."

"I hope so. I mean, maybe I'm wrong but she seemed genuine."

For his sake, Jules hoped her son was right. "You need some money? You've certainly earned some for all the work you did today. I'm already going to have to pay you royalties on *Man of the World*."

He laughed. "As much as I hate to say yes, I actually could use a couple of bucks."

"Maybe I should just hire you as my assistant producer and put you on the payroll for real." The thought had just come to her, but it wasn't an impulse. He was helping her out more than she could have imagined possible.

He stared at her for a second, brows raised. "Seriously? Like for real and not just because I'm your son?"

"For real. You're doing so much for me. And toward making this album a reality. I'd be paying anyone else who was doing it. There's no reason you should do it for free just because you're my son."

"Wow. That would be really great."

"Come see me before you leave, and I'll give you an advance on your first paycheck."

Grinning, he got up and hugged her, sandwiching her guitar between them. "Thanks, Mom."

"You're welcome, sweetheart, but you earned this." As he let go, she got up and took her guitar off and set it aside. "See you downstairs, okay?"

"Okay."

She went out through the sliders and down the spiral steps to the second floor. She didn't go in just yet, instead settling onto the couch in the screened area. She kicked her feet up onto the coffee table and pulled out her phone to see if she'd missed anything.

Billy, whom she'd called earlier about getting the rights to cover the Johnny Cash song, hadn't responded yet other than to say he was working on it. She wasn't surprised. Things like that didn't happen overnight.

There was a text from Jesse, too. Perfect timing, she thought as she tapped the notification to read it.

Cash did great today. Meant to tell you earlier, but I've been swamped.

No worries, Jules typed back. *He did great here, too. Helped me write another song for the album. Kind of surprised me with how good it was.*

Doesn't surprise me, Jesse answered. *The kid is smart and hard-working. Why didn't he do better in CA?*

Jules shook her head. *I don't know. Except, maybe I do.* She hesitated, choosing her words carefully. *I think he was trying to follow in his father's footsteps. Rock and roll.*

Now things make sense. He's got a country soul.

Jules smiled. *Yeah, he kind of does.*

Cash had always been much more like her than Lars, his dad. Fender, on the other hand, he was his father's son. Maybe too much, sometimes.

Any chance I'll get to see you tonight? I could slip out for an hour. Maybe grab some dinner?

I'd love that. Something casual? She had no interest in getting dressed up.

Do you like Korean barbeque? Kang's is outstanding.

I've never had it but I'm game.

It's closer to you, so meet me there at 7?

That gave her almost two hours. *Perfect. It's a date.* She sent a smiley face, too.

The sliders that went into Claire's bedroom opened and Claire stepped out. She was rubbing lotion into her hands and she was wearing a bright teal tunic with white leggings and a white tank top underneath. "I didn't know you were out here."

"Just chilling for a bit. You look amazing. What are you all dressed up for? Have I seen that outfit before? I love it."

Claire smiled. "I'm not all dressed up but thank you. This is new. Sort of. New to me." She laughed. "I did a little shopping today. With Roxie, if you can believe it."

"Really?" Jules patted the cushion beside her. "How did that happen? And what do you mean 'sort of' new?"

"After the whole insurance check mess, we had a talk and just decided that we really are on the same team and that we need to act that way. I certainly didn't know about her, and she definitely didn't know about me. There's no point in us being angry at each other. Bryan's the one who deserves our anger."

"That's for sure," Jules said.

"Roxie offered to take me to the grocery store, since she had to go anyway, and Kat was going to need the car to take herself and Trina to the beach. Roxie and I got to talking, I mentioned how I could really use some new clothes but didn't want to spend the money, and she told me about one of her favorite places to shop."

"Cool. Where?"

Claire's eyes widened ever so slightly and she lowered her voice. "It's a thrift shop."

Jules snickered. Claire said the word "thrift" like it was four letters and not six. "'Thrift' isn't a dirty word, you know. I've found some amazing stuff at thrift stores."

Confusion filled Claire's eyes. "You shop at secondhand places? But you have money."

Jules shook her head. "It's not about having money. It's about finding unique and interesting pieces that nobody else has. A lot of my stage wear is vintage stuff. In some cases, it's better quality. Things aren't made the way they used to be. And getting something custom made these days, which I've done, will cost you a fortune."

Claire sat back. "I had no idea. Does Mom know?"

"That I shop at thrift stores?" Jules shrugged. "I have no idea. I can honestly say it's never come up in conversation."

"Well, don't tell her. I don't think she'd like it very much."

Jules made a face. "Claire. You're a grown woman. You're allowed to shop wherever you want."

"I know. But you know how Mom is."

Jules nodded. "Yeah, I do. I guess I've just lived my own life for so long that I don't care as much as you do. But you shouldn't be ashamed of where you shop. You shouldn't care what anyone thinks, either. Buying from thrift stores is a smart way to save money. I don't see what the big deal is."

"I just..." Claire sighed. "I don't want to hear about how I'm wearing other people's hand-me-downs. Or whatever she might say."

"Don't worry. I won't say a word." Jules grinned. "So long as you tell me where this place is."

Claire laughed. "How about I take you there, because I'm curious to have another look myself. This whole outfit was twelve dollars. Tank top, leggings, and the tunic. You should see the rest of the stuff I got, too."

"Twelve bucks?" Jules blinked. "Oh, we are going there. And soon." She hooked a thumb over her shoulder, gesturing at Claire's bedroom. "Now, let's go inside."

"Why?" Claire asked.

"Because," Jules answered. "I want to see the rest of your haul!"

Chapter Thirty

Trina was glad she'd brought clothes to change into. She felt much better than if she'd been sitting around in a damp bathing suit with only her shorts and T-shirt over them. She'd not only washed her hair but dried it thanks to the blow dryer in the women's locker room at the fire-house. They'd had shampoo, conditioner, and body wash dispensers, as well, along with towels.

She put a little makeup on, then helped Kat with some makeup, too, because Kat hadn't thought to bring any. She'd French-braided Kat's hair for her, after it was mostly dry, leaving little whisps out around her face. Trina was pleased with how they both looked. Cute but casual. Like surfer girls who'd just spent a fun day riding waves.

The guys had showered and changed into shorts and T-shirts.

Now the four of them were sitting at an outdoor table at Coconuts, which was right on the beach. The thatched roof overhead and the tropical music coming through the speakers made Trina feel like she was on vacation. The sand on the floorboards and view of the water helped, too.

"I like this place," she said to Miles.

He smiled. "So do I. It's like being on vacation."

She laughed. "I was just thinking that." She looked at her menu. "What's good here?"

"I like everything I've tried," he said. "But the coconut shrimp is sort of their specialty. They're really good. That's just an appetizer usually, but you can get them as a dinner, too."

"I've heard of coconut shrimp, but I've never had them," Trina confessed. "Isn't coconut more for dessert?"

"I guess so, but it works with the shrimp. And they give you this sweet pineapple chili sauce to dip them in, which is sweet, obviously, but also spicy." He laughed. "I think I just talked myself into an order."

"Can we share them?" Trina asked. "I'm not sure I'll like them."

"Yeah, of course," he said. "But I bet you'll love them."

"I can't wait to try them. I think I'll get the chicken sandwich for my dinner."

"I'm getting the grouper sandwich."

Trina looked across the table. "Kat, what are you getting?"

Kat glanced at her menu. "I'm getting the Coconuts salad. And we're getting an order of coconut shrimp."

"So are we," Trina said.

Miles pointed at a server going by with a tray of food. "There's the coconut shrimp now."

Trina lifted up in her seat to see better. The shrimp were fat and bumpy with a golden-brown crust. They looked really good. She still wasn't sure she'd like the taste, but she was willing to try them. "They look nice."

"They taste better," Miles said.

"What are you getting, Alex?"

He grinned. "Fish tacos with tater tots."

"What?" Trina said. "You can get tater tots instead of fries?" She looked at her menu again to check the list of sides.

Alex laughed. "It's one of the main reasons we come here."

"I am totally getting them, too."

"Same," Miles said. He looked at her again. "Hey,

you want to come over and see a movie at my place sometime?"

"Sure," Trina said. Then she shook her head. "You know what? You should really come to my place soon. Meet my mom and my grandmother. They would love to meet you."

"Yeah?" He smiled. "You think they'll like me?"

"I think they'll love you." If they liked Miles half as much as Trina did, he had nothing to worry about and she had no reason to think that wouldn't be the case.

"Okay. Cool."

"I'll text you with some dates after I get home. Make sure there's nothing else going on that interferes."

"Sounds like a plan."

Their server came back with their drinks. The boys had gotten beers. Trina had ordered a peach daquiri and Kat had gotten a mango one. They put their food orders in and handed over their menus to their server.

"The sun will be going down in about an hour or so," Miles said. "Sunset should be pretty nice. Maybe we can go for a walk after dinner."

"I'd like that," Trina said. She was happy to do just about anything with him.

A pretty girl walked by their table, then suddenly stopped and backed up. "Miles?"

He looked over and Trina could have sworn he sighed. "Hey, Liz."

Trina paid closer attention. The girl was probably around her age and had good blond hair. The kind with highlights and lowlights and a root shadow. That was time and money, right there. She was in a cute blue top that showed off her shoulders and little white shorts that showed off her legs. She wasn't just pretty with good hair. She was fit.

Even her makeup was on point. There was basically nothing wrong with her that Trina could see.

Liz gave Miles a big grin. "What are you doing here?"

Miles narrowed his eyes and bent his head, his expression clearly skeptical that she couldn't figure it out. Instead of answering her, he put his arm around Trina. "Liz, this is my girlfriend, Trina Thompson. Trina, this is an old friend of mine, Liz Stewart."

Liz laughed like Miles had just told a hilarious joke, displaying even white teeth. "I'm not that old and I wasn't just a friend. Nice to meet you, Tina."

"Trina," Trina corrected her. "Nice to meet you, too." So this was who Miles used to date? Liz looked pretty perfect. Trina had to wonder why they'd broken up.

Liz looked at Alex. "Nice to see you, Alex. Is this your girlfriend as well?"

Alex nodded. "Where's Kent?"

Liz's smile faltered for a split second. "Kent and I aren't dating anymore." She lifted her shoulders and fluttered her lashes. "I'm really enjoying the single life, though, you know? It's so freeing."

She put her hand on the table and gave Miles another coy look. "Well, it was lovely to see you. I better be getting back to my table, or my friends are going to start a search party. You be good now."

She sauntered off without waiting for Miles to respond.

Alex shook his head. "I'm so glad you stopped dating her."

Miles nodded. "Me, too."

Trina looked at him. "Why did you stop dating her?"

Miles exhaled loudly. "A lot of reasons. For one thing, she thought I should go back to school to become, in her words, a 'real' doctor."

"Why?"

"Me being a paramedic wasn't good enough for her, I guess. She comes from money and maybe her parents thought so, too. I don't know. And I don't care." Miles tensed up, and a muscle in his jaw twitched.

Trina sensed she'd hit a nerve. "I think you being a paramedic is amazing. You save lives all the time. You're a first responder. That makes you one of America's heroes."

He visibly relaxed and took her hand, giving it a squeeze. "Thanks, babe."

Trina couldn't get the image of Liz out of her head. "She's awfully pretty."

He shrugged. "She's all right on the outside but the inside ruins it. You, on the other hand, you're pretty all the way through."

Trina smiled as his words sent warm, happy feelings down her spine. "Thank you."

He leaned in and kissed her cheek. "Don't give her another thought, okay?"

Trina nodded. "I won't." She would try. It was going to be hard not to think about Liz a little bit. She was a beautiful woman that Miles wasn't interested in. That alone was something to ponder, even if he had explained why.

But then their server returned with their two coconut shrimp appetizers and Liz was forgotten.

Trina caught a whiff of toasted coconut off them.

"They do smell good."

Miles put a shrimp on one of the small plates the server had also brought and handed it to her. "Wait until you taste it. Make sure you try that sauce. But give it a second. I think they're pretty hot."

Trina laughed. "I think *you're* pretty hot."

That got Miles to laugh and Alex to groan. Miles leaned over and kissed Trina again, this time on the lips. "Feeling's mutual."

Smiling, she picked up her shrimp and dipped it in the sauce, then took a careful bite. It was crunchy and sweet, but savory and spicy, too. In a word, it was one of the best things she'd ever eaten.

Even if it was a little hot.

"What do you think?" Miles asked.

She nodded as she chewed, then swallowed. "So good. I could eat that whole plate. And I'm not just saying that because I'm starving from surfing. Those are delicious."

He grinned. "I told you." He pushed the plate toward her. "Go on. I'll get another one."

"No, no. I can't eat all those or I won't eat my sandwich." But she was touched by his kindness all the same.

When he was getting one of the shrimp for himself, Trina glanced in the direction Liz had gone. She was at a table with three other women, all of them laughing.

Except for Liz, who was watching Miles.

Chapter Thirty-one

Claire was in a buoyant mood and not just because she felt so good in her new outfit. That helped, of course. But the main lift in her spirits was because she was having dinner with Danny, his daughter, and his father and that genuinely made her feel like part of the bakery business.

Which wasn't to say she hadn't felt like part of it before, but this was a new level of inclusion. They were essentially having a family meeting about their new family business. And she'd been invited.

If that didn't fill her with warmth and confidence about how they saw her, nothing would.

Because no matter what her title was, no matter that she was going to be one of the investors, Mrs. Butter's Bakery was still a Rojas brainchild. It was still their family's new venture.

It had been Danny and Miguel's idea years ago. Claire had just come along at the right moment with the right ideas to spark them into action. She was perfectly fine with that, too. She would have been happy just to be a senior employee.

But Danny had insisted she be more. He wanted her to be more. He wanted her to get her fair share of recognition for the ideas and recipes she was contributing. She'd be putting in a lot of hard work, too.

So would Danny, but when it came to the kitchen, she'd be in there more than anyone. And she was a hundred percent ready for it.

She took a quick glance at herself in the mirror to make sure nothing was amiss, then picked up her new little purse and tucked her phone into it. The only problem with the leggings she had on was they didn't have a pocket to put her phone in. Otherwise, she wouldn't have taken a purse at all.

She went out to the kitchen, got the tin of cookies she'd made that day, and headed for the elevator. She was a little nervous about this new batch of cookies. They weren't anything she'd invented.

They were something much more important: One of the Rojas family recipes. A cookie called a *mantecadito* that was really just a traditional jam thumbprint. Instead of jam there was guava paste, which hadn't been hard to find, thanks to the extensive International Foods aisle at the Publix.

She stepped into the elevator. The recipe wasn't all that complicated, but that made getting it right even harder. The simplest recipes were the trickiest, because simple meant everything had to be perfect for the recipe to shine.

But this recipe also had a long history behind it and memories attached. Because of that, and because Danny had told her they'd had a hard time making his mother's and grandmother's recipes taste right when they'd followed them, Claire's first step had been to research the cookie before anything else.

The internet was a glorious thing. She'd found several old versions of the recipe and had compared them to the yellowed recipe card that had been in the collection of recipes Danny had turned over to her.

After much deliberation, she'd made only two changes to the recipe as it was printed. She'd used lard instead of vegetable shortening, since all of her research had said that was more traditional, which made sense, because lard would have been more readily available. She'd also added a teaspoon of vanilla extract along with the teaspoon of almond extract that was called for. She'd done that to add a depth of flavor.

She'd tried one of the cookies and thought it had turned out pretty good. But she wasn't the one who'd grown up with the recipe. Danny and his family would be the real judges.

As she got out of the elevator and walked toward Danny's house, she could only hope she'd gotten close.

Faint music reached her ears as she went up the steps to the front door, the Latin beat putting a smile on Claire's face. Ivelisse must already be here, because there was a car she didn't recognize in the drive. She rang the bell, and the door was soon opened.

Ivelisse smiled at her. "Hi, Claire. My dad's just in the kitchen putting the finishing touches on a few things. Come on in."

"Thanks." Claire stepped inside. "Nice to see you again."

"You, too." Ivelisse glanced at the tin in Claire's hands, her eyes bright with curiosity. "Did you bring us another new creation?"

Claire shook her head. "Not this time. More like an old creation."

"Now I'm really interested to see what you have in there."

They walked into the kitchen together where Danny was at the counter, adding sliced cucumbers to a big salad bowl. Miguel was sitting at the kitchen table, a soft drink in front of him. The table was set, so they were obviously eating inside, which was fine with her.

The kitchen smelled of whatever savory dish was cooking on the stove. There was one big pot, one medium one, and a large frying pan, now empty.

"Smells so good in here," Claire said.

"*Pollo guisado*," Danny answered. "Nothing fancy, just chicken stew with rice and plantains." He smiled as he saw Claire. "Don't you look nice. That's a great color. What did you bring us this time?"

"Thanks. Something that I hope I got right," Claire said. She put the foil pan on the counter. "*Mantecaditos*. If I'm even saying that right. The recipe is from the collection you gave me. I made two small changes, so I'm not sure what you're going to think of them."

Danny's mouth fell open as he sucked in a breath.

"*Mantecaditos*! I haven't had those in so long. Not the homemade ones anyway." He rinsed his hands, then dried them off on a towel. "Normally, I'd say no dessert before dinner, but for this, we're making an exception."

"Bring me one," Miguel called out.

"I will, *Abuelo*," Ivelisse answered him.

Claire took off the foil cover, revealing the colorful little cookies. On top of the guava paste, which had been added as a cube but had then melted during baking, she'd added a sprinkle of multicolor nonpareils, the way she'd seen the cookies decorated online.

"They look perfect," Ivelisse said.

Danny nodded, then he closed his eyes and inhaled. "They smell right, too."

Ivelisse took two, carrying one to her grandfather. Danny helped himself as well.

Claire waited while they all tasted them, wondering just how close she'd gotten. Maybe she shouldn't have changed anything the first time. Maybe she should have followed the recipe exactly.

"These are..." Danny shook his head.

"Like a taste of my childhood," Miguel finished. "These could be from my mother's kitchen."

Claire exhaled in relief and smiled. "Really?"

"So good," Danny said. He nodded. "They're the best version of these I've had in years."

"I agree." Ivelisse let out a happy sound of deliciousness. "You are some kind of kitchen wizard, Claire. I've made that recipe. They *never* tasted like this. What did you do?"

"Not much," Claire said. "I used lard instead of vegetable shortening and added a teaspoon of vanilla along with the almond essence."

Ivelisse popped the last bite into her mouth. "Of course. Lard makes so much sense. It's what my *abuela* would have used. And the vanilla is subtle, but it pulls the whole thing together." She looked at her father. "We have to sell these in the bakery. We have to."

He nodded. "No argument from me." He leaned over and kissed Claire on the cheek. "If I wasn't impressed with you already, I would be now. Well done."

"Thank you." She was smiling a lot, but she couldn't help it. She'd been worried about the changes she'd made, but she should have trusted her instincts.

"Take a seat," Danny said. "I'm about to serve everything up. I hope you're hungry."

"I am," Claire said. And she meant it, too, now

that the nervousness about the cookies was out of her system. "But I can help, if there's anything that needs to be done."

He shook his head. "You're our guest. Go relax."

She took a seat across from Miguel. Ivelisse brought her a big glass of ice water and a bowl of sliced bread for the table, then went back for the plantains.

Danny set the big pot on a trivet in the center of the table. "Watch out, this is hot." He returned and added the second pot. "This is the rice."

He took his seat at the end of the table and smiled at them all. "This is really nice." He reached over and took Claire's hand. "I'm so glad you're here with us. And that you're going to be a part of this new business."

Claire could only smile back. "So am I."

Chapter Thirty-two

*R*oxie hadn't wanted to leave her mom alone, so she'd invited Ethan over for dinner, which wasn't anything fancy, since they were ordering pizza. It wasn't exactly a date, either, because they had a few things to talk about concerning the salon.

Mostly Roxie wanted to be sure that they were on track with everything they needed to be doing.

He showed up before the pizzas and salad were delivered. He'd brought a six-pack of bottles. Hoppy's Old-Fashioned Cherry Soda. He held them up. "I thought Willie might like something non-alcoholic to drink. It's made right in Pensacola."

Roxie had explained about Willie being hungover. "Very kind of you." She greeted him with a quick kiss on the cheek. "Thanks for coming over."

"Hey, you say 'meat lovers pizza' and I'll show up." He grinned.

She laughed. "Good to know you're that easy."

He shrugged. "When it comes to you, I don't need a lot of persuading."

"Now you're just being sweet." She kissed him again, because why not.

"Is that Ethan?" Willie called out.

"It is," he answered.

They both went through to the living room. He showed Willie the soda. "I brought you some of my favorite cherry soda. Goes great with pizza. Would you like one?"

"That was nice of you," Willie said. "I'd love to try it."

Ethan took the six-pack over to the counter. "It's even better as an ice cream float."

"That does sound good," Willie said. "Too bad we don't have any ice cream."

"Maybe after dinner, I'll run out and get some," Ethan said. "I'm sure the convenience store up the road will at least have vanilla."

"I won't be here after dinner," Willie said.

Roxie looked at her. "You won't? Where are you going?"

"Over to Miguel's. I'm having dessert over there."

Roxie sighed. "You know I invited Ethan over here because I thought you wouldn't want to go out."

"I don't," Willie said. "But going to Miguel's isn't going out. It's right next door."

Roxie was in the kitchen, getting plates out. She glanced at Ethan and mouthed the word, "Sorry."

He came over, setting the six-pack on the counter. "Don't be. I don't mind coming over and we can go for a walk on the beach afterwards. If you want."

She nodded. "I'd like that. Thanks for being so understanding."

"Not a big deal, I promise."

The doorbell rang.

"Pizza!" Willie called out gleefully.

"Will you get her a glass of ice for that soda while I grab those?" Roxie asked.

Ethan nodded. "I'm all over it."

He came back behind the counter as she went to the door. The kid waiting there took out the two boxes of pizza from the insulated pack before handing her the bag with the salad in it. She gave him cash with a nice tip included. "Thanks."

"Thank you. Have a good night."

She closed the door and returned to the living room. The pizza smelled great, but she wasn't having more than two slices. One if they were big. "Dinner is here. Meat lovers and a plain cheese. Plus salad."

"Two pizzas?" Ethan said. "I hope you didn't order all of that because you thought I'd eat a lot."

"I ordered the plain cheese because it was a special for only five bucks and we like leftovers."

"Good," he said.

She glanced at her mother. "Two slices, Ma?"

"Yes. Just cheese. And some salad."

"Okay, give me a second, Ma, and I'll make you a plate."

"Thanks, honey."

"What kind of dressing do you want?"

"Italian." Willie was occupied watching a game show that looked unnecessarily complicated to Roxie.

"What can I do?" Ethan asked.

Roxie glanced over. "Get yourself some food and find a spot on the couch. I'll be over to join you in a second."

"Don't you need a drink?"

She shook her head as she put helpings of salad into three bowls. "No, I have a water over there."

"Okay."

She smiled. "But thanks. Italian dressing okay for you? Assuming you want salad."

"I do and it is."

In a matter of minutes, they all had their food and were sitting down to eat.

Ethan, who'd helped himself to two slices of meat lovers, grinned at her, then said softly. "I feel like I'm in high school, having a date at your house and being chaperoned by your mom."

Roxie laughed. "It does kind of feel that way."

Ethan had another slice of meat lovers, but Roxie only had seconds on the salad. Willie ate what Roxie had served her and no more. After they were done eating, Roxie cleaned up, which didn't take much.

Not long after that, Willie got a text. "That's Miguel. He asked me to come over. You two behave while I'm gone."

"Ma." Roxie shook her head. "We're going for a walk on the beach."

"That sounds nice." Willie got up and headed to her room. A moment later, she was in the elevator and waving goodbye. "Thanks for that cherry soda, Ethan. It was very good."

"You're welcome," he said as the doors slid shut.

Roxie looked over at him. "I thought we'd get a chance to talk about the salon."

"We can," he said. "If that's what you want."

What she wanted was to walk on the beach. "I

guess you'd tell us if there was something we needed to do, right? Or some decision you were waiting on us to make?"

"I would. And you're in good shape. How's everything coming along with getting supplies and all of that?"

"Good. Sign people should be there soon to take final measurements."

"Excellent. What about hiring? Has Trina thought about doing that yet? At this rate, the salon will be open in a couple of weeks. We're really moving along."

"We talked about it, but I guess we didn't think it was time yet."

"You definitely could. In fact, if you wanted to set up a card table and a couple of chairs in the front of the shop, you could do interviews right there," Ethan said. "The painting will be done in another day or so. Maybe sooner, since Trina's keeping so much of the white. It'll be fine to be in there."

Roxie nodded. "I'll tell her. She'll be excited to start that process."

"If I could make a suggestion?"

"Sure."

"Tell Trina to put a notice in the *Gulf Gazette*. They'll put it in their paper, but they'll also put it on their online jobs board. They send out a notice to all subscribers when new jobs are posted. That's where she'll get the most responses from."

"Hang on." Roxie got up and grabbed the notepad and pen she kept in the kitchen. "If I don't write it down, I'll forget." She jotted down a reminder, then left it in the middle of the counter so that she'd either remember or Trina would see it. "Okay, thanks. That will help. Ready for that walk?"

Ethan got to his feet. "You bet."

She turned off the television but left the lamps on either side of the couch lit, then took his hand. Together they headed outside and down the steps. At the edge of the pool deck, they toed off their shoes and stepped into the sand.

Ethan let out a sigh as if he'd been waiting for this all day.

"Happy?" she asked.

He pulled her close. "You have no idea."

Then he kissed her.

Chapter Thirty-three

Kat felt bad about yawning during the movie they were trying to watch at his place, but Alex had just laughed and brushed it off.

"Surfing can wear you out," he said. He had his arm around her, and she was leaning into him. It was a very comfortable position to be in.

She would have been asleep in another ten minutes. Maybe less. She nodded. "Apparently, because I am beat. I'm sorry. I really want to hang out longer, but I think I'll end up falling asleep."

"It's okay," he said. "We had a *great* day."

"Yeah, we did," she answered.

He lifted his arm off her shoulders to lean forward and pause the movie. "Come on. I'll run you home."

"I could call an Uber."

He frowned. "You will not. No girlfriend of mine is paying for her own way home when I have a perfectly good car right outside."

She grinned. Being called "girlfriend" had such a sweet ring to it. And he was so good to her. She grabbed her purse, and they went outside to his car. He got her door, then went around to the other side.

She and Alex had said goodbye to Miles and Trina after their dinner at Coconuts. Miles and Trina were off to walk the beach, then Miles was taking Trina home.

Alex got in behind the wheel.

"Thanks for today," Kat said. "I really loved it. And I definitely want to do it again. I'm even thinking about buying my own board, once I get my first check from Future Florida. So long as you help me pick it out, because I have no idea what kind to buy."

He backed out of the driveway. "I'd be happy to help. That would be so cool." He laughed. "I've never had a girlfriend that surfed with me before. A lot that liked to sit on the beach and watch, but this is better."

"Well, it's going to take me a while to get close to being as good as you."

"Babe, you got up today. More than once. You're going to be great before you know it. You're a natural."

She smiled. She never would have thought of herself as a surfer. Certainly not a natural one. She wasn't really all that athletic. "It's weird to think of myself surfing. I never really played sports that much as a kid. I did some dance, a little gymnastics, but I never was great at any of it."

He shrugged. "Maybe that's just because you hadn't tried surfing yet."

"Yeah, maybe." She adjusted her purse on her lap. "I like thinking of myself as a surfer. It makes me feel like I could do anything. Sort of like..." She tried to explain what was going on inside her. "Like I'm a different person than I thought I was, I just never realized it. Getting this job at Future Florida is part of that, too. It's as if I've only just now appreciated what I'm capable of. Weird, right?"

"Not weird," he said. "First of all, being in the water, especially salt water, can alter your brain's whole setup. See, there's all of these ions in the air when you're at the beach, and they promote a very different way of thinking."

"For real?"

"Seriously. Look it up. But that aside, you did

something today that a lot of people will never do. And I'm not just talking about surfing. You took a chance, and you conquered some fear. That levels you up as a human being. It builds character."

She nodded. "I suppose you're right." A question came into her mind. "What was it like the first time you went into a burning building?"

He snorted softly, his eyes focused on the road. "I was terrified."

By the tone of his voice, she could tell he meant it. "It sounds terrifying. I don't know how any of you do it."

"We train for it. And that training is supposed to help with the fear, but being faced with a live situation wasn't the same. I had a moment where I thought I was going to turn around and just walk away. Our natural instinct isn't to head toward fire, it's to go in the opposite direction."

"But you didn't. Obviously. How did you get through it?"

"I reminded myself that I was there because I wanted to be. That I knew it was going to be hard, but it was what I'd chosen to do. In that case, we had two people unaccounted for. The longer I stood there, the less likely they were to be saved."

Kat realized she was holding her breath. She let it go. "That had to be an awful feeling."

He nodded, his eyes holding a darkness that looked like memories. "I put one foot in front of the other and before I knew it, I was inside. My commander yelled for me, and it was like that was all it took for my training to kick in. I went into action."

"You weren't afraid anymore?"

He laughed. "No, I was still terrified, but I was able to push that fear down enough to do my job."

She was almost afraid to ask the next question. "Are you still afraid?"

"Yeah," he said solemnly. "I am. I think the moment a firefighter stops being afraid is the moment they start being reckless. Fire is like a living, breathing thing. You have to respect it, or it will kill you."

A lump formed in her throat. She swallowed it down before reaching out and putting her hand on his arm, needing to touch him. "I hope nothing ever happens to you. I don't think I'd deal with that very well."

He gave her a quick look and smiled. "I don't take chances, I promise."

"Good." But she knew that just because he was

careful didn't mean he might not get hurt. Her thoughts went in all different directions, not all of them good. She looked out the window and prayed that neither Alex nor Miles would ever get hurt. Or any of the crew at the firehouse.

Alex pulled into her driveway and got out to get her door. As he opened it, and she climbed out, a familiar voice called out to her.

"You're *dating*?"

She looked in the direction of the voice and saw Ray stumbling out from underneath the beach house where the shadows were the thickest. She stared at him in disbelief. "What are you doing here?"

Alex stood in front of her and a little off to the side. Over his shoulder, he said, "Who is this guy?"

"My ex-fiancé," Kat answered. She sighed as she looked around. There was no sign of his car. He must have parked further up the street so she wouldn't see it. "Seriously, Ray, you shouldn't be here."

Ray took a few more unsteady steps toward her. "You haven't answered my texts or my calls."

Because she'd blocked his number. "We have nothing to say to each other. And you seem drunk."

"Of course I'm drunk," he said. "I'm miserable. You broke my heart."

Kat took a breath and tried to stay calm. "Ray, you slept with one of your nurses. And I caught you. In my bed. If you want to place blame, you need to look at yourself."

Ray jabbed a finger at her. "You did this to us. You and all your...your...indecision."

Alex put his hands up like a shield. "Listen, buddy. Why don't I take you to a hotel in town and we can get you a room where you can sleep this off?"

"Are you sleeping with my fiancée?" Ray blurted out. He came closer. "Are you the reason she left me?"

Kat was quickly getting fed up. "Ray, shut up. *You're* the reason I left you."

He looked like he'd been crying. He wiped at his face with the back of his hand. "Just give me one more chance, Kat. Please. I'm dying without you."

"I doubt that very much. You need to call a ride and get out of here."

Alex still had his hands up. "The woman wants you gone, friend. Time to act on that."

Ray blinked a few times and seemed to finally focus on Alex. Ray looked him up and down. "I don't take advice from Ken dolls."

Alex said nothing to Ray but spoke to Kat again over his shoulder. "You say the word and I'll get him out of here."

She didn't know what to do. He obviously couldn't drive. "Ray, you've really made a mess of things, you know that?"

Ray started sniffling. "I just want you to love me."

"You should have thought about that before you slept with Heidi. Speaking of, if you were sleeping with her, why aren't you two a thing now?"

The tears began for real. "She broke up with me, too."

"All right," Alex said, pulling his phone out. "I'm getting you an Uber on my dime. I'll have him take you to the Best Western in town. They should have a room available."

"*No*," Ray shouted. "I'm not leaving without Kat." He swatted the phone out of Alex's hand, then lunged toward Kat. "Just talk to me."

She shrieked and jumped back.

Alex, ignoring his phone on the ground, grabbed Ray by the shoulders and held him away from Kat. "That's enough."

Ray swung wildly at Alex, missing. "You dumb piece of—ow!"

Alex moved so quickly Kat wasn't entirely sure

what he'd done or how he'd done it, but he had Ray's arm up behind his back, which had effectively made it impossible for Ray to do anything else.

Lights came on next door at the Rojases' place.

"Babe, can you grab my phone? Just need to hit Send on that Uber request."

Ray was sobbing and mumbling and complaining that Alex was hurting him. She picked up Alex's phone, but shook her head. "I'll call one. You don't need to pay for this idiot."

Her mom and Danny appeared on his front porch.

"Kat?" her mom called out. "Is that you?"

"Yes," Kat called back while she brought up the Uber app on her own phone.

Danny and her mom came down the steps and walked over. Danny nodded. "Is this the ex?"

"Yep." Kat typed in the Best Western as a destination.

"Did he put his hands on you?" Danny asked.

"No," Kat answered.

"He tried," Alex said. "But he was too drunk to make contact."

Her mom put her hands on her hips and stood directly in front of Ray. "You should be ashamed of yourself, young man. After what you did to my daughter, you have the nerve to come here? How dare you? I considered you family, once upon a time."

Ray cried harder.

Danny waved a hand in front of his face. "I can smell the alcohol. Good job containing him, son."

Alex nodded.

"That's Alex, by the way. Alex, this is Danny Rojas, our next-door neighbor, and my mom, Claire. Although this was not how I wanted you to meet."

"Thank you, Alex," her mom said. "I'm glad you were here. It's nice to meet you, despite the circumstances."

"Nice to meet you, too, Mrs. Thompson." Alex glanced at Kat. "When is that Uber coming?"

"Sorry, still working on that."

Danny ran his hand through his hair. "Why don't we throw him in my truck and take him wherever he needs to go? He's in no shape to drive."

Alex nodded. "I was going to send him to the Best Western in town."

"Sounds good," Danny said. "I'll grab my keys."

"You boys don't have to do that," her mom said.

"It's no trouble," Alex said.

It was Kat's turn to snort. "It's all kinds of trouble."

"Kat," Ray whined. "Why won't you talk to me?"

Her mother rolled her eyes. "Oh, for the love of Pete. Ray, you drunken fool, snap out of it. You cheated on her and it's over. Permanently. Kat has moved on. Do you understand me? You need to do the same. If I ever see you on this property again, I will call the police."

Kat rolled her lips in to keep from laughing and looked at Alex, whose eyes were as wide and amused as her own must be.

Danny returned with his keys and took Ray's other arm. "All right, let's load him up."

Alex relaxed his grip and the men walked Ray off. Alex gave Kat a smile. "Back in a bit."

"Thank you."

Her mother stood next to her. "It's a good thing your grandmother didn't know he was down here. She would have called the cops."

"Is Grandma home?"

Her mom nodded. "She's watching one of her crime shows. Except now she calls it 'doing research.'" Her mom looked at Kat and smiled. "You didn't tell me Alex was so handsome. Or that fit."

"He *is* a firefighter, Mom."

Her mom slipped her arm around Kat's waist as

Danny's truck pulled out of the driveway. "Those are two very capable men right there."

"Yes, they are." She put her arm around her mom's shoulders.

"Your grandmother said she has something to tell us later. Want to go up and see what it is?"

Kat nodded. Danny's taillights faded from view. "Sure."

Chapter Thirty-four

Margo looked over as the elevator opened and her eldest daughter and granddaughter stepped out. "Are your evenings over so soon?"

The two women exchanged knowing glances.

Margo's brows bent. "What is that all about?"

"Yeah," Jules said from her spot on the couch. Toby was next to her, snoring softly. "What's going on? I was bummed Jesse only had an hour to spare for dinner, but now I see I would have missed something if I'd been out longer."

Kat nodded at Claire. She sat next to Jules and started scratching Toby's head. "Go ahead. You tell them."

"Well..." Claire took the other chair. "Danny and Alex just escorted a very drunk Ray off the property."

"What?" Jules laughed. "Are you serious?"

"That's ridiculous," Margo said. She'd always thought Kat could do better. This just proved it. "What did he hope to accomplish?"

"He was trying to win Kat back," Claire said.

"Not like that," Margo said. "The nerve. What a lunatic."

Jules tucked her feet under her, obviously riveted by the news. "Drunk, huh?"

"As a skunk," Kat said. "He was crying, too." She winced. "It was actually pretty sad."

"Sounds sad," Jules said. "So Danny and Alex stepped in?"

"Like heroes," Claire said.

Margo pursed her lips but managed not to roll her eyes.

"Tell me everything," Jules said.

So Kat did, filling them in on what had just transpired. "Danny and Alex will be back after they get him a room."

"And probably after they make sure he gets into that room and into bed," Claire added. Then she looked at Margo. "You want to share your news now? You said you had something to tell us."

"That's quite a hard tale to follow up," Margo

said. She lifted her chin slightly, preparing herself for their reactions. "But I bought a house today."

"You what?" Kat said.

"You bought a house." Jules stared at her mother.

Claire opened her mouth but said nothing at first. Then she cleared her throat softly. "You said you were going to get your own place. I didn't think it would be quite so fast."

"Neither did I," Margo said. "But an opportunity presented itself and I had to act. It's a private sale and a very good deal. I'd be foolish to pass it up."

"Um, where is this place?" Kat asked. "Are you going to be close by? How big is it? How did you find out about it? When are you moving in?"

"One question at a time, Kat." Margo smiled. "It's not far. About ten to twelve minutes. Probably faster if your aunt is driving. It's a twelve-hundred-square-foot ranch, three bedrooms, two bathrooms. It has a pool, nothing fancy, but a pool all the same. Two-car garage, as well. It needs a decent amount of cosmetic work. Parts of it are very dated, so I'll be here until that's reasonably taken care of."

Toby let out a big sigh. Jules scratched his belly. "What kind of cosmetic work? You mean painting? Stuff like that?"

Margo nodded. "Painting. New flooring. New countertops in the kitchen. The master bath is a total redo." The second bath was stuck firmly in the Seventies as well, but she'd decided she could live with that for a while. Painting the walls and cabinets would go a long way in there.

"Can we help?" Claire asked. "We could at least paint."

"Yeah," Kat said. "And maybe pull up carpet? Or, I don't know, whatever needs doing. I could probably get Alex to help, too. I don't know how handy he is, but he's strong."

Margo smiled. "Any help would be gratefully appreciated." She hadn't even had to ask. She should have known better than to think otherwise. Once again, Conrad was right. It was time for her to have more faith in her family. "Thank you all for offering. It's a lot of work to take on by myself."

"Mom," Jules said. "You won't be doing it by yourself, I promise. Cash is all yours, whenever you need him."

That made Kat and Claire laugh.

"Thank you, sweetheart." Margo's breath seemed to come easier.

"Are you selling your place in Landry then?" Claire asked.

Margo nodded. "Yes. I have to. I have some savings, of course, but not enough to want to pay two mortgages and handle the remodeling. I'll probably be getting a storage unit for my things."

Jules shifted to see her mother better. "You can't put them in the garage at the new house?"

"Maybe," Margo said. "It all depends on the timing of things. When the current owners move. That sort of thing."

"And how did you find out about this place?" Kat asked.

"The house is in Conrad's neighborhood." Margo readied herself for their comments. "He knows the people who are selling it."

Jules got a big smile on her face like Margo had just told them all a big secret. "Isn't that cozy?" She laughed. "Good for you, Mom."

"I'm not sure what you're implying but there's nothing untoward going on."

Jules snickered. "Mom, I think it's great. Be as untoward as you want. You're both consenting adults."

"*Julia.*"

"What?" Jules said with an exaggerated smile, proof of how amusing she found herself. "You're allowed to have fun in your life, you know. If you want to live next door to your boyfriend, go for it."

Margo almost said, "He's not my boyfriend." But that was exactly what Conrad had become. Denying it would be a lie.

Claire's mouth bent in a smug little smile. "I mean, I am, and look how that's working out. Pretty darn good."

Kat laughed. "This is not a conversation I ever thought we'd be having."

"Nor I," Margo said. She tightened her lips together, but she wasn't really that upset. Her daughters were certainly full of ideas, though. "Perhaps we should just watch the show. This is research for me now, you know."

Claire leaned back. "How is the book coming?"

"It's going all right," Margo answered. "We're happy with how the draft is developing. I just hope we can maintain our progress. It's harder than you think."

"I'm sure it is," Claire said. "I can't imagine trying to write a book. I hope it's a runaway success. I can't wait to read it."

"Me, too," Kat said.

"Thank you," Margo said. "That is very kind of

you both. If you can be honest, we'd appreciate feed-back when we get to that point."

"We'll be honest," Kat said. "Even if it's hard. Although I'm sure it'll be great."

Margo could only hope.

Jules was still grinning. "I can't believe we're going to have an author in the family. That's pretty cool."

Claire sat up again. "Hey, can we see the house?"

"Yes," Margo said. "But not in person until the deal is done. I don't want to bother the Clarkes by traipsing my whole family through the place. I did take pictures, though, and I'd be happy to show you those."

They all gathered around while she scrolled through the photos on her phone. There were a lot of comments, mostly positive, but also affirming just how much work she had ahead of her.

After that, they all settled in to watch the show and as the closing credits were rolling, the elevator doors opened. Danny and Alex stepped off. They didn't come any further in than just the front of the elevator.

"All hail the conquering heroes," Margo proclaimed.

Danny nodded at them. "Ray is taken care of. We got him a room and made sure he was in it. He'll have to come back over here tomorrow to get his car, but I'm happy to supervise that so Kat doesn't have to interact with him again."

Kat got to her feet. "Thank you so much. I really appreciate both of you helping me like this." She went to Alex's side.

Claire stood and went to Danny. "I guess we can finish our evening now."

He nodded. "I'd like that."

She gave Jules and her mom a wave. "See you later." Then she and Danny got in the elevator.

Alex got in, too, with Kat pausing at the doors to look back at her grandmother and aunt. "I'm going to say goodnight to Alex, then I'll be back."

The doors closed. Margo sat watching the screen as the next episode began, but her mind was on the future. What would it be like to live so close to Conrad?

Would they have dinner together? Take strolls through the neighborhood? She'd already decided to convert the smallest of the bedrooms into her writing studio. How often would they work at her place? The lanai at the new house had a nice, covered area. They could work out there when the weather was right.

She knew it would all sort itself out, and while she was still worried about everything that had to be done, she had a lot more peace about it, too.

Chapter Thirty-five

*W*illie settled into one of the chairs by the outdoor firepit. Miguel had brought her a throw in case she got cold, but she was perfectly warm. The night air did have a little coolness in it, but the firepit put off a surprising amount of heat.

He'd gone inside to get them dessert and see if Danny was back yet. She heard footsteps but didn't bother turning. She recognized his gait.

He put a small tray on the table between their chairs. It held a plate of cookies, two plates of cake, forks, napkins, and cups. He added a thermos beside the tray.

She looked at him in wonder. "You carried all of that down?"

"I took the elevator. It was no problem. I made

some decaf for us, but the good kind, already fixed the way we like it."

She laughed. "So it's strong and sweet."

"Is there any other way?" He sat down and opened the thermos. He filled their cups with the milky coffee.

"What kind of cookies are those?" They looked good, but then so did most sweets, Willie thought.

"*Mantecaditos*. Claire made them. They're an old family recipe and very delicious. We're going to sell them at the bakery."

He put a cup of decaf coffee on her side of the table. It smelled good. She picked it up with both hands and took a sip. It tasted even better. She rested the cup on the arm of the chair and reached for a cookie.

She took a bite. The sharpness of the jam combined with the sweetness of the biscuit made a good combination. She gestured with the remaining half of the cookie. "What did you say this was again? Manti-something?"

"*Mantecaditos*."

"*Mantecaditos*," she repeated. "And what kind of jam is this?"

"Guava. Do you like it?"

"I do. I've just never tasted anything like this before. It's really good. Different. To me, anyway."

"Guava is a very popular fruit in my country. We have a guava tree on the side of the house here. When they have fruit, their perfume is the best smell in the world."

She ate the last bite of her cookie, then sipped some more coffee before reaching for her plate of cake. She couldn't have asked for a nicer evening. Miguel put his feet up on the edge of the firepit, so she did, too. She tried the cake next, nodding almost instantly. "I can see why you like this. It's very tasty."

"*Tres leches* is the best."

The warmth from the fire was making her drowsy, but in the most comfortable way. "I love this firepit. We need one of these at our place. I'll have to mention it to Roxie and Trina, see what they think."

Silence stretched out between them as they ate cake and drank coffee, both of them seemingly mesmerized by the dancing flames.

"Are you happy?" Miguel asked.

Her brows bent as she glanced over at him. "I'm very happy. Why? Don't I seem like it?"

"No, you do. I just wanted to be sure."

He looked like he had more on his mind, so she didn't say anything, just let him be.

He put his coffee cup on the table. "I know you remember that I asked you to marry me when I thought you were going to be without a place to live."

She nodded. "I do. It was one of the kindest things anyone has ever offered to do for me."

He took a deep breath as he kept his gaze on the fire. "I cannot stop thinking about it. About what might have been."

She stayed quiet, looking at him, but wondering if maybe she shouldn't. She didn't know what to say. She wasn't sure what he was saying, actually. She thought she might have an idea, but she didn't want to assume.

He glanced at her. "Have you thought about it?"

"Of course."

"I love you, Willie. I know we've only known each other a short while, but does that mean my feelings are wrong? At my age, if I don't act quickly, I may not get to act. How much time does either of us have left? We can't know. But what I do know is I want us to spend that time together."

"We are together."

He shook his head. "I mean as husband and wife. Officially, before God and everyone." He bowed his head slightly. "I know that you have become a very wealthy woman recently. I want none of that money and I'll sign paperwork promising not to touch a cent of it. All I want is you."

Her mouth opened. "Are you asking me to marry you?"

"Not yet. When I do that, you will know. Right now, I am telling you how I feel and asking if you feel the same. If there is a reason for me to plan a special night to ask a more serious question. Be honest with me, Willie. I am heartsick over you."

She smiled. "Miguel, you are the sweetest man. You take such good care of me." He was right about neither of them knowing how much time they had left. It frightened her to think that way sometimes, but mostly she was at peace with it. She had lived a very good life. And now, her daughter and grand-daughter would be taken care of long after she was gone.

So why shouldn't she also be taken care of? "I think I love you, too."

He looked up. "You do?"

She nodded. "I've been in love enough times to know my feelings." A sixth husband. Was she insane? Maybe. Love did that to a person. "It doesn't bother you that I've been married so many times?"

He shook his head. "The only thing that bothers me is that you are not currently married to me."

She laughed, reaching out across the table for his hand. He took it and she wrapped her fingers around his. "I can't think of anything I'd like to do more than spend the rest of my days with you. Plan your special evening, Miguel."

His eyes sparkled, throwing back the fire's light. "You mean that?"

"I do."

He grinned and said something in Spanish she didn't quite catch before leaning down to kiss her knuckles. "You have made me a very happy man. What kind of a ring do you want, my darling? I will buy you anything. Just tell me."

She glanced at her hand. At her slightly gnarled fingers and spotted skin. "I don't need anything fancy."

"Yes, you do. You are my queen. I won't have people thinking I didn't buy you the kind of ring you deserve."

He was so cute. And obviously not going to rest until she gave him an answer. "In that case, I'd like a nice sapphire set in yellow gold. A real pretty blue one with a couple of diamonds around it. Doesn't have to be big, doesn't need a lot of diamonds, but that's what I want."

He nodded. "I can do that."

She narrowed her eyes a bit. "Does Danny know what you're doing?"

"Do you mean will my son be upset?"

"Well, I guess. I just want to know if he knows. I want to know how much of a surprise this is going to be to your family."

"You aren't concerned with what your family will think?"

"Honey, I've already been married five times. I don't think a sixth is going to throw them for that much of a loop."

He smiled. "I have told my son how I feel. He knows the desires of my heart. But he also thought you would say no."

"Really? Why?"

"Because we haven't known each other very long, but when he gets to be our age, he will understand that time is not the friend it once was."

"That's for sure." She got to thinking. "In fact, we should get married right away. We don't need a lot of people there. We can do it right here on the beach, don't you think?"

He nodded. "That would be nice."

"It would be. I'll have to find a dress. Maybe we can get Claire to make us a cake. Do you have something to get married in?"

He smiled. "White linen, I think. Pants and shirt. Is that all right?"

"It sounds just fine."

There was a lot to think about and a lot to plan for, even for a small, simple wedding, but how hard could it be? She'd done it enough times to know what mattered and what didn't. "How do you feel about a honeymoon in Puerto Rico?"

His grin widened. "That is exactly where I want to go. We could even see some of my family who are still there."

"I better learn to speak some Spanish then."

"I will teach you." He held her hand a little tighter. "Thank you for not thinking I was *loco*."

She laughed. "I think we're both *loco*." She winked at him. "But in the best possible way."

Chapter Thirty-six

*A*fter her mom turned in, Jules wasn't ready to go to bed. And since Cash was out on his date, she decided to head upstairs and work on her music. Quietly. This wasn't the time of night to be rocking out.

She took the steps, pausing on the rooftop deck to gaze out at the beach and the stars. Such a pretty night. She went inside, turned on one small light, and settled down on the couch with her notebook, leaving her phone on the cushion beside her.

She left her guitar where it was next to her, not really in the mood to play anything just yet. She only had four songs so far. Five, if she got permission to cover *Folsom Prison Blues*. But that still left four more to create.

She tipped her head back and stared at the ceiling, thinking through her own emotions for a point of inspiration. But the truth was, she was feeling a bit melancholy. Not because of her music. That was going very well.

Cash and Jesse had just about set everything up necessary for her to record her demo at the Dolphin Club. But she was missing Jesse. She would have loved to be out with him tonight. He was great company and a lot of fun.

Dinner had been great, but it had been too short.

The club was a big responsibility. His responsibility. She understood that. She wouldn't want to take him away from his business. The thing was, if this song and this album took off like her agent thought it would, she'd be touring again.

There would be months of her on the road and nothing to connect them but video calls and text messages. That was a hard thing for a fledgling relationship to go through. And she liked Jesse enough to care what happened to them. Not just because he'd done so much for her, either. She was falling into deep like with the guy.

Enough that love might not be far behind.

The last thing she wanted was for him to think she'd used him in any way to further her career. She hadn't, of course, but the idea that he might wonder about that made her sick. She really wanted to talk to him. Face to face would be better, but if there was a show at the club tonight, he might be too busy.

She picked up her phone and sent him a quick text. *How's it going tonight? Busy?*

She could probably guess based on how long it took him to respond and how detailed his response was.

She'd written one new line down before he answered. Couldn't have been more than two minutes. She looked at her phone.

Busy enough. I'd rather be with you.

She smiled. *Same here. Is there a show tonight?*

No, just live music. What are you doing?

Working on lyrics.

How are they coming?

She glanced at the page. She'd barely started. *They're coming. Just noodling.*

I'd ask you to noodle here but it's not fair that you have to come to me all the time. Probably not the best writing environment, either. I wish we could spend more time together. There. I said it. I miss you.

She let out a little laugh. *I miss you, too. That's why I texted.*

I really need to hire a manager who can do my job. At least most of it.

Do you really think that person exists?

I'm not sure, but I hope so. Placing an ad tomorrow.

She sat up. She thought he'd been kidding. *You're serious?*

Very. How else am I going to see more of you?

She hadn't been expecting that. At all. *I'd love that.* She started to type more, about how if the song took off, she'd be going on tour and that would mean time away, but she deleted everything and just stared at the screen.

That was a conversation better had in person. Instead, she wrote, *Maybe we could do breakfast tomorrow? I'd really like that.*

So would I. How about my place? Ten okay?

She'd never been to his place. She nodded as she typed, *It's great. See you then.*

He sent back a one-line address along with a thumbs-up. She knew he was just up the street, but she hadn't known exactly which house.

Breakfast at his place was the perfect time and place to talk about what the future held. She wasn't looking for any major commitment. She just wanted to know where his head was at concerning them, although if he was hiring someone so that he could have more time off to spend with her, that was a pretty good indicator right there.

She worked a little more on the song but was

preoccupied thinking about Jesse. There were worse things to get stuck on. She closed up the third floor and went back downstairs to get ready for bed. Toby was still on the couch, but he hopped down when she came in. "Let's go do one more pee-pee before bed."

She grabbed his leash and took him down in the elevator. He went straight to the grass and did his business, then kicked his back feet a few times, throwing a little grass over the spot. She laughed. "All right, time for bed."

She took him up, wiped his feet off, then hung his leash in the laundry room. He looked longingly at his food bowl. She peeked into it. There was still some kibble in there, but the bottom was visible. She shook her head. "I know you think if you can see the bottom then the dish is empty, but that's not true, Tobs. Eat what's left."

The bedroom light was on when she opened the door. Her mom was sitting up in bed, reading.

"Good book?" Jules asked softly.

"Not bad." Her mother looked over. "But you can't really tell with a thriller. Sometimes they fall apart in the end. Were you working on lyrics?"

Jules nodded. "A little. I didn't get much done. Which is fine—I'm making good progress."

"I thought maybe you'd go over to see Jesse tonight."

She got her sleep shirt out of the dresser. "We're having breakfast in the morning."

"How's all of that going?"

Jules sat on the side of her bed. "You mean me and Jesse?"

Her mom nodded.

"It's going pretty well. I like him a lot. He's been incredibly helpful. He's making it possible for me to record the demo that Billy wants. He got musicians and backup singers, and he's providing the studio space. I'd be in a fix without him."

Her mom set her e-reader down. "Do you like him for what he can do for you? Or do you like him for him?"

"I like him for him. I really do. But I'm worried he might think the former. That's something I plan on talking to him about tomorrow. That and where we're going."

Her mom frowned. "You're not getting serious with this man already, are you?"

"I don't mean like that. I mean about what's going to happen when I go back on tour, because that might be happening pretty soon. Depending how this song goes over." Jules sighed and leaned back. "I don't want my going on tour to mean the end of us, but you know how hard long-distance is. Especially that kind of long-distance."

Her mother's eyes narrowed, but there was compassion in them. "You really like him, don't you?"

"I do."

"Then ask him to go with you."

Jules's mouth came open. She hadn't been expecting that at all. "There's no way. I mean, he's got the club to look after. And Shiloh."

"You take Toby on the bus. What's one more dog? Unless they don't get along."

"No, they do. But what about the Dolphin Club?"

"Jules, if there's one thing I know about men is that they can make the impossible happen when it's something they really want to do."

"Sure, but this is his livelihood we're talking about."

"I understand that. But there's nothing that says he has to accompany you on the entire tour. But maybe for a few weeks of it, here and there."

Jules thought about that. It would be amazing to have him along. He was so good at making things happen and getting stuff done. A person like that on tour with her would be invaluable. And he'd just mentioned hiring someone to take over his job to spend more time with her.

Could that person be up to speed by the time she had to leave? Would Jesse have enough confidence in that person to really let them handle things? She had no idea, but it was certainly interesting.

"It's worth thinking about, isn't it?" her mother asked.

Jules nodded slowly. "It is. Enough so that I'm already trying to figure it out."

Chapter Thirty-seven

Trina woke up feeling like she'd used muscles she didn't know she had. Which was pretty much exactly what had happened. Trying to stay on the surfboard, all of that paddling, and jumping up, combined with the beating she'd gotten from the waves had apparently taken its toll. Miles had warned her she'd be sore from surfing, though, and she was prepared with Advil and plenty of water.

In fact, she'd left them on her nightstand. Now, as daylight peeked through the blinds, she reached over for the pain relievers and the bottle of water. She took two Advil with a big gulp of water, then laid back down and closed her eyes.

Nothing wrong with giving the painkillers a little time to kick in.

She pulled the covers over her head to block the

light and thought about last night and how nice it had been to walk hand in hand with Miles on the beach. They'd walked for a while, then gone back to his house for a snack of ice cream bars. They'd sat on the couch together, eating their ice cream and snuggling close as they watched a movie.

When she'd gotten tired, he'd bought her home. It had been late. So late her mom and grandmother had already been in bed, but she knew she'd see them this morning, so she'd been super quiet as she'd gone to bed herself.

She sighed into the covers. She should get up and moving. Today was going to be busy, but she was happy enough to ignore what lay before her for a little while longer. Although coffee sounded pretty tempting, too.

She'd be in the salon today, setting up some things in the employee breakroom and waiting on the arrival of the sign people, who were coming to measure, as well as doing some cleaning and whatever else she could accomplish.

The more that could be done, the quicker the salon could open. Of course, she still needed to hire stylists. Her goal was to open with at least three, herself included. Four would be better, but realistically, she understood that unless those stylists brought clients with them, the shop wouldn't have enough customers initially.

She'd also like to have at least one dedicated shampoo person, as well as two receptionists. Eventually, she might even hire someone to do makeup.

As for her mom, Trina wanted her as an assistant salon manager. Trina's second set of eyes and ears. Making sure everyone was being taken care of, that customers were happy, that stylists had the supplies they needed, and that the shop wasn't running out of anything.

Basically, helping Trina run things enough that Trina could still concentrate on her first love, which was doing hair and making people feel good about themselves.

She also didn't want her mom working full time. Part-time was more than enough. And if they got busier, which was obviously what Trina hoped would happen, she'd just hire more people. Another receptionist. Maybe a part-time cleaner to keep up with sweeping the floors, washing tools and towels, and making sure the rest of the salon was in good shape.

With a soft grunt, Trina tossed the covers back. She really couldn't stay in bed. There was too much to do and she needed coffee so she could sit down and make a list of what she hoped to accomplish today.

She got up and went out to the living room in her shorty pajamas, doing her best to keep quiet while also ignoring her aching muscles. She got a pot of coffee going, then went back to her room for her salon binder, her notebook, a pen, her laptop, and her phone.

Hands full, she went out on the back deck and took a seat on the couch. Might as well enjoy the fresh air before she ended up inside again. She put everything on the table, then checked her phone and found a message from Miles.

How are you feeling today?

A little sore, she typed back. *But I took Advil like you said.*

Good. Stay hydrated. You'll feel better soon, babe. Have a great day.

"Babe" made her smile. *You, too. Yesterday was great!*

So are you.

She sent a heart back to him. How nice was it to be involved with a guy like Miles who wasn't just sweet and considerate, but an actual adult? She'd dated too many guys who'd seemed like overgrown children. No more of that.

As she put her phone down, her mom came up the outside steps, dressed in her gym shorts, sports bra, and tank top.

"Hey," Trina said. "I didn't know you were up already."

"Up and just finished two miles." Her mom pushed her sunglasses on top of her head as she came through the screen door. She wiped a little sweat off her forehead. "Please tell me you put coffee on."

"I did. Waiting on it myself. Although it might be ready now."

Her mom smiled. "Did you have a good time yesterday?"

Trina nodded. "Surfing was so much fun. I actually managed to stand up a few times! Only for about a second, but I still did it. Only downside is I am *sore* today. Surfing uses way more muscles than you might think. Especially my core. Man. I might be moving slowly until this Advil kicks in."

"The best kind of exercise is the kind you don't know you're doing."

Trina laughed. "That's exactly what it was like." She put her stuff aside. "Let's go see if that coffee's ready."

They went inside, the aroma of freshly brewed coffee greeting them.

Trina inhaled. "That is seriously the best smell."

"I agree." Her mom got cups down from the cabinet.

Trina leaned against the counter, feeling every muscle as she moved. "How was pizza night with Ethan?"

"Really nice. Your grandmother headed over to Miguel's not long after we ate, so Ethan and I went for a walk on the beach. We ended up sitting by the pool for a while and just talking. It was nice. Oh! Kat's ex showed up. But that happened when we were out walking the beach, so we missed all the drama."

Trina straightened. "Ray was here?"

"Yep." Her mom nodded. "Claire actually texted me to apologize about the noise, which was how I found out. Danny and Alex ended up escorting him off the property. They took him to the Best Western in town and made him get a room. He was pretty drunk, apparently."

"Wow. Kat must have been upset."

"I think she was all right. Danny and Alex acted pretty quickly." Her mom filled her cup, then filled Trina's.

"Still," Trina said.

"I know." Her mom got the creamer out and set it on the counter by the sugar. Roxie wasn't using sugar lately. She'd switched to packets of the fake stuff.

"What time did Mimi get back?"

"No idea." Her mom popped the top of the creamer bottle and splashed some in. "But it was after I went to bed."

"And before I came home." Trina fixed her coffee, too. "She certainly enjoys her time with Miguel, doesn't she?"

"She does. Makes me happy. She's got new life in her." Her mom sipped her coffee. "That is good. Not that your grandmother was in a bad place or anything like that, but she's just got a pep in her step, you know?"

"I do." Trina tipped her head toward the porch. "Let's go back outside so we don't wake her."

"Okay."

They got situated out there, her mom in one of the chairs, and Trina back on the couch. Her mom sipped her coffee for a few minutes, just looking out at the water.

After a while, she let out a happy sigh. "I'm so glad we're staying here. I really love this place. Not just this house but look at that water. There is nothing in Port St. Rosa that compares to this view."

Trina looked up from her list-making and thought about that. "That's for sure. There's nothing in Port St. Rosa that compares to Ethan, either." Or Miles, for that matter.

Her mom laughed. "Very true. And I just remembered Ethan said you can pretty much start holding interviews at the salon if you want. He said you could set up a card table and some folding chairs in the reception area and work out of there."

"Really? That's great, because I was just thinking I need to get started on the hiring end of things."

"Why don't you swing by the CVS on the way in and see if you can pick up a sign for the window that says Help Wanted? You could add your phone number to it and start taking names and numbers. We can get an ad online, too. Ethan said the *Gulf Gazette* has an online job board that's pretty active."

Trina nodded enthusiastically. "I definitely want to do that." She grabbed her laptop and opened it up, giving it a couple of seconds to come to life. "I'm going to see about putting an ad on there right now."

She did a quick search for the *Gazette*'s website, then clicked on it and found the job board. She registered an account, verified it, and opened up a form to place her ad. "New Salon Hiring All Positions," she typed as the headline.

In the body of the ad, she put, "Stylists, Receptionist, Shampooer, and Assistant." Then, "Competitive wages, fun environment, brand new everything! Text or call." She added her number and read what she'd written to her mom.

"Sounds good to me. I bet you get calls today."

"That would be amazing." Trina hit Publish. "And I've just realized I need to set up a Facebook page for the salon. I'm not doing a website, but I should at least have a Facebook page, don't you think?"

"I do."

Trina clicked over to Facebook and started setting that up. "I'll at least get it started. I won't be able to do too much until I have some photos. I need to figure out our operational hours, too."

"It'll all come together very soon."

"Sooner than you think," Trina said.

The sliders opened and Mimi came out with a big mug of coffee and an even bigger smile on her face. "Morning, my girls. How are you this beautiful day?"

Trina glanced at her mom. "Good, Mimi. You seem chipper."

"I am." Her grandmother took a seat, letting out a sigh that matched the smile on her face.

"Any particular reason why?" Roxie asked.

Willie's smile got slightly bigger. "Let's just say I have some news."

Chapter Thirty-eight

*R*oxie looked at her mother. "News?" She could only imagine what her mother had to tell them. Willie led a very interesting life. "Does this have anything to do with last night and Miguel?"

"It does," Willie answered. "And I know you're probably going to be shocked, but hear me out before you decide I've lost my marbles, will you?"

A little tingle of panic zipped through Roxie's stomach. "This sounds perfect for a first thing in the morning conversation."

"Well, it's something you both need to know," Willie said.

"What is it, Mimi? The suspense is killing me," Trina said.

Willie paused and took a long sip of her coffee, no doubt using the moment to build suspense. Roxie almost laughed. Her mother was so predictable. About *some* things. About others? Not so much.

"That is good coffee," Willie said.

Roxie huffed out a breath. "Ma, please. Like Trina said, we're dying."

Willie smiled. "Miguel asked me to marry him."

"I know," Roxie said. "You told us that."

"No, not because he thought I needed a place to live. He asked me for real this time. Or he's going to. He just wanted to know if I felt the same way."

"What?" Roxie needed more coffee.

Willie lifted her chin. "He's going to ask me officially very soon. And I'm going to say yes."

Trina looked a little distraught. "Mimi, you just met the guy. I know you like him and he's very nice but—"

"But nothing, my girl. I am an old woman, and I don't have the luxury of time. A long engagement might end in a funeral."

Roxie grimaced. "Don't say things like that, Ma."

"Well, it's true," her mother shot back. "And I know it's not something any of us want to think about, especially me, but I have to. If Miguel and I want to have a life together, we have to start now."

"Wow," Trina breathed out. "You're really getting married?"

Willie took another sip of her coffee. "We are. We'd like something simple. Right here on the beach. Just the two families. Claire and her group, too, if they'd like. Wouldn't be polite not to invite them."

Roxie knew better than to argue with her mother when her mind was made up. "Where are you going to live?"

"We talked about that. I think we're going to have a look at a place called Dunes West. It's a fifty-five and over community. Only about fifteen minutes away, according to what Miguel told me. They have all kinds of models to choose from and depending on what package you pick, they take care of everything. From your yard to your pool to cleaning the inside, too. Sounds like my kind of living."

Roxie pursed her lips. "And who's paying for this new place?"

"Both of us, missy. Miguel's got his own money. He doesn't need mine. Doesn't want it, either. He's already told me he'll sign one of those prenup thingies. He's in this for me, not my millions."

Roxie sighed. "That's good to hear, I guess. You really love this guy, Ma? I mean, it's not just some infatuation that's going to pass?"

"I've been married enough times to know the

difference between infatuation and love. This is love." Willie smiled. "I want to be with him all the time. And he feels the same way about me."

"Then I think it's great, Mimi," Trina said. "It'll be weird not to have you around, though. I'll miss you."

"Now don't go getting all weepy on me." Willie reached over and patted Trina's knee. "I won't be far away. And we'll get a big enough house that you can even stay over sometimes if you want. But you're going to be busy with the salon! You might not even have time for your old Mimi."

Trina frowned. "Don't say that. I will always have time for you."

Willie smiled. "I know you will. But I want you to be busy. Besides that, Miguel and I are going on a long honeymoon."

"You are?" Trina asked. "Where?"

"Puerto Rico," Willie replied. "We're going for a month. We're going to rent a place near where most of his family lives. He's got a grandniece he's never met."

"Wow, Ma, you've really thought a lot about this."

Willie looked over at Roxie. "We talked it all through last night. As much as we could, anyway. I hope you can be happy for us. I know it's happening fast, but we don't know how much time we have left, so why wait?"

"I am happy for you." But Roxie felt a little sadness, too, because she knew her mother was right about the time part of it. "Whatever I can do to help, you just say the word."

"Thank you. I would love your help picking out a dress. I'll need some flowers, too. And we'll have to find a priest to do the ceremony. Miguel's Catholic, so he'd like a priest."

Another question popped into Roxie's head. "Does Danny know about this?"

"He does," Willie assured her. "And he's fine with whatever his dad wants to do."

"Okay. That's good," Roxie said. The last thing they needed to pull off a fast wedding was Miguel's son working against them. "What about food?"

"We'll get it catered. There's a restaurant Miguel and I both like, Papi's. I need to call them and see if they can do it."

"When do you want to do all of this? How soon?"

Willie smiled, but there was a tentativeness in her expression. "Soon. Like next weekend."

Roxie blinked. "That *is* soon. I guess if the restaurant can make it happen and we can find a priest and get the marriage license, the rest will be easy enough."

"Miguel and I are going to get the marriage license this morning. Do you think you could call the restaurant for me? Oh, and talk to Claire about making us a cake? I'll pay her, obviously. Doesn't have to be anything too fancy, either. A beach theme might be nice."

Roxie felt a little overwhelmed, but she nodded. "I can do that. What about a dress?"

"I want to go to that fancy boutique in town. Lady M's. I know it's expensive, but I've never been able to shop there because of money and now I can. I certainly don't need a white dress, but I do want something pretty."

"We can go after you get back from getting the license," Roxie said. "We'll have to get an Uber, because Trina will have the car."

"Maybe I could come back as soon as I'm done and go with you? Please?" Trina grinned. "I would hate to miss out on wedding dress shopping with my Mimi."

Roxie smiled. "Of course you can. We need you there. Why don't you text us when you get there and see how much work you have to do? Then you can maybe estimate a time to be home."

"Okay, perfect."

Roxie pressed her hands against her knees. "Well, we have a busier day ahead of us than I had anticipated. Let's get some breakfast going so we can get started."

"I can help," Trina said.

"No, that's okay." Roxie pushed to her feet. "I'm going to get the bacon started, then scramble some eggs and make some toast. Nothing fancy. You keep working. In fact, if you finish the salon stuff, you can start a list of wedding things for your grandmother. That will help a lot."

"I can do that," Trina said. She got her notebook out. "All right, Mimi. Let's write down everything that needs to be done."

Roxie went inside. She still needed to shower, but she'd have time to do that after they ate. Trina would be at least a few hours. Roxie got the bacon out. She couldn't believe her mother was getting married.

Except she could. Willie loved being married. It was a familiar state that she thrived in. For the most part. She'd had her share of divorces, too, but Roxie had a feeling that wasn't going to be the case this time.

Married. Roxie shook her head. She really hadn't

expected her mother to do it again. Not at this point in her life.

But Willie clearly knew what she wanted. And who.

Roxie could only hope to be that sure about her own life someday.

Chapter Thirty-nine

Kat was dressed to walk on the beach, but she wasn't quite ready yet. She went out to the back porch and looked toward the street. From this angle, in the light of day, she could see Ray's car. It was still parked on the opposite side of the street, waiting for him to show up and drive it home.

Kat really wanted a word with him before he left. Maybe it wasn't the smartest thing to do, but she knew Ray. He'd be humble and contrite this morning. He'd listen. At least that's what she expected, since he'd also be hungover.

She only needed enough time to get it through his head that they were done. And she planned to do that by giving him his ring back. If that didn't underline just how over things were between them, there was no hope for the man.

As she was watching, a car pulled up. She leaned forward, trying to see better. Was that Ray getting out of the back? It was. And he looked awful.

She ran to her bedroom and grabbed the engagement ring from the ceramic box on her dresser, then hustled down the steps and toward the street. "Ray."

At the sound of his name, he turned, squinting against the sun. Dark circles shadowed his eyes. He looked haggard. He hadn't shaved, which didn't help.

She held the ring out, pinched between her two fingers. "Here. Take this with you."

His miserable expression got a little worse as he realized what she was holding. "I don't want that."

"Neither do I." She stopped a few feet away from him. They were both standing in the middle of the street. "Just take it. Consider it a reminder that we are done."

He blinked, staring at the ring.

"You do know that, right? That you can't come back here? That you can't call me or text me anymore? That there's no reason for us to talk?"

"Was what I did really that bad, Kat?" Hurt filled his gaze. "Everyone makes mistakes. Why don't I get a second chance?"

"Because you cheated and that's not something you should have *ever* done." He still hadn't taken the ring, so she set it on the hood of his car. Up to him now. "I've moved on, Ray. You should, too. I don't want anything to do with you, but I don't wish you any ill will, either. Just get on with your life."

He finally picked up the ring and shoved it in the pocket of his creased khaki pants. There was dirt on them, probably from the tussle last night. His shirt was wrinkled like it had been slept in, which it probably had been. "I know you've moved on. You made that pretty clear last night. At least your new boyfriend did."

She wasn't going to deny that's who Alex was. She was proud of him. And proud of herself. "What did you think I was going to? Sit in my room and pine for you? For what might have been? I've changed, Ray."

"Yeah, you can say that again. You couldn't have fixed your hair and makeup like that when we were together?" He fumbled for his keys, no longer making eye contact. "You won't see me again."

"Good." She stepped back out of the road but stayed on the sidewalk. Something inside her said she should watch him leave. Partly to make sure he did, and partly because it felt like closure.

He got his door open, but he just stood there. "Is

he really that much better than me? He looks like a beach bum."

Kat shook her head. Was that what Ray was hung up about? What Alex looked like? "Yes, he really is that much better than you. He's not a cheater, for one thing."

Ray snorted. "Give him time. All men cheat. Look at your father if you don't believe me."

Kat's insides went icy. "Get out of here before I call the cops."

Ray leaned one arm on the roof of his car. "A day will come when you'll regret leaving me. Mark my words."

"No, it won't. I am very happy. Happier than I've ever been." She pulled her cellphone out of the pocket of her leggings, ready to make good on her threat. "Now get in your car and drive."

He looked at her one more time. "I hope you get everything you deserve."

She laughed. Was that supposed to be some kind of cryptic threat? "Same to you. And Heidi."

He got in the car, slammed the door, and drove off, tires squealing.

Kat realized she was shaking. She didn't like confrontation, but she thought she'd handled that pretty well. She turned and went inside, taking the elevator up this time. Reminding herself to breathe. Reminding herself she'd never have to talk to him again.

Her mom was waiting for her in the kitchen. "Sorry for eavesdropping but I saw most of that from the porch. Are you okay?"

Kat nodded. "I don't mind that you were eavesdropping. I just needed to make sure he understands we are completely over."

"Sounded like he did. I had Danny's number up and ready, just in case you needed him to remove Ray again."

"Thankfully, I didn't, but I appreciate that you were on the ball." Kat glanced at the coffeemaker. She was hyped up enough already that her first cup could wait until after they got back from walking. "I gave him the engagement ring back."

"You did? Good for you."

"I thought that would be a great way to illustrate what I was trying to tell him. He didn't take it. I had to put it on the hood of the car. Then he took it."

"Same result." Her mom hugged her. "I'm proud of you, honey. That was a hard thing you did. But I'm proud of you for more than that. For getting the new job and taking care of yourself and not letting this stuff with your dad shut you down. You're a strong, brave woman and I'm proud to be your mom."

Kat smiled. "Thanks. I'm proud of you, too. With moving forward and not being afraid to let Danny into your life and the bakery stuff. All of it."

Her mom shrugged, her cheeks rosy. "Danny was the easy part. Speaking of, we still need to do a double date. I'd like to get to know your Alex a little better than just meeting him in the driveway."

"Yeah, I know. He's up for it, too. We just need to work out the timing." Kat's smile slipped off her face as Ray's words rang in her head. "Ray said all men cheat and that Dad was an example of that. Do you think that's true?"

Her mom shook her head. "Not at all. I think weak men cheat. Men like Danny and Alex? Those aren't weak men."

"No, they're not," Kat said, feeling better already. "Ready to walk?"

"Very much so. Let me just grab my visor."

"Yeah, I need my sunglasses, too. Meet you on the deck."

A few minutes later, they had their feet in the sand and were making progress toward their two-mile goal.

Kat kept her eyes ahead, watching all the other

walkers out on the beach. "What are you baking today?"

"Nothing," her mom answered. "Today I'm taking your aunt to the best new shopping destination I know of. A thrift shop called Classic Closet."

Kat glanced at her mother to be sure she hadn't been swapped with a clone. "*You're* going to a thrift shop? What does Grandma have to say about that?"

"Nothing, because she doesn't know, but I don't care, either. I found great stuff there yesterday. Roxie took me. And today I'm taking Jules, after she gets back from her breakfast with Jesse."

"Wow." Kat couldn't imagine her mother at such a place. Aunt Jules, yes. Her mom? Not in a million years. "Could I tag along?"

"You really want to come?"

"I do. Why not? It'll be fun."

Her mom nodded. "It will be." Then she laughed. "So long as you don't invite your grandmother."

Chapter Forty

"You were right," Margo said to Conrad. "I owe you an apology. The girls offered to help without me even asking." She sighed. "I really must learn to have more faith in people."

"You have faith in me, don't you?" Conrad asked. He'd just picked her up and was driving them back to his house, although they were making a stop for breakfast first.

"I do. In fact, you've helped restore my faith in people."

"But not completely."

She chuckled. "I am a cynical old woman, Conrad. You can't expect me to change overnight."

"That would be asking a lot of anyone." He pulled into the parking lot at Digger's Diner and turned off the car.

They went inside and found a booth along the front wall. A server, a young woman named Patty, had menus for them before they were even fully seated. "Can I bring you both some coffee? Or would you like something else to drink?"

"Coffee would be fine," Margo said. "I'd like a glass of water, too."

"Same," Conrad said. He leaned in toward Margo. "We have a big scene coming up today."

"I know. I've been thinking about it." They were killing someone today. A witness to their villain's murderous ways.

"So have I," Conrad said. "What are you thinking? Because I'm not sure I like what I've come up with."

She sighed. "I'm in the same boat. I was thinking poison, but we did that already. I don't like the idea of repeating the method. I think our girl is smarter than that."

He nodded. "Yes, exactly. She'd do it in a way that would not only leave her blameless but maybe even cast suspicion on someone else."

Margo sucked in a breath. "It's got to look like a suicide."

Conrad sat back. "That's brilliant. That's exactly

what we're going to do. Any ideas about how to make that happen? What kind of suicide?"

"Well, we've got a female witness. Women usually choose pills."

Conrad thought a moment. "True. But isn't that a little close to the poisoning we already did? Is it wise to kill two people off with such similar methods?"

The server came back with their coffees and waters on a tray, her gaze holding some concern, which led Margo to believe that she'd overheard part of their conversation. Patty put a cup of coffee and a glass of water in front of each of them.

Margo laughed. "I promise you we aren't talking about doing anyone real in. We're writing a book. A murder mystery. We're just figuring out our next chapter."

Patty grinned as she added a dish of creamers. "That's a relief. I was a little worried for a second there. But that is very cool that you're writing a book. I like a nice romance once in a while myself. But mysteries are very popular."

Margo nodded. "They are, but we have to finish the book first."

"Good luck. I can't even imagine writing a whole book." Patty took out her order pad. "Have you decided what you'd like to eat?"

Conrad shook his head. "Sorry, we haven't even looked yet. Are there any specials we should know about?"

"We've got two this morning. The Farmer's Plate, which is three eggs any way, three strips of bacon and a split buttermilk biscuit covered in sausage gravy. Then there's the Dieter's Delight, which is an egg white veggie omelet served with fresh fruit and whole wheat toast."

"Thank you," Margo said. She reached for two creamers and added them to her coffee, along with a pink packet of sweetener. "I still need a minute."

"Same here," Conrad said.

Patty nodded. "Take your time. I'll be back in a bit."

Margo smiled at Conrad. "We'd better be careful what we say or someone's going to call the police on us."

"Wouldn't that be something?" He laughed. "Probably be the first time I made it into the *Gazette* as the subject of an article instead of the writer. Although, you know, that wouldn't be a bad way to promote the book once it's out. Imagine the buzz we'd create."

She rolled her eyes but all in good humor. "You

would think that getting arrested might lead to sales."

Smirking, he looked at his menu. "We'd better figure out what we're going to eat."

She picked up hers and had a look as well. "I'm in the mood for something unusual. Something that I wouldn't normally get." Her gaze strayed to the pancakes, but that was a bad idea. All those carbohydrates would make her sleepy *and* go straight to her lower half.

Sadly, the pineapple upside-down cake pancakes sounded even more delicious.

She sighed. "What are you getting?"

"The Breakfast Sampler."

She found that on the menu. Two eggs, two slices of bacon, and two pancakes, any style. "That does sound good." Maybe she'd do that, too. Better two pancakes than a stack of three, which was what came in a regular order. And having them with some protein would help.

She put her menu down. "I'm getting the same thing. What kind of pancakes are you getting?"

"Blueberry. You?"

"Pineapple upside-down cake."

His brows shot up. "You are living on the edge

today. Is that what the prospect of murdering someone does to you?"

Patty returned at that very moment. "I did it again, didn't I?"

They both laughed. Conrad nodded. "Yes, you did and, yes, we were talking about the book again, I swear."

They ordered their meals and went back to talking.

Conrad sipped his coffee. "So your conversation with your daughters about the new house went well?"

She nodded. "Far better than I anticipated. Telling them about my plans has helped a lot. I still think it's a lot to take on. In fact, I know it is. But I no longer feel like it's such an impossible task. I'm truly excited about it now. Eager, even."

He turned his head slightly, giving her a dubious look. "Does that mean you'd rather shop for decorating selections than write?"

"No, not at all." She smiled. "But I wouldn't be opposed to taking a quick trip this afternoon to that tile place you mentioned yesterday."

He laughed. "Good, because I wouldn't mind having a look around there, either. All this remodeling talk has got me thinking that it's finally time to redo my master bath. I've wanted a walk-in tile shower for years. Not sure what I'm waiting for."

"That is exciting." She'd only seen his master bathroom once, when he'd first given her a tour of his place, but she remembered it being a standard, one-piece insert sort of thing. "What colors are you going to do?"

"Neutrals, probably. Maybe white and gray. I like that with a touch of blue. Not sure if my budget includes Carrera marble, but wouldn't that be nice?"

"It would." She lifted her coffee cup. "Here's to writing and remodeling, then."

He picked up his cup and clinked it against hers. "I'll drink to that."

"It'll be good motivation to get our writing done," she said before taking a sip.

He nodded. "I agree. It gives us a bit of a deadline, too, and I know from personal experience that I work better with a deadline."

Margo wasn't sure she loved the pressure of a ticking clock, but what was done was done. "I guess I'll know today if the same is true for me."

Chapter Forty-one

Jules arrived at Jesse's place exactly at ten. She'd dressed casually but comfortably in a pair of white knit capri-length joggers and a cute blue and white striped T-shirt with a vee neck. Flipflops and a small amount of makeup and jewelry completed her outfit.

He opened the door in an old pair of corduroy board shorts and a Chauncey's Surf Shop T-shirt with a band of hibiscus blooms across the front. Shiloh was next to him, smiling her doggy smile and wagging her tail. The welcome scents of bacon and coffee drifted out.

Those smells put Jules into an even better mood than she'd been in two seconds ago. She grinned as she looked him over. "All you need is a mustache and a Detroit Tigers hat and you'd be Magnum, P.I."

He laughed. "Yeah, well, I don't have a Ferrari, either." He stepped back so she could come in.

"Neither did Magnum. That belonged to the guy who actually owned the house." She walked in, stopping in front of him and giving Shiloh a scratch on the head. "Morning, pretty girl."

"I forgot he didn't own that car," Jesse said. "What do you think? Should I buy one?"

"Only if I get to drive it." She grinned. "Morning to you, too."

He leaned in and kissed her. "Morning. Hungry?"

"Yes. What's on the menu?"

"Quiche."

She blinked in surprise. "Wow. I did not expect that."

He held his hands up. "Don't be too impressed. In the interest of full disclosure, I bought it premade from Publix. All I'm doing is heating it up."

"Ah," she said, amused by his confession. "That seems much more realistic."

"Hey," he said as they walked through the foyer and into the rest of the house with Shiloh leading the way. "I can cook. But not quiche. That seems more complicated than burgers on the grill."

"Safe assumption, but I don't mind that it's not

homemade. I'm sure it'll be good."

"I've got some cut up fruit and I'm making some bacon, too—which I need to check on—then I'll show you around the house, if you'd like."

She nodded, already looking around. "I'd love a tour. This place is amazing."

It was different than what she'd expected. For some reason, she'd thought his place would be modern. All glass and steel cable railings and white everything.

But it wasn't like that at all. It was an eclectic mix of old and new, with some modern pieces, but a few that might have been mid-century. Except for the obviously well-used dog bed in one corner and the antique jukebox against the far wall, there was a kind of hip, cosmic age, Sixties surfer thing going on with lots of lime green, turquoise, and wood tones. Accents of brushed gold brought more of that feeling, as did the sleek lines of both the new and antique pieces.

She gestured toward one of the walls. "I love the starburst clock. That has to be vintage, right?"

"It is," he said. "It used to hang in my grandparents' living room, if you can believe that. I was also so impressed with it as a kid that they passed it down to me."

"Very cool."

"The chandelier over your head was theirs, too."

She looked up and saw a satellite-style light fixture that immediately brought to mind the same vibe as the rest of the design scheme. "I love it. Very groovy."

"That is exactly the right way to describe that light." He was flipping the bacon over. "Kind of *Jetsons*-meets-*I Love Lucy*." He laughed. "I know. I have strange tastes."

"Not strange at all. Very hip and cool and you."

"Thanks."

The living room, dining area, and kitchen were one big space that faced the water, which was easy to see, because the entire back wall of his house was glass, floor to ceiling. Those panels of glass were currently open, allowing easy access to the partially-covered big back deck that overlooked his pool below and the beach beyond.

On the shaded part of the deck, there was a glass-topped table with four chairs. On the other side, there was an elevated dog bed with a ragged stuffed animal on it. Further out in the sun, the deck held two lounge chairs and a few spiky potted plants that added a bright spot of green.

His place was more than nice. It was magazine

worthy.

She had to ask. "Did you decorate this place yourself?"

"A little bit, but my mom helped a lot. It's sort of what she does. More as a hobby than as a job, but it keeps her busy."

"She's really good. I might need to hire her when I buy my place."

"No promises, but I can probably get you the friends-and-family discount."

She laughed. "Thanks."

"Come on this way and I'll show my office and the guest room."

"Okay." She followed him through the living room and past the dining room. Naturally, Shiloh tagged along, tail wagging the whole time.

He pointed toward the left side of the small hall. "That's the guest room. Then there's a bathroom, then my office."

She looked in the open door. The guest room had a guitar mounted on the wall over the bed, Fifties-looking wallpaper featuring old vinyl records, and nightstands made from antique speakers. Framed posters from several Elvis movies decorated the other walls. "I love the music theme."

"Thanks. Again, my mom helped with that." He

pushed the bathroom door open and turned on the light. "Bathroom looks old, but it's completely new. You'd be amazed at the companies making reproductions these days."

She grinned at the blue and white color scheme, tiles, fixtures, and accessories that could have been straight out of a 1960s home. "It's really fun. I like it a lot."

"And then my office." He opened that door next.

It was a pretty simple setup. An L-shaped desk ran along two walls and held dual computer monitors, some speakers, and a keyboard. But the walls were covered with framed gold and silver records, some signed, along with other music memorabilia, like concert posters complete with tickets, autographed album covers, and headshots, most of them signed, too. The room had another dog bed.

"This looks like the Rock & Roll Hall of Fame." She pointed. "Is that Willie Nelson picture signed?"

"It is." Jesse smiled. "What can I say? I love music."

She nodded at the keyboard. "Do you play, too?"

"A little. Just enough to embarrass myself."

She chuckled. "I love how much you love music. I mean, you really own your appreciation for music and, as a musician, I find that very appealing."

He looked pleased. "Thanks. Music really has gotten me through some hard times. Let me put the bacon on some paper towels to drain and I'll show you the upstairs."

"Okay."

A couple of minutes later, they were following Shiloh up the steps to an open area with a big comfortable couch and a massive TV setup with some kind of gaming system. A blanket on the couch had dog hair on it. Small, square Bose speakers were everywhere.

He laughed softly. "Welcome to the man cave."

"You play video games?"

He nodded sort of sheepishly. "I do. I hope that doesn't change your opinion of me."

She chuckled. "Not at all. Just don't tell Cash or he'll be begging to come over."

Jesse's brows lifted. He patted Shiloh's side as she leaned against his legs. "Yeah? Because I would love to have someone to game with. I have a couple of groups I play with online, but it's different than having someone actually hanging out with you. Do think he'd like to play sometime?"

"He'd love it." She grinned. "But seriously, you've been warned. You won't get rid of him."

"I knew I liked that kid." He opened a set of

double doors that led into a room at the back of the house, which was the side that faced the beach. "This is my bedroom."

The back wall was glass, just like the downstairs, and it, too, opened onto a deck, this one about half the size of the first floor's deck and completely open. The bed was positioned so that it looked toward that wall of glass, meaning Jesse woke up to an incredible view of the beach and water beyond. The scheme here was simple. Blue, white, and tan with hardwood floors. A beautiful, modern fan whirled slowly over the bed, its three long blades reminiscent of a futuristic plane prop. The whole space had the feel of a very expensive hotel suite on some distant tropical island. Except for, once again, the well-used dog bed in the corner.

"Beautiful space," Jules said. "More of your mom's doing?"

Jesse nodded. "Yep. Although I picked out the fan."

Of course he had. "I love it." Jules's stomach rumbled. She put her hand on it to cover the noise.

He laughed. "Come on. Let's go get you fed."

They went back downstairs, Shiloh rushing ahead of them like she knew there might be bacon for her. He got the quiche out of the oven while Jules fixed them each a cup of coffee. He sliced the quiche, then made up plates for them with fruit and bacon, which Shiloh got a small piece of, then he carried them to the outside table.

Another trip for napkins and utensils and they were set. Shiloh lay down in the sun a few feet from the table.

They tucked into the food. Jules tried the quiche right away. Ham and cheese with some broccoli and onions. "This is great. It's just perfect."

"Thanks."

She thought about how his house reflected his love of music. And about how she'd been thinking about asking him if he'd like to accompany her on part of her tour.

But now she wasn't sure. Did that love of music mean he was married to his club? Or that he'd actually want to come with her? She knew he wanted to spend more time with her, which was why he'd mentioned hiring someone to take some of his responsibilities.

But that didn't mean he'd want to leave his business completely. Or want to accompany her on tour.

She couldn't decide whether to ask him or not. So she didn't.

Chapter Forty-two

As much as Claire loved to bake, it was nice to have a day off from it. Especially the cleaning up part. After she and Kat had breakfast—just the two of them, since Margo and Jules were already gone and Cash was still sleeping—she took a leisurely shower. The hot water felt great after the walk they'd had.

She spent more time fixing her hair and makeup. Even if they were just going out to shop at Classic Closet, she wanted to look nice.

That was all part of the new her. Putting more time and effort into herself. Looking as good as she could. Caring about her appearance. Taking care of herself. Getting more exercise. Eating better. Trying new things.

Like shopping at a thrift store. She laughed. She'd tell her mother about that eventually, but not just yet. Her mom had enough going on with buying a new house.

After Claire was ready for the day, she went to see if Kat was ready, too. Claire had a couple of things she wanted to accomplish before they headed out for the day. For one thing, she wanted to rewrite and better organize some of the lists she was working on for the bakery. She wanted to categorize them by item. Cookies in one list, bars in another, cakes, pies, and so on. It would help her get a better visual image of what the display cases would look like once they were filled.

She was even thinking about trying to draw out the display cases and where the various items would go, even though her artistic abilities were pretty limited to stick figures and doodled flowers.

But first, there was the matter of getting the house in Landry emptied and up for sale. The sooner, the better.

She found her daughter dressed and in her room, sitting on the bed, looking at her laptop. "Busy?"

Kat looked up. "Sort of. But it's nothing I can't put aside for a minute. What's up?"

"I was going to ask if I could borrow your

computer and maybe look up what it would cost to rent a truck to move our stuff."

Kat smiled. "I'm already working on that." She patted the empty space next to her on the bed. "Come on. We can look at it together."

"Okay." Claire went over and sat on the bed beside Kat. "What have you found so far?"

"Two different places. U-Haul, naturally, but the other one is a smaller company called U-Move-It. Both are about the same price, but U-Move-It seems a little more flexible." She showed her mom the company's website. "I really just need to talk to Cash and see what day he can go with me. Alex, too. Although he said he'll switch his shifts with someone else if he has to."

"And we'd be renting the truck in Landry?"

"Yes," Kat said. "Renting it there, returning it here. Have you decided if you're going to go with us?"

"I think I have to," Claire said. "There's just too much stuff to go through. You can't do that all on your own. It's going to take days."

"It can't take days. Not more than two, anyway," Kat said. "I need to be back here, organize whatever comes with me, and be ready to start work. I know it seems daunting, but there just isn't a whole lot in that house we need to keep. Other than the few antiques you want, our clothes, and whatever sentimental items there are."

"And my baking things."

"Right."

Claire exhaled, doing her best not to get bogged down by the weight of having to clean out that house. "I need to focus on minimalizing and not getting caught up in the process. Because the sooner that house is sold, the better. That money will help a lot."

"All you need to do is identify what you want to keep. Then you can pack up your baking stuff, your clothes, and personal items in your car and come back here. Me and the boys will take care of the rest."

"It's so much for just three of you."

Kat smiled. "Mom, I can do this. Those two men are very capable. And I've already been in contact with the local veterans association. They have a thrift store that will take pretty much anything we want to give them. They are ready and waiting with a truck."

"Really?" Claire shook her head in wonder.

Kat nodded. "And I hope you don't mind, but I reached out to Nick Walker."

Claire blinked in confusion. "Who?"

"You know, that guy who advertises he's the number one realtor in Landry? I figured if anyone was going to sell the house fast it would be him. I asked him to come by the house and give us an idea of what it could sell for and what would need to be done to get the best price. Like painting. Have the carpets shampooed. Stuff like that."

"Wow. You are really on top of things."

"Just trying to help, because I know you're busy."

"Thank you for doing all of this." Claire was amazed at how her daughter had taken charge of this big job. Kat had really grown up lately and Claire was thrilled to see it.

"I'm happy to do it. Happy the guys are going to help me, too."

"So am I. That's very kind of them. Alex isn't even family. By the way, are we any closer to having a dinner date for the four of us?"

Kat sighed. "No, I forgot to ask him about that. I will, though. Promise. There's just been a lot going on."

Claire had a feeling her daughter meant because of Ray. "No worries. We're going to be here a long time. We'll make it happen."

"How are things going with the bakery?"

"Good. Dinner last night was great. They loved the cookies I made and we talked a lot about different ideas for promotions and who we need to hire and when we're going to get that underway...all kinds of stuff. Thankfully, Danny's daughter, Ivelisse, is handling a lot of the ordering. She's getting us bags, product boxes, and nice Mrs. Butter's Bakery aprons for all of the employees to wear. Danny's handling the equipment side of things. But I'm in charge of the edibles."

Claire's lists of items to be made got longer every day, but the lists were also keeping her sane.

"You're really going to be swamped, aren't you?"

Claire tipped her head back and forth. "I don't know about swamped, but as we get closer to opening, I foresee some long days in my future. Maybe some long nights, too. Getting a bakery up and running is no joke. The amount of product we'll need for opening day is kind of staggering."

"I bet. You really need the cases full, don't you? I mean, there's something appealing about abundance, isn't there?"

"Yep. You said it. And we'll have to do our best to anticipate which products we'll sell the most of so we can be ready to restock. The cookies and the popcorn bars won't be too hard to keep up with. I'll have extras of them, no problem. But cakes, pies, cupcakes—those things all take longer. Especially when they have to cool before being decorated."

Kat looked at her. "I literally can't imagine the amount of work and planning you have ahead of you. I'd be a nervous wreck."

Claire laughed. "I probably would be if I let myself think about it too much. Which I'm not."

"Is that why we're going shopping today? Because you need the distraction?"

"Maybe. It won't hurt. But it's mostly because Jules liked everything I got and wanted to go herself."

Kat nodded. "Well, I'm glad we're going. I could use a few things myself."

"Do you have to dress up for Future Florida?"

"It doesn't seem super business-y, but sort of smart casual. I think nice work-appropriate pants with cute tops and maybe a light jacket or cardigan would be fine. Although I could use some better shoes. All I have here is sandals, flipflops, and sneakers. But I'll be bringing all my shoes back from Landry, so I don't need to buy more."

"That reminds me," Claire said. "I'm going to need some really comfortable shoes for working in the bakery. I'm going to be on my feet a lot."

"You know what you should look into? Nurse shoes. Those Danish clog things."

Claire nodded. "That's not a bad idea. Lots of chefs wear clogs like that. There's a health-care workers shop in the same strip mall as Classic Closet. Maybe we can stop in there and have a look."

"Definitely," Kat said. "You have to have good shoes. If your feet hurt, so will the rest of you."

Her words, as innocent as they were, sent a small wave of doubt through Claire. "Am I too old to be doing this?"

"Mom. What are you talking about? Of course you're not too old." Kat laughed. "If anything, you've aged in reverse since we got here. And eating right and exercising will help keep that process going. Look, I can't speak for people your age, because I'm not there yet, but I know you and I have no doubts about your ability to do this. Neither should you."

Claire smiled. "Thanks. I needed that."

"You've worked tirelessly over the last few decades as a mom and a wife. Now it's time to put that same kind of work into your own business. It might even be easier. You won't have me or Dad to clean up after."

Claire snorted. "No. Just customers." And, hopefully, lots and *lots* of them.

Chapter Forty-three

*T*rina found a Help Wanted sign at the CVS, just like her mom had suggested. She bought a fat black marker as well. Once she was back in the car, she wrote her phone number in the space provided.

When she got to the salon, she realized she had nothing to hang the sign with, but one of the guys working inside gave her a roll of blue painter's tape. It worked just fine. After taking down some of the paper covering the windows, she got the sign posted. She just hoped someone noticed it.

Then she went back to her car and got her notebook and binder so she could stay on top of what had been done and what still needed doing. Back inside, she used a big box that had apparently held a cabinet as a table. It was better than nothing and with no reception desk, she didn't have much choice unless she wanted to put her stuff on the floor. Which she didn't.

Not long after that, her phone chimed. She took it out and found a notification telling her that the ad she'd placed on the *Gulf Gazette*'s online job board was live.

"Excellent." She'd definitely get some calls now.

A couple of the men who were there working were actually cleaning up from the painting they'd finished. Two more were putting up the wallpaper.

Trina stood back, admiring the paper, and picturing how the salon was going to look. She still couldn't believe it was happening, but that feeling wasn't likely to go away anytime soon. That's just how it was with dreams that came true.

She couldn't believe Mimi was getting married again, either, except that she kind of could. If there was anything her grandmother liked, it was being in love. Trina smiled. How fun would it be to go wedding dress shopping this afternoon?

She borrowed the big push broom from the workers and started sweeping the floor. There was a lot of dust and debris, and she knew it would have to be done again. Ethan had told her the floor would be cleaned and polished before the salon opened, but she couldn't help herself. She wanted things to look tidy.

She had a big pile of stuff swept up and was only half done when Ethan came in carrying a large box. "Hey, Trina."

She stopped sweeping. "Hi, Ethan. What's in there?"

He smiled. "One of the new light fixtures. The shop called to say they were in so I just picked them up. I'm going to get them hung today."

"Oh, wow. All of them?"

"All but the chandelier that goes in the reception area. That won't be in for another day or two."

"Still, that's awesome. I can't wait to see them."

He nodded. "I've got that shelving unit you wanted for the storage room, too. I'll put that together this afternoon as well."

She couldn't have been happier. "The place is really coming together."

"It is." He glanced at the broom. "You know the floor isn't going to stay clean, right?"

She laughed. "I know, but I can't help myself."

"You're the boss. Whatever makes you happy." He gave her a wink as he carried the box to the back.

The boss. Wasn't that something? She'd never

thought that title would apply to her. And yet, here she was. In charge. Life was something, wasn't it?

Her phone chimed again, this time with a text message.

She read it. *Saw the ad, interested in the receptionist position, would love to see the place and chat more!*

Wow, her first potential employee! Trina answered with the salon's address, then a quick note. *Come on by, I'll be here until noon.*

That seemed like long enough to wait. The sign guy was due any minute and she wanted to get back and go wedding dress shopping, which reminded her that she needed to let her mom and Mimi know. She sent them a text with her estimated return home. She was about to put her phone away when the potential employee answered.

Sounds good. See you soon!

Trina tucked her phone into her back pocket and glanced down at her outfit. She'd dressed sort of casually today in just capri jeans and a T-shirt. She hadn't thought she'd actually be interviewing anyone today.

Nothing to do about it, though. Hopefully, they'd understand the salon was a work in progress and she was there working. She finished her sweep-ing. She carefully used a scrap of cardboard as a dustpan and dumped the pile into the big plastic trash can the guys had set up. She did her best not to get dirty.

Ethan brought in more boxes of lights. He set them carefully on the floor near the wall before putting the ladder up.

She went over to talk to him. "Maybe I could work on putting the shelving unit together? Unless you think it's too big of a project. I'm eager to get that set up. I'll have product coming in soon."

"You're welcome to give it a go, but there are no windows in the storage room and I'm going to have to kill the power for a bit so I can get the lights wired up."

"Oh." Trina made a face. "About that. I have someone coming in shortly to interview for the receptionist position. I might need the lights on for that."

He nodded. "I'll get this light up, then turn the power back on. I can work on the shelving unit until your interview is over."

"Okay, thanks. I'm going to run out to the car. I brought two of our folding chairs to set up for interviews. I hope no one thinks that's cheesy."

He smiled. "If people come in for an interview, their main goal is to impress you. Even if they think the chairs are cheesy, which they won't, they won't say anything."

"Good point." She went out to the car and got the chairs. They were the metal frame and canvas kind that they used at the beach. In fact, as she opened them, sand came off of them. She brushed the seats with her hand so they were totally sand-free, then set the two chairs up facing each other in the front of the salon.

The area would eventually be the waiting lounge with sleek black leather furniture and a drinks station and a gleaming chrome and marble table in the center. A selection of interesting and current magazines would be available for her clientele to look through while they waited.

There was nothing worse, Trina thought, than going into a salon that had nothing to read but dated magazines that were in terrible shape. A Cut Above would have new ones all the time. And not just *People*. Celebrities were interesting enough, but there was so much other stuff going on in the world. She wanted *National Geographic*, at least one home decorating magazine, maybe an older ladies' magazine, too. *Good Housekeeping*, *Real Simple*, or something like that.

After all, those were the women who had money.

Maybe she'd get something for the men, too. *GQ* or *Sports Illustrated*. Women liked sports. Some did, anyway. She made a quick note in her notebook to research magazine subscriptions.

The interior lights went off and Ethan came out of the back. There was still plenty of light in the building. Even with paper over the front windows, lots of sunlight filtered through. Ethan climbed the ladder and began to work.

A knock on the door was followed by it being opened. A middle-aged man came in wearing a Bright Signs polo shirt. "Hi. Are you Trina?"

"I am. You must be the sign guy."

He smiled. "I am. Tim Bright, at your service." He handed her a business card, which she took. "I'm going to take some quick measurements then I'll be on my way. We're doing the building sign, road frontage sign, and a window sign, is that right?"

Trina nodded. "That's right. Thank you."

"Thank you. Once I confirm the measurements to you in an email and you sign off, we'll go into production. I'll have an installation team out here next week."

"That fast?"

"Yes, ma'am. We do everything in-house, so we

work quick. Not many people want to wait for their signs."

"Makes sense."

He nodded. "You have a good day now."

"You, too." She made a note in her binder and stuck his card into one of the pockets. She needed one of those inserts that was made to hold business cards. Probably from Amazon.

She watched Tim measuring the front window where the shop name and new logo would go.

"Almost done," Ethan called out. "I'll have the lights back on shortly."

"No worries." The sun had gone behind some clouds, making the interior a bit darker, but Trina wasn't bothered. She pulled out her phone to look for the business card thing, then more knocking on the door interrupted her.

She turned to see a familiar-looking young woman peeking in through the door. Trina couldn't believe her eyes. "Liz?"

The door opened the rest of the way. Miles's ex-girlfriend came in, pushed her sunglasses off her face, and blinked in the dim interior. Suddenly, the lights came back on.

She screwed up her face. "Tina?"

"*Trina*," Trina corrected. "What are you doing here?"

Liz stepped further inside, lifting her chin. She was in white pants and a cute little blouse, a small Louis Vuitton handbag on her arm. "Probably for the same reason you are, I imagine. To interview for the receptionist position."

So this was who had texted about the job? "No, I'm not here for that—"

"Don't tell me you're a stylist?" Liz laughed like that was hard to believe.

Trina wasn't amused by Liz's attitude, but she understood she was the one in power here. Not Liz. She held the young woman's gaze. "I *am* a stylist, but that's not why I'm here. I'm here because—"

"Pretty nice, huh?" Ethan walked up, gesturing to the new light fixture he'd just installed. "But what really matters is what you think, boss. You like it?"

Trina smiled and glanced at the chandelier, but not before she caught sight of some of the color draining out of Liz's face.

Trina focused on the new fixture. Sparkling with light, the chandelier was gorgeous and classy and already setting the tone for the kind of chic vibe she hoped to accomplish. "I love it. It looks beautiful, Ethan. Thank you."

"You're welcome." He smiled as he glanced at Liz. "I'll go work on that shelving unit, then. Let me know when you're ready for me to put the rest of the lights up."

"I will." Trina turned back to Liz. "As I was about to say, I'm not here for a job. I'm here because I own this salon. I'm the one doing the interviewing. Are you still interested in applying for that job?"

Liz swallowed, then nodded. "I am. If you're still interested in talking to me."

"Can I assume that your patronizing attitude is a thing of the past and that it won't extend to anyone else if you become an employee?"

Liz nodded. "Yeah. I mean, yes. Sorry about that."

Trina smiled and gestured toward the folding chairs. She wasn't sure hiring Miles's ex-girlfriend was such a great idea, but she wasn't going to let Liz know that. "Then have a seat and let's talk."

Chapter Forty-four

*K*at followed her mom's directions as she pointed them out, but Kat had set her GPS, too. Not that she didn't trust her mom, but Claire had only been to the thrift shop once and Roxie had driven. Kat decided to err on the side of caution.

She saw the shopping center up ahead, so she got into the right lane. "I think we should go in the health-care place first and get your shoes taken care of. Then we can wander without pressure in the thrift shop."

From the backseat, Jules replied, "I like that idea. Get the boring stuff out of the way before the fun."

"Buying shoes isn't boring," Claire said. "It might not be the most exciting thing, but they're still shoes. Maybe they'll be cute."

"They're nurse shoes," Jules shot back. "I'm not sure cute is really going to be a factor. But it doesn't matter. Just so long as they'll give you good support. No one's going to see your feet behind the bakery counter anyway."

Claire made a face. "Danny will. I don't want him to think I'm wearing orthopedic clodhoppers."

Kat laughed. "What now?"

"You know," her mom said. "Old lady shoes."

"Well," Jules started. "You are an—"

"Julia Bloom," Claire interrupted. "If you know what's good for you, you will not finish that sentence."

Kat looked in the rearview mirror to see her aunt's eyes lit with amusement.

Aunt Jules said, "I was going to say 'exceptional baker.'"

Claire stared at her sister through the visor mirror, mouth twitching with barely contained laughter. "Sure you were."

Kat snorted. Hanging out with her mom and aunt was always a good time. "Okay, settle down. We're here." She parked and they all got out.

They headed for Scrubs and More, the healthcare supply place, and went inside. Her mom went directly to the shoe display. Kat hung back, looking at the racks of scrubs. There was a lot more to choose from than she'd imagined. Some really cute prints, too.

"Hey," her mom called out. "What do you think of these?"

Kat and Aunt Jules walked over to see what Claire was holding up. They were black clogs with a pattern of colorful cupcakes on them.

Kat grinned. "Those are actually pretty perfect. I never thought you'd find something baking-themed."

"Me, either." Jules took the shoe from her sister. "Wow, they're lighter than I expected."

Kat picked the shoe up to feel the weight. "Totally." She turned it over and looked at the price, which made her blink. "Did you see how much these are? Almost a hundred and fifty dollars."

"Yikes," Jules said. "But I guess you can't expect this kind of hard-working shoe to be cheap."

Claire took the shoe back. "Maybe I should just get sneakers."

Kat shook her head. "Mom, have you priced sneakers lately? They aren't going to be cheaper."

"Okay," Claire said. "Let me see if they have my size."

They did, and ten minutes later, they were

headed back to the car to drop off the box before going into the thrift shop.

"That's the fastest I've ever spent a hundred and fifty dollars," Claire said. She laughed. "I know it was worth it, but I hope to spend a lot less and get a lot more in Classic Closet."

"Me, too." Kat unlocked the car so her mom could put the shoes in. She didn't have that much hope that she'd find anything suitable for her new job, but she was keeping an open mind. She could always use new casual clothes, so anything she found would be fine.

"I don't mind spending a bit," Aunt Jules said. "Not if it's something really cool and unique that I can wear on stage. I can write that off, you know."

"Really?" Kat shook her head and locked the car again. "Must be nice."

"It is," Jules said as they walked toward the shop. "But it can really only be worn for the stage if I do that."

Claire opened the door, and they all went inside.

"Oh, wow," Kat said. "This place is bigger than I thought it would be."

"That's what I thought the first time I was here, too," Claire said. "But it's pretty well organized, so it's not hard to find things."

Kat rubbed her hands together. "What do you say we divide and conquer?"

Her mom laughed. "Okay, but I want to see any good stuff you find."

"Deal."

"Oh, one more thing," her mom said. She pointed to the sign overhead. "Today all red dots are buy two, get one free. You'll find the dots on the tags."

"Even better," Jules said.

"Let's get shopping." Kat headed into the rows of clothing, eager to see what she could uncover. Since she wasn't looking for anything specific, she just skimmed through the racks, going through the selections in her size.

The first thing she found was a cute blue and white skirt in a bandana print. She could see it with a white top and maybe a tan jacket. Or a blue top and a white jacket. Or maybe casually with just a white tank and white flipflops. She picked it up and looked it over, expecting to find a stain or something to explain why it had been donated.

Nothing jumped out at her, though. She looked at the price. Eight dollars. That wasn't bad at all, not for something she could wear to work. Then she realized the tag had a red dot. Now, that made things interesting.

She hung onto the skirt and looked with more intent. Maybe she could put a whole outfit together. Her next find was a pair of salmon pink ankle pants. They weren't something she'd ever choose, but they were a good brand and could be nice for work if paired with the right top. Besides, she was trying to get some bolder pieces into her wardrobe. What was bolder than salmon pink?

She kept digging and found a cropped tan jacket that would have been perfect other than a missing button. It was marked down to three dollars, and for that price, she could put new buttons on it. By the time she made it to the dressing rooms, her arms were full.

There was no way she was buying everything, but some of the items would eliminate themselves based on fit and how they looked on.

Her Aunt Jules arrived with a similar armful as Kat was about to go into one of the rooms. "You found a bunch of stuff."

Kat nodded. "So did you."

"Yeah, look at this." Aunt Jules riffled through the load she was carrying and pulled out a red suede jacket with long fringe down the sleeves and on the hem. The fringe was so long it nearly reached the floor. "Can't you just see me in this on stage?"

Kat laughed. "I totally can."

Her mom showed up. She didn't have quite as much as either of them, but she still had quite a number of things. "Time to try on?"

Kat and her aunt nodded.

"Let's show each other the keepers," her mom said.

"Aunt Jules already has one."

Jules hefted the suede jacket again. "For the stage."

"Nice. That's very you," Claire said with a smile.

They all picked a dressing room and went in. Kat hung all her finds on one wall, then began the task of trying them all on. She started with the blue and white skirt and tan jacket first. They were both very cute. "Mom," she called out. "Is it any harder to change jacket buttons than regular buttons?"

"No," her mom answered from the room next door. "You just have to make sure you get the right size and sew them on with sturdy thread."

"Okay." Kat could do that. Might take her an entire evening, as she wasn't the most skilled at that kind of domestic chore, but she could do it.

"Do you not like the buttons on something?"

Kat stepped out. "I like them just fine, but one's missing. Come look."

A couple of seconds later, her mom came out in a bright pink and green printed shift dress. "That's a very cute outfit. But you know, sometimes jackets have extra buttons sewn inside for that reason."

Kat glanced down. "They do?"

Her mom took hold of the jacket and opened it up. She tipped her head toward Kat. "There."

Kat looked down. Sewn to the right-hand seam were two extra buttons, one the same size as those on the front and another that matched the ones on the cuffs. "How about that? I'm definitely buying this now."

"You should. It looks great on you."

"So does that dress on you," Kat said. She grinned. "This is fun."

"It is," her mom said. "Do you think we dare bring your grandmother here?"

Aunt Jules came out of her dressing room in slim black pants, a black western shirt and the red fringe jacket. "Oh, please, yes. In fact, let's not tell her where we're taking her. Let's just make it a surprise."

Kat snorted. "That'll be a surprise all right. I bet you good money she doesn't buy a thing."

Aunt Jules hooked her thumbs into the belt loops. "I'll take that bet, partner." She laughed. "Although I already have a feeling you're going to win."

Chapter Forty-five

Margo and Conrad had not only finished the chapter they'd been working on, but started the next. Apparently, deadlines, no matter how small, did help their motivation. Margo had certainly felt the pressure to perform, but that hadn't been entirely bad.

Now, as she stood in the midst of one of the tile shop's many display rooms, she was surprised to learn that looking at tile made her remarkably happy. It was just so interesting and each new color or pattern or texture sent her mind off thinking about the possibilities.

Didn't even matter that none of this was for her soon-to-be house, although she had an eye out for that, too. Just in case something spectacular appeared.

Which it might. This shop had so much more to

choose from than the Home Depot. Nothing against the big-box store, but they couldn't possibly be expected to offer the kind of variety that a place specializing in tile did.

"This place is marvelous," Margo whispered to Conrad.

He nodded. "And they give a discount to military. Veterans included."

"Do they? Isn't that nice." That would help with the prices, which were also a bit more than Home Depot, but then again, you got what you paid for. Margo knew that very well. "See anything you like?"

"I see too much that I like."

She laughed. "I agree. Each one is nicer than the last. There are some amazing tiles here."

He glanced behind them to the showroom they'd just come through. "Those ones from Italy were something."

She nodded. "Couldn't you just feel the Tuscan sun looking at those? Glorious."

"I've never been to Tuscany." He gave her a coy smile as he slipped his arm around her waist. "Maybe we should go. Once you're settled in your new place and my bathroom remodel is finished."

She hesitated, giving in to that idea for a

moment. "Maybe we should. But not until the book is done, too."

He nodded. "Good point. Then we could work on our next one while we're in Tuscany. *Murder in the Tuscan Hills.* Or something like that. What do you say?"

"I say we have a lot on our plates already." She smiled. "But it is a lovely idea. I'd love to see Italy again."

"Does that mean you'll consider it?"

She nodded. "I will." She knew for her, it would mean getting to know him better first. Taking a trip with someone was a big commitment. But getting to know him better was already part of her future plans. That would be even easier to do when she only lived a few minutes away.

"Maybe we'll make a mint off the first book and be able to afford a whole month in Tuscany. Wouldn't that be something?"

She chuckled. "It would be, although I don't know how realistic it is. Even so, I like the way you think. Come on, let's see about picking out some tile for you. Then maybe we could get some lunch. That little Greek place we passed looked nice."

"Olive Grill?" He nodded. "Yeah, let's do that. I

haven't been there in a while, but they have great food."

"First, your tile."

"Right." He rubbed his hands together. "Let's get serious. I want a nice white and gray mix."

"Small tiles?"

"For the shower walls, that seems the way to go. With bigger tiles on the floor. Although I'm going to have them price out the Carrera marble, too. Just for comparison's sake."

"Smart." She looked around "You'll need two selections of tile then." She pointed to a slate-colored tile on the other side of the room. "What about that? It's very masculine. Is it too dark?"

"Not for the floor, no."

She nodded. "Good. I know you said you want to use blue as an accent color. That gray definitely has blue undertones."

He narrowed his eyes. "Gray has a blue undertone?"

"Well, that one does. Some of them skew greener."

"We're talking about gray, right?"

She smiled. "This is why you need a woman's help. Come on, let's look at that one more closely and if you like it, we'll find a smaller tile blend to go with it."

After much searching, Conrad found two mosaic panels that he liked. Instead of deciding on them, one of the salesmen signed out all three samples for him to take home and look at in the space.

Conrad carried them out to his car. "That was nice of them, huh?"

Margo went ahead to open the trunk for him. "Very. I like the idea of being able to live with the samples and see them in the actual room they're going in. That's very helpful."

He put the samples in the trunk. "I'll say. I have a feeling I'm still going to need you to help me decide."

"That's what I'm here for."

He shut the trunk. "I'd say you're here for a lot more than that." He kissed her, a quick peck on the mouth. "What would I do without you?"

"The truth is, I feel the same way about you. Thanks for that," she said softly. She meant it, too. He'd really given her a safe way to experience the world again. His fearlessness made everything seem possible.

"Can I buy you some lunch?"

She shook her head. "You buy me lunch too

often. We should go Dutch. Or you should let me pay."

He took her hand. "I like treating you. Maybe that makes me old-fashioned, but I think the man should pay, so long as he's able. And I am able. Besides, you're not working."

"I don't need to work. I'm very comfortable." She had quite a nest egg built up from her late husbands' insurance. He went around and opened her door for her. She shot him a look as she got in.

He seemed to ignore it. "Yes, but I don't need to work either, which means I not only get a paycheck from the *Gazette*, but I also have my military retirement. I've made a few decent investments, too." He went around to his side and got in.

"Fine." She put her sunglasses on. "We'll go Dutch."

He sighed like he was exasperated, but she could tell from the gleam in his eyes that he was just pretending.

She laughed. "Drive, Marine. I'm hungry."

"Yes, ma'am."

The Olive Grill was just a short ways back, so it wasn't long before they were sliding into a booth. The restaurant was charming, with blue and white checked tabletops and a cheery green olive leaf border around the walls.

A server quickly greeted them with glasses of water and menus and left them to have a look.

"You know," Conrad said. "We still need to decide on a pen name. And figure out what our author photo is going to be."

Margo looked at him over the edge of her menu. "Yes, I suppose we do. But isn't that putting the cart before the horse a bit?"

"Maybe. But it's still a detail that needs to be addressed."

"Can't we write under our real names? *The Widow* by M. Bloom and C. Ballard? Something like that? Then we could do a photo of the two of us." She grinned. "In black leather jackets, leaning against a brick wall. Very noir. You know the kind."

He laughed, nodding. "I do. I don't own a black leather jacket, though."

"Neither do I. What do you think about us writing under both names?"

"It would be the most equitable. If you're good with it, so am I. It would make finding the book easier for the small following I have through the paper."

"Good point. Then that's settled."

"As for the photo, I think I could get Bo Lindquist to take it. He works for the *Gazette* as a staff photographer. Probably wouldn't even charge us and if he did, it wouldn't be much."

"I'm fine with that, too." She put her menu down. She already knew what she wanted. "We don't need to take the photo for a while, though."

He shrugged and put his menu on the table as well. "We could do it anytime. You know what you want for lunch?"

She nodded. "Greek salad with chicken. You?"

"Same."

"Good," she said. "Maybe if we both eat onions it won't bother us."

He laughed. "Maybe. Do you want to talk any more about getting yourself moved over here?"

She exhaled. "We can, but I don't think I can do much until the Clarkes are ready to move. One of my girls suggested I use the garage at that house to store my things, but being in the tile shop made me think the workers might need that space for some of their supplies."

"They might. Why not just get a storage space? It'll only be for a month or two."

"I could. And I would like to get my house sold as

soon as possible. Foremost, I'd like to get my car. It's not fair that you always have to pick me up."

"I don't mind doing it, you know that. But if you really want your car, why don't we go tomorrow? We can leave first thing and be back before you know it. That will give you a chance to bring a few things back with you, too, if you want."

"Tomorrow." She thought about that. "It would mean no writing."

"Not necessarily. If I drive on the way there, you could write longhand. Then I can type it in when we get back."

"You have a solution for everything, don't you?"

He smiled. "I'm a Marine. It's what we do."

"I would very much like to have my car. You sure you don't mind driving me to Landry?"

"Not at all. Be happy to."

"You have to at least let me pay for your gas. And your lunch, because we'll have to eat."

He gave her a tight smile. "As much as I would love to argue that, I won't."

She laughed. "Then it's a deal. Tomorrow we'll get my car." She reached across and took his hand. "Thank you."

"You're welcome." He leaned toward her. "You

realize I'd do just about anything to get you moved over here permanently."

She squeezed his hand. "Your enthusiasm is appreciated."

It was such a treat to be wanted the way Conrad wanted her. She'd missed it more than she'd realized. Spending time with him seemed to be all the grief therapy she needed. Which was how she already knew that the trip to Tuscany would be happening.

She didn't know when, but they'd figure that out.

Chapter Forty-six

*R*oxie parked as close to the Lady M boutique as she could, then she, Willie, and Trina got out and went inside. Roxie had only been in the shop once, just to look. It smelled as good as she remembered. The music was soft and pleasant, and the carpeting was so plush, her flipflops sank into it.

Trina whispered, "This place is fancy."

Willie nodded. "Let's hope they have something."

Roxie didn't think that would be a problem. The racks were full of clothes, some of them covered in frills and bling. Lady M was known in Diamond Beach as the place to shop for any special occasion, but there were some women who dressed like this all the time.

"Good afternoon, ladies." A woman of about

Roxie's age approached them. "Can I help you find something today?"

Roxie nodded. "My mother is looking for something she can use as a wedding dress."

The clerk's eyes widened as she looked at Willie. "You're getting married?"

"Yep," Willie said. "Believe it or not."

"Congratulations," the clerk replied. "That is fabulous. I'm Lisa, by the way."

"Nice to meet you," Trina said. "That's my mom, Roxie, and my Mimi, who goes by Willie." She laughed. "And I'm Trina."

"Nice to meet all of you. Is this your first time into Lady M?"

"It is," Willie said. "We never had the money to shop here before but now we do."

Roxie rolled her eyes. "Ma, you don't have to tell people that."

Lisa laughed. "It's okay. I know we're a little expensive, but we carry unique and special designs for a very discerning woman. What sort of dress do you have in mind for your wedding gown?"

"The ceremony is going to be beachside," Willie said. "So nothing too fancy. But fancy enough that I look like a bride."

Lisa nodded. "Would you like to look around the

shop? Or would you like me to make some suggestions?"

"Can't we do both?" Roxie asked.

"By all means," Lisa said. "Feel free to wander. If you find anything you like, I'll take it back to the fitting room for you. In the meantime, I already have a couple of dresses in mind that I'd like to show you."

"Great," Willie said. "Let's shop, my girls."

Roxie stayed with her mom, as did Trina. Roxie was worried that her mom might get tired out, but her energy seemed to be just fine. If Willie needed a boost, Roxie figured she could always send Trina down to Java Jams for a mocha latte. That would pick Willie up for sure.

"There's a lot to look through," Trina said.

Roxie nodded. "There is. I never realized how big this place was." It was no Classic Closet, but then again, what was? She found a floral print dress that looked nice enough. She checked the tag and nearly gasped. Four hundred dollars.

She knew her mother had money now and probably wouldn't think twice about a price tag like that, but it still made Roxie pause. All the same, she took the dress off the rack and held it out. "What do you think of this one, Ma?"

Willie looked over. "Looks like something Laura Ingalls wore on *Little House on the Prairie*."

Roxie rolled her eyes. "So no, then."

Willie grinned. "It's my wedding day. The last one I'm ever going to have. I want to look beautiful and sexy, not like I'm capable of plowing the back forty."

Trina giggled. "Mimi, you'll look beautiful in anything you wear."

"That's sweet of you to say, Trina, but if there was ever a time to be particular, it's now."

Trina nodded. "I agree. Let's keep looking."

Lisa came over and showed them a dress she'd picked out. It was a long dress with spaghetti straps but had a matching jacket. The whole thing was swirls of pale blue and lavender on a white background and the pattern was accented with iridescent sequins. The fabric was light and flowy. "What do you think of this? I picked it because it matches your hair."

Willie sucked in a breath. "That is gorgeous. It looks like something a mermaid might get married in. I love that. In fact, it might be perfect. Definitely going to be too long for me, though."

Lisa shook her head. "We have a seamstress who

can take the dress up, so don't worry about that. Shall I put this in your changing room?"

"You bet," Willie said. Then she looked at Roxie and Trina. "Find me more like that. I need some bling."

They went to work, sorting through the shop's many racks. They ended up with a few more dresses, one skirt-and-top outfit, and a linen suit in a beautiful shade of periwinkle. To go under that, Roxie had found a matching periwinkle shell completely covered in sequins. Lisa had added a few more dresses as well.

Willie went back to find a changing room stuffed with options. "This is going to take me all day."

"You want a mocha latte, Mimi?" Trina asked. "I'll run down and get you one."

Roxie nodded. "I was just going to suggest that."

"That would be just the ticket," Willie said. She glanced at Lisa. "Do you mind if I have a drink in the store? I'll be careful with it. But a little sugar and caffeine might be the only things that get me through trying all of this on."

Lisa nodded. "That would be fine."

"Be right back," Trina said.

Willie headed into the changing room, which was large enough to accommodate four people.

Roxie took a seat right outside in one of the plush pink chairs meant for that purpose. "What are you trying on first, Ma?"

"That mermaid gown." Willie grunted. "I should have brought a long-line strapless bra. You know the kind I mean?"

"I do," Roxie said. "Do you even own one of those?"

"No, but I might have to get one. Can't have the tatas unfettered on the day of. Wouldn't be Christian."

Roxie snickered. "I'm sure we can order one on Amazon. Although they might sell them here. They have a lingerie section. Hang on. I'll go check. I know your size."

Roxie returned a few minutes later with the bra Willie had requested. She handed it through the curtain.

"Thanks," Willie said. "This will do nicely." Not long after that, Willie pulled the curtain back. "What do you think?"

Roxie smiled. "Oh, Ma. Those colors are beautiful on you. It's a great dress. Definitely too long, but she said they can fix that."

Lisa reappeared. "If I might make a few adjustments?"

"Sure," Willie said.

Lisa reached into a nearby basket and pulled out a few plastic clips. She moved around Willie with practiced efficiency, tightening the waistline here, adjusted the straps there, nipping and tucking and when she stood back, the dress looked like it had been made for Willie.

At least from the front. From the back, most of the clips were visible.

Lisa gently turned Willie toward the big mirror. "What do you think?"

Willie smiled. "I probably shouldn't like the first dress I try on, but I do. I really like it. This might be the one."

A soft chime sounded, then Trina joined them carrying Willie's mocha latte. "Oh, Mimi. You look gorgeous."

Roxie nodded. "You do, Ma. I know it's the first dress and you should totally try on the others but that one's a winner."

Lisa smiled. "Why don't we add a few little touches to it and really get the whole picture?"

"I'm game," Willie said.

"I'll be right back," Lisa said.

Willie made grabby hands at Trina. "While she does that, let me have my drink."

Trina brought it over. "Here you go, Mimi. That dress is really you."

Lisa returned with another small basket. From it she took a hair clip with some crystals, sequins, and a puff of white tulle. She set it on an angle in Willie's hair. Then she pulled out some long dangly earrings of white and crystal glass beads and clipped them onto Willie's ears. She gave her a bracelet that matched, too. Then she stepped back. "How's that?"

Willie stared at herself for a long moment without saying anything. Then she took a breath. "I look like a bride. All I need is a bouquet. And my groom."

Roxie felt an unexpected surge of emotion. She sniffed as tears built. They were happy tears, though. She hoped her smile reflected that. "I've never seen you look more beautiful, Mama."

"Thank you, sweetheart. You think Miguel will like it?"

"I think he'll love it."

Trina nodded, seemingly speechless.

Willie dabbed at her eyes before turning to face Lisa. "I don't want to try anything else on. This is my dress."

Roxie clapped, her smile so big her face hurt. "She said yes to the dress!"

Chapter Forty-seven

illie grinned and held up her finger so that Lisa didn't go running off. "We're not done yet, though."

Lisa stayed put. "I'll be happy to help with anything else you need."

"Thank you," Willie said.

"What else *do* you need, Mimi?" Trina asked.

"Two more dresses," Willie said. She'd been planning for this moment, hoping she'd have enough energy to keep going and she did, in part because she'd found her dress so quickly and in part because of the mocha latte Trina had gotten her.

Roxie looked confused. "Ma, I thought this was going to be a simple wedding. What are you going to do with two more dresses? That's crazy. If anything, you might want to look for shoes."

"For one thing, I'm going to wear those silver

sandals I have. They'll do just fine," Willie said. "For another, I wasn't talking about two more dresses for me. I was talking about dresses for you girls."

Roxie got up and came over. "Ma, do you have any idea how much this dress is that you've got on?"

"Yes, and I don't care. I don't care how much any of this costs. I want you both to have new dresses for the wedding. Now go shop while I get out of this thing and put my clothes back on."

Lisa stepped up. "Would you mind keeping it on until the seamstress gets here? She's only a few minutes away. I can take the clips off, though. She'll do her own pining when she does the fitting."

"Sure," Willie said. "What do you need me to do?"

"Just turn around, I'll take the clips off and unzip you, then you should be fine."

Willie turned. She looked at her girls through the mirror. "Off with you. Go shop. Or I'll pick your dresses out and you might not like that."

Both of them did as she commanded, smiling.

Willie exhaled. "Thank you for your help, Lisa. I thought I might get a bad reaction coming in here. That whoever was working today might not think I was classy enough to shop in here, but you've been very nice. Above and beyond, really. I appreciate that."

Lisa removed the clips then unzipped the dress. "Making customers happy is all that matters to me. When you spend this kind of money on clothes, you should be treated with the utmost respect. Actually, it shouldn't matter how much or how little you spend. Everyone deserves respect until proven otherwise."

"Do you work on commission, Lisa?"

"No, ma'am. But I'm well compensated, I assure you."

"I hope so." Holding the dress in place with her hands, Willie turned. "You're a smart woman, Lisa. I bet you had a good mother."

"The very best." Lisa smiled. "And she still owns this shop."

Willie grinned. That explained why she was well compensated. "A family business. I like that a lot. We're starting something like that ourselves. My granddaughter, Trina, is opening her own hair salon."

"That's wonderful. If she'd like, she can leave some business cards with us. We do have women in here looking for hairdressers."

"I'll tell her, thank you. Now, I'd better get out of

this." Willie went off to the dressing room and pulled the curtain shut.

Lisa called out, "I'll take the dress up to the counter for you. I'll put everything else away, too."

"Thank you." Willie got the dress off then handed it out through the curtain. "I want all the accessories, too, but I'll bring those out when I'm dressed."

"No problem."

It took Willie a minute or two to get herself put back together. She came out, accessories in hand, but Lisa wasn't there. Willie put them on the little table where her drink was, then sat down to rest and have some more of that mocha latte.

Trina was the first one back. She had a couple of dresses over her arm. "I found some things."

"Good," Willie said. "Let me see them on you."

As Trina went into one of the dressing rooms, Lisa returned. "Let me clear out that changing room then I'll be back for the rest."

"Take your time," Willie said.

Lisa scooped up everything Willie hadn't tried on and took it away. Willie admired the woman's work ethic.

Roxie arrived then, arms full. "I really liked that linen suit we picked out for you. I hope you don't mind, but I got one in my size to try on. Unless you think that's too dressy for a wedding guest?"

"Why would I mind? I'm not buying it for me. And if that's what you like, then it's not too dressy. Are you thinking it's something you could wear again?"

"Maybe. Ethan asked me the other night if I'd like to come to church with him sometime. Might be nice for that, don't you think? Without the sequin top underneath."

Willie nodded. "It would be very nice."

Roxie nodded. "Yeah, I think so, too. Okay, off to see how it looks." She went into the dressing room Lisa had just emptied.

Willie leaned back in the chair, resting her old body, and sipping on the delicious drink Trina had brought her. Lisa came back for the accessories and took them away, promising to have them all boxed and ready shortly.

Then Trina came out in a short baby-pink dress that had a pleated skirt and a smattering of rhine-stones on it. "What do you think?"

"It's pretty enough," Willie said. "But I don't know." She sipped her drink. Something about the dress looked both too old and too young for Trina.

"Hang on," Roxie called out. "I want to see." She

stepped out in the periwinkle suit with the sequin shell underneath. She looked at Willie. "Too much with the sequins? I mean, I'm not the bride."

Trina let out a little squeal. "You look great, Ma."

"Thanks." Her gaze went over Trina head to toe. "You look nice. But I'm not sure that dress is you. It looks more Vegas brunch than beach wedding."

"Yeah," Trina said. "It's not right, is it? No big deal, I have more." She went back in. "Next!"

Roxie went to put on her next outfit, too.

When Trina came out again, she was in body-hugging strapless dress that stopped just below her knees. The dress was made up of fabric that looked like a million little flowers, all in shades of pink with accents of white. The centers of the flowers were small clear sequins so that the dress sparkled with every movement Trina made.

"Wow," Willie said. "You look like a movie star."

Trina grinned. "You like it?"

"I love it. If I had a body like yours, I'd wear that to get married in."

Roxie came out of the dressing room again, this time in a mint-green tank dress with beading. "Oh, Trina. That might be the prettiest dress I've ever seen you in. You should get that. That is your dress."

Trina nodded, biting her lip as she looked in the

mirror. "It is really pretty." She glanced back at Willie. "Maybe with some strappy high-heeled gold sandals?"

Willie nodded. "You'll look like you just stepped out of the pages of a magazine."

Trina laughed. "Maybe I can wear it to the grand opening of A Cut Above, too."

"That would be perfect," Roxie said. "Honestly, you have to buy that."

Trina made a face. "It's not cheap."

"Neither am I," Willie said, laughing at her own joke. Then she pointed at Roxie. "The suit was better."

"Yeah, Ma," Trina said. "That periwinkle suit was beautiful on you. Go put it back on so we can see it again."

Roxie did that, coming out just as Lisa returned.

Lisa smiled at Willie. "The seamstress will be here any moment to fit your dress."

"Thank you," Willie said.

Lisa smiled at Roxie and Trina next. "Don't you two look lovely. Any adjustments needed?"

Both Trina and Roxie shook their heads.

Willie gestured at them with her cup while speaking to Lisa. "We're taking those outfits, too."

"Very good," Lisa said. "You're all going to look so beautiful. I hope I get to see a picture."

Willie nodded. "I promise to come back and show you one." She sipped her drink. "All right, my girls. Let's get this show on the road. I'm about ready for a nap."

Roxie laughed. "Okay, Ma. We won't be much longer. Just let us change."

Lisa smiled. "I can take those outfits up to the register as well and have you all taken care of shortly."

"Sounds like a plan." Willie had no idea how much she was about to spend, but she didn't care. Although there was some irony in the fact that her last husband was making it so easy for her to marry her next husband.

She lifted her cup in a silent salute to Zippy, may he rest in peace. She hoped she got to tell him someday just how much he'd done for her family.

Chapter Forty-eight

Claire was exhausted. They'd spent nearly two hours at Classic Closet and between the three of them, had bought enough stuff to fill Kat's trunk.

Jules had spent the most, but then the fringed suede jacket had been sixty-five dollars. That seemed like a lot to Claire, but she was still learning about how thrift shops priced things. Jules had sworn it was a steal.

Jules was so happy, she'd promised to make dinner for all of them. A healthy chopped veggie salad with grilled chicken, homemade vinaigrette, and parmesan shavings on top.

Claire would have eaten anything at that point and been grateful. The shopping had really worn her out. It was all the trying on. Something about getting dressed and undressed a hundred times sapped a person's energy.

Now she was sitting on the couch refining her lists for the bakery and organizing them into types of product. Her mom, who'd gotten home a few minutes after them, was in her chair, watching a show about a missing persons case. Kat was organizing her closet with her new things. Jules and Cash were in the kitchen working on dinner.

Roxie and her family were getting ready for dinner downstairs, too. Claire knew, because she'd run down there to say thanks again to Roxie for introducing her to Classic Closet, telling her all about the fun day they'd had there.

Roxie had in turn filled Claire in on Willie's big news.

Claire couldn't believe Miguel and Willie were getting married next weekend. Then again, the Rojas men seemed to charge forward when they made a decision about something, so maybe it wasn't that surprising after all.

Roxie had asked Claire about making a wedding cake, something simple with a beach theme. She'd offered to pay, too.

Claire had agreed but refused payment. Instead, she'd told Roxie that the cake would be her wedding gift to Miguel and Willie, but she'd made it clear that fancy cakes were not her thing, so simple was the best she could do.

Roxie had said that would be fine and was grateful that Claire had agreed to make the cake on such short notice.

Claire already had some ideas. Mostly graham cracker crumbs for sand, some chocolate molds that she could use to make gum paste shells and starfish, and a decent quantity of edible glitter. She thought Willie would like that bit the most.

Claire planned to scour Pinterest later to see what else she could come up with. She knew she wanted two tiers, and each tier would be three layers, so that would be a lot of baking, but she'd get the cakes done early. That would give her plenty of time to perfect the decorations.

She'd need to get pans, though. Even if she brought back what she had at the Landry house, she didn't have pans large enough for the bottom layer. It wasn't a big deal. She'd use them again, so whatever money she spent wouldn't be wasted.

A suitable bride and groom topper probably wasn't something she'd be able to purchase, however. Those generally didn't come with gray hair and wrinkles. But Claire was thinking about doing two beach chairs and putting an M on one and a W on the other.

She smiled just thinking about it. Beach chairs would be a super cute cake topper. Large shells with their initials was another option.

Her only hope was that the outside of the cake looked as good as she was imagining. She wasn't worried about the flavors. Willie wanted pina colada, something Claire knew she could easily achieve. It was just a matter of deciding whether to combine the flavors or do a coconut cake with pineapple buttercream.

Or maybe she should do a pineapple cake with a coconut buttercream filling and then a vanilla buttercream for the exterior layer. She wasn't a fan of fondant-covered cakes. Yes, it made a nice smooth surface for decorating, but it generally tasted like sweetened moist cardboard.

Not a great thing to eat on your wedding day. Or any day, really.

And while she might not be able to get buttercream as smooth as fondant, the beach theme would be pretty forgiving. The ocean wasn't a flat surface, after all.

The doorbell chimed and Claire looked over at her mom. "Who could that be?"

Margo shook her head but kept her eyes on the screen. "Maybe they ordered takeout again."

"They were heating up leftover pizza when I was down there earlier." Claire went back to her lists. So far, she had four kinds of cookies and wanted to add three more. Two of those should be something from the Rojas family recipe collection, but she wasn't sure which ones. She had more experimenting to do.

She had four types of popcorn crispy bars, with an additional plain bar that would be completely coated in chocolate and served on a stick. Those would be individually wrapped in cellophane and sold near the register as an impulse buy.

They'd have one display case dedicated to cupcakes and muffins. The muffin flavors, something she had yet to finalize, would lean toward the tropical. Pineapple, coconut, guava, banana, mango, those sorts of things. The cupcakes would be half traditional and half not. Another category she needed to tackle more thoroughly.

Pies wouldn't be a big category, but she was thinking about offering a pie of the month. Something seasonal. She was also toying with the idea of doing a sour orange pie as a shop signature. Sour orange pies were an old Florida tradition that had fallen by the wayside. Mrs. Butter's might be just the place to help bring them back.

She was jotting down that idea when Roxie called up the steps.

"Claire? Can you please come down here?"

This time, Claire's mother looked at her, brows raised. "Now what?" Margo said softly.

Claire shrugged and put her notebook down. "Coming," she called back. She got to her feet.

Jules gave her a look, too, as Claire walked past her sister in the kitchen. "Sounds serious."

"No idea," Claire said. "But if I'm not back in time for dinner, come and get me."

Cash snorted. He was chopping vegetables.

Smiling, Jules nodded as she whisked ingredients for the vinaigrette in a bowl. "You got it."

Claire grabbed a slice of carrot, popped it in her mouth, and crunched it up on her way to the first floor. She started down the steps. Roxie was at the bottom with someone else, who was standing in the foyer but too close to the front door for Claire to see clearly.

She swallowed the carrot, slowing as she reached the last step. The other person was a young woman, holding an infant in her arms. The woman had long chocolate-brown braids pulled back in a knot and dark skin. She reminded Claire of Danny's daughter, Ivelisse, a bit. Both of them were very beautiful. But this woman was younger. Maybe late twenties?

The infant was sleeping, wrapped in a light blue blanket.

Claire looked at Roxie. "What's going on?"

"This is Paulina." Roxie crossed her arms and looked at the young woman. "Go on. Tell her what you told me."

Paulina sighed. "I don't understand."

Claire didn't either.

"Go on," Roxie said again. "Just tell her."

Paulina looked at Claire. "I'm looking for anyone related to Bryan Thompson. I know he owns this house. That's why I'm here. I'm trying to find some of his family. I know he's passed away, but this is very important. Do you know any of them? Please. I need to get in touch with them."

Claire stood very still, hoping all the thoughts worming their way into her brain were wrong. "Why do you need to talk to them?"

Paulina patted the infant's backside. "Because I'm Bryan's wife, and this baby is his son."

Mantecaditos
Puerto Rican Thumbprint Cookies

Ingredients
1 cup lard, at room temperature
1 cup butter, at room temperature (2 sticks salted butter)
1¾ cup granulated sugar
3 egg yolks
1 tsp almond extract
1 tsp vanilla extract
1/2 tsp salt
4 cups all-purpose flour, sifted
guava jelly or paste
nonpareil sprinkles for garnish

Instructions

1. Preheat the oven to 350 degrees F. Cream together the lard, butter, and sugar in a bowl. Blend with an electric mixer until the mixture has lightened.

2. Add the egg yolks, almond & vanilla extracts, and salt. Mix until thoroughly combined.

3. One tablespoon at a time, add the flour into the lard/butter mixture. If the dough is too sticky, add more flour, one tablespoon at a time.

4. Use small cookie scoop to make dough into balls, about 1 ½ teaspoons each.

5. Create an indent in each cookie with your thumb.

6. Add a small cube of guava jelly or paste (about 1/4 teaspoon). Top with sprinkles.

7. Bake for 15-20 minutes at 350 degrees F or until edges are golden.

8. Cool on cookie sheet for 5 minutes. After that, cookies can be moved to a wire rack to finish cooling.

Want to know when Maggie's next book comes out? Then don't forget to sign up for her newsletter at her website!

Also, if you enjoyed the book, please recommend it to a friend. Even better yet, leave a review and let others know.

About Maggie:

Maggie Miller thinks time off is time best spent at the beach, probably because the beach is her happy place. The sound of the waves is her favorite background music, and the sand between her toes is the best massage she can think of.

When she's not at the beach, she's writing or reading or cooking for her family. All of that stuff called life. She hopes her readers enjoy her books and welcomes them to drop her a line and let her know what they think!

Maggie Online:

www.maggiemillerauthor.com
www.facebook.com/MaggieMillerAuthor

Made in the USA
Middletown, DE
30 August 2023

37656115R00235